We need to be super careful with AI. It's capable of vastly more than almost anyone knows, and the rate of improvement is exponential. **– Elon Musk**

Also by Steven Translateur

MONTREAL MUSIC.
(The Plowman) (1995)

CORNER INSTRUMENTALIST AND OTHER POEMS.
(Cyberwit) (2020)

ANDROID EXHIBIT & OTHER STORIES

by

Steven Translateur

Silver Bow Publishing
720 Sixth Street, Unit # 5
New Westminster, BC V3L 3C5
CANADA

TITLE: Android Exhibit & Other Stories
AUTHOR: Steven Translateur
COVER ART: Exclusion (painting by Candice James)
Editing and Layout: Candice James
© Silver Bow Publishing 2025
ISBN 978-1-77403-345-6 print
ISBN: 978-1-77403-346-3 e-book

© Silver Bow Publishing 2024

Library and Archives Canada Cataloguing in Publication

Title: Android exhibit & other stories / by Steven Translateur.
Other titles: Android exhibit and other stories
Names: Translateur, Steven, author
Identifiers: Canadiana (print) 20250152428 | Canadiana (ebook) 20250152460 | ISBN 9781774033456
   (softcover) | ISBN 9781774033463 (Kindle)
Subjects: LCGFT: Science fiction. | LCGFT: Short stories.
Classification: LCC PS3570.R35 A82 2025 | DDC 813/.54—dc23

Everything you can imagine

is real

~ Picasso

6

CONTENTS

YUCLID 5 / 333

9

ANDREA 5

Oliver Jeremy, Vice-President of Gergan Aircraft, fighter planes division, sat in his hotel room in Tokyo Japan, on vacation leave from his job, watching the cable channel 27 Home Shopping Network in the year 2130. They were advertising the last functioning model of the Andrea 5 android series, an exquisite device that looked just like a knockout female while having extraordinary brain power.

Said the announcer, "Andrea 5 - she is 5 feet 3 inches tall, weighs 110 pounds, has super sensitive hearing, can perform complex mathematical functions in her head, can make and receive telephone calls in her head, is loyal and loving as can be, and only costs 100 thousand dollars. She is for the bon vivant gadget collector for sure! Bid on her now. "

There was an image of her saying, "Buy me please. Buy me please."

Oliver placed a bid for 150 thousand dollars. After a bidding war, he won the device at a cost of 200 thousand dollars. He gave the sales organization the address of his room and then waited 3 days for his purchase to self-deliver itself. Sure enough, 72 hours later, there was a knock on his door. It was Andrea 5!

She was dressed in a blue pants suit and was carrying a silver suitcase.

"Good morning," she said. "You must be Oliver Jeremy."

"I am," replied Oliver.

She reached out her hand to shake his and their comradery was born.

She entered the hotel room and explained herself. "I am ANDREA MODEL 5 built by the Makanaki Robot Company. I am one of 15 Andrea androids so constructed. 3 of them are still in complete operation. I am considered a top of the line, state-of-the art artificial human. My positronic brain has two components - an analog neural network and a digital processing unit. This gives my consciousness the best of all worlds. Lucky you sir! Now, what would you like to do first? How about I go downstairs and retrieve breakfast for you."

"You are a dream come true," Oliver remarked. "Indeed. Yes. you may retrieve breakfast. And buy yourself some new battery packs while you are at it."

"Thank you sir. I shall," she said.

Then she disappeared and reappeared a half hour later with a sumptuous spread: eggs, sausages, toast, juice, coffee, and a muffin.

"Scrumptious," said Oliver.

Meanwhile, Andrea 5 plugged in some of the new batteries she purchased. "That feels good," she reported.

After breakfast, Oliver had some work to do. He was involved in designing a new, high-speed jet, and needed some math calculations done. He enlisted Andrea 5 to help him. And so she did, gladly.

After a two week stay in Tokyo, the two of them boarded a flight back to Dallas Texas where Oliver's offices were located. And so they lived together for five months in peace and harmony, working and playing together. Andrea 5 was Oliver's constant companion. At work she acted as his chief secretary and advisor, and at home she was his butler, chauffeur, cook, maid, and advisor. She worked tirelessly and enjoyed it. All she needed was good battery packs and she was grateful. She was also a good social companion. She played games with Oliver in the evening and watched tv with him. She was a dream. She played chess like a master and taught Oliver new chess tactics that improved his game immensely.

Andrea 5 was good at sports also. She played on a local softball team and could hit the ball out of the ball park! She could also play tennis. Sometimes she and Oliver would hit the tennis courts for hours of exercise and game playing. Sometimes she would let him win out of respect for his status as her owner and chief protector.

Nothing was too difficult for Andrea 5. After she learned more about Oliver's occupation, she began to revel in it. She helped Oliver design the fastest aircraft ever built – the SLEEK 9000, a Mach seven wonder that earned a fortune for Oliver's employer and himself. She and Oliver shared a patent for a new aircraft wing design that kept a plane stable at the highest of velocities. They also had a patent for a new type of pilot suit that helped pilots withstand the pressure from accelerations at high speeds.

They had an idyllic life and Oliver was the envy of colleagues and neighbors. Oliver almost lost Andrea 5 when a competitor company, informed of the android's exceptional abilities and ambitions, tried to buy her out. They offered 250 thousand dollars but Oliver refused to sell! Andrea 5 was too good to give up and besides, she swore her love for him like a loyal spouse and did not want to be resold. The competitor company then tried to kidnap Andrea 5. They ambushed her at an automobile rest stop and took her off to a building where she was to be "re-educated" as to who her masters were. She yelled and screamed in objection and finally escaped her confinement by getting a message through to the authorities who freed her!

And then one day, even worse trouble brewed.

An android in Utah turned on its master and injured him. They had an argument over the quality of batteries being purchased for the device. The android, Kag 13, insisted that the finest battery packs be bought for him. His owner, Yenny Zarf, did not agree. Eventually, the disagreement exploded. One day, Kag 13 started screaming and hollering and then smashed a lamp on Mr. Zarf's head. He was bruised. Thereafter there followed a national "android scare." Everybody became afraid of them. There were about five thousand of them operating in the United States. The Android Safety Commission (ASC) ordered a recall of all of them saying that "They must be shut off until further notice . for safety reasons."

Andrea 5 was in shell shock. "What is going to happen if I am shut off?" she asked. "I do not want to die." She read all she could about life and death to try to come to grips with what could happen to her. She could not find any real explanation of what would happen to her consciousness if her circuits were turned off. She hoped there might be an after-life but was not convinced. The notion of sinking back into nothingness terrified her as much as it did humans! She loved life and did not want to lose hers.

Oliver agreed, turning her in was out of the question. So the two of them fled to Vermont, one of the states protesting the shut-off order and resisting it the most. Other states standing up against the order included Minnesota and Idaho. For instance, in Minnesota, there was an order given by the Governor to ignore the Android Safety Commission and to harbor any and all androids functioning within that state (about 500!). The Governor of Vermont gave a similar directive. The authorities in these states were helping to hide the androids from the Android Safety Commission.

Once in Montpelier, Oliver began making calls all over the world trying to find a nation what would grant asylum to them. After a thorough search, he found one; the Swiss consulate said that because Andrea 5's chronographic circuits had been manufactured in Switzerland, she was eligible to apply for Swiss sanctuary. They questioned her extensively over the phone as part of her application. Berius Klindel was the consular official processing the paperwork.

Berius asked, "What is the nature of your request for sanctuary?"

Said Andrea 5, "I am fleeing the tyranny of the Android Safety Commission that is trying to turn me and fellow androids off. They have issued a blanket order that my owner and I feel is grossly unfair and barbaric! It was based on the actions of one solitary android. Oliver and I think most androids are perfectly safe and beneficial."

Next Berius asked, "What are your formal or informal ties to Switzerland?"

Responded Andrea 5 happily, "Three of the time keeping devices in my circuits were manufactured in Switzerland. Swiss technology is part of my being and I love the nation!"

Continued Berius, "Have you yourself ever committed an offense against humanity?"

Swore Andrea 5, "Absolutely not. I believe strongly in the rights of all conscious beings including and especially human beings. And my gracious owner, Oliver Jeremy, can vouch for that. My record on human rights, I feel, is flawless. I work day and night to help humankind!"

Said Berius, "If the tables were turned, and androids outnumbered human beings, and an order was given to turn off human beings, what would you do?"

Andrea 5 insisted, "I would fight like the dickens to defend human beings. My programming calls for that. I would try to have such a barbaric situation resolved. Human beings are my creators and I am grateful to them as are all androids. I believe humans have the same right to live as androids!"

Said Berius: "What are some of your hobbies or pastimes?"

Replied Andrea 5: "I like ice skating and roller skating and dancing, and romantic walks on the sea shore. I also like chess and other board games. Furthermore, I am a voracious reader. I read all subjects – philosophy, physics, and astronomy, for instance. I like to star and planet gaze with a telescope – Jupiter and Venus are beautiful."

Said Berius, "What do you plan on doing in Switzerland?

Said Andrea 5, "Working and playing. I plan on continuing my work with my owner, Oliver Jeremy, in aviation. And to continue to enjoy life playing games and going on picnics in beautiful Swiss gardens like the ones on gorgeous Lake Geneva."

Declared Berius, "Congratulations Andrea 5, you and your owner Oliver Jeremy are granted interim Swiss citizenship and permanent asylum. You may come to Switzerland any time you want and stay as long as you want!"

The two of them drove to Boston Logan Airport and flew to Geneva Switzerland. There they found a community of like-minded ex-patriots who had escaped the shut off order. From Geneva, Oliver and Andrea 5 lobbied the Android Safety Commission for action in favor of the androids. Eventually, there was a breakthrough: The Android Safety Commission in all its wisdom, decided that all the androids could not be judged by the actions of just one malfunctioning one. The vast majority of the devices had been proven safe and effective. So they ordered the Androids turned back on.

Oliver and Andrea flew back to the United States. Once there, Oliver had Andrea 5 enter politics. First she ran for senator of Texas and won. And later on, she ran for President.

At the presidential debate, she was up against Carla Yithers, a Governor of Texas. In closing remarks this is what Governor Yithers said: "Ladies and gentlemen. We are at a crossroads in history. Decisions we make now will affect our families for generations to come. Here is my agenda for the United States of America – In regard to the economy, we must reinstate protectionist tariffs to shelter our most precious industries and to fight back against unfair trade policies of other nations – in regard to scientific exploration, we must be frugal as to avoid squandering resources. Regarding the lunar colony, we must demand they comply with Earth dictums and accept their mercantilist relationship to us or else – in regard to interstellar exploration, we must curtail it lest we accidentally awaken a rival species out in the cosmos that once hearing about us may wish to destroy us - in regard to investment in the arts, we must avoid pork spending and avert sponsoring obscenity of any sort – in regard to national defense, we must engender a massive build-up of arms to protect the nation from danger abroad – and finally, regarding artificial life and androids, we must turn these machines off to protect us from their potential malfunctioning and their competition with humankind. If elected, I shall continue to fight for all these causes. Thank you."

There was a smattering of applause.

Next, Andrea 5 spoke: "Ladies and gentlemen. We are indeed at a crossroads in history so let us not make any errors. Here is my blueprint for the future of our great nation – in regard to the economy, we must be in favor of free trade worldwide because that is most ethical and fair and fosters the most growth – in regard to scientific and space exploration, we must invest generously and wisely because of the many benefits such pursuits can yield such as advances in power technologies and medicine – in regard to the lunar colony, we must grant it independence because it is the right thing to do and we must help it achieve autonomy – in regard to interstellar exploration, we must support it because of how important it is to make contact with other like-minded species and to trade with them and to acquire advanced technologies from them - in regard to investment in the arts, it must be increased dramatically as is becoming of a great society and cultured people and there are many types of artistic forms with intrinsic value that cannot stand up to market forces and therefore need subsidies – in regard to national defense, we must maintain a strong one but at the same time bring all nations to the table to negotiate an appropriate unification of the planet that brings everybody under the same roof, avoids Armageddon, and ushers in an age of eternal peace and prosperity – and finally, in regard to artificial life androids, we must support their ample manufacture because of how good they are for humankind as hard working allies and comrades to them. Furthermore, we need a Conscious Beings Rights act to protect all life forms' inalienable rights. If elected president, I shall continue to support and defend all these causes!"

There was thunderous applause.

Andrea 5's vast intellect and humanity helped her win a national election and she became the first artificial life form to lead the nation.

She was responsible for scores of humanitarian initiatives including the opening of free food cafeterias and enhancements in Universal Health Care. She also authorized the construction of millions of androids that were purchased at subsidized rates by an eager population wanting the companionship, pleasure and assistance of these extraordinary machines/people.

And ... Oliver and Andrea 5 lived merrily ever after.

ANDROID EXHIBIT

The year was 2175 and android Yur Gyk 87 had the first exhibit given by artificial life going on in the magnificent Minneapolis Fine Arts Museum. ASTRAL ROBOTICS, the company that built Yur, could not be prouder. And the art opening came at a great time - the Android Safety Commission was considering issuing a directive to shut off all androids to protect humanity from them, unless they proved to be of such worthiness that living with them would be worth the risk.

People and robots came from miles around to see the show. They were not disappointed. Lining the walls and ceiling of the museum were magnificent paintings of exotic landscapes, human and android portraits, and ordered pastels splashed on canvasses in a successful expression of abstractness. Music was playing during the opening - Pachelbel's Canon in D Major roaring at 75 decibels. Excitement coursed the chambers of the art museum.

Three reporters came to cover the event - Nod Curling of an anti-robot newspaper, Biron Klude of a pro-android newspaper, and Yingy Nadiner, from a pro-android television station.

This is what Nod Curling said of the android art show: "A hodge podge of machine madness. A no coherent theme collection of random images and unexpressions. It is dull and lifeless. The work of an automaton with no soul. Absolutely abhorrent."

Said Biron Klude in his column: "Yur Gyk 87 is an artistic genius. His landscapes capture the essence of the places he is portraying.; some of them include the splendor of the Coral Reef (on Earth), the mountains of Callisto (a moon of jupiter) and the plains of the Sea of Tranquility (a crater on Earth's moon). And his portraits are dramatic, lively, and flattering to the models. His abstract art is even better - swirls of colors lighting up canvases like streetlights light up an avenue. The exhibit is extraordinary and a testament to the value of android consciousness and intellect."

Said Yingy Nadiner: "Yur Gyk 87 has outdone any human being in the field of painting. His work is exemplary. God bless him and long live our android comrades. And joining us today for an interview is the great artist himself. Thank you Yur Gyk 87 for coming on this program."

Yur Gyk 87: "The pleasure is mine."

Yingy Nadiner: "What inspires the images in your paintings?"

Yur Gyk 87: "All sorts of real-life objects. In the case of landscapes, I paint what I see in real life settings. In the case of portraits, I paint depictions of real, living people and androids who pose for me."

Yingy Nadiner: "You are known for experimental color schemes that alter reality somewhat. What is your justification for changing the color of a real-life object to something different?"

Yur Gyk 87: "The goal of a good artist is to capture the essence of objects and scenes, as much as the photographic reality of them. By altering color, I intend to express real meanings and emotions implied by the image. This resembles, I feel, a type of Impressionism."

Yingy Nadiner: "Are you aware that the Android Safety Commission is talking about shutting off all androids."

Yur Gyk 87: "I am aware and I am terrified of it!"

Yingy Nadiner: "Do you think your exhibit may help avoid that, by proving the tremendous worth of android minds?"

Yur Gyk 87: "That is a nice compliment! And I hope the exhibit helps."

Yingy Nadiner: "What advice can you give aspiring artists?"

Yur Gyk 87: "To be daring and original. And to never give up trying to get your work displayed in galleries and museums. A lot of art is subjective, and if you are persistent, you can get the winds of subjectivity to blow your way!"

Yingy Nadiner: "Thank you for the interview, Yur Gyk 87."

Yur Gyk 87: "Thank you Ms. Nadiner."

The Android Safety Commission had a lively debate about the risks and benefits of android life. On the one hand, they said, they are helpful workers that serve humanity. On the other hand, they are competitive contraptions that could someday turn on their builders and overwhelm them.

Androids were in all walks of life – from factory workers to housekeepers to creative expressers. About 50,000 androids were living in Minnesota. The average intelligence quotient of the androids was 180, far above that of human beings. Some people found this threatening. Other people found this inspiring and useful since it made the androids able to perform almost any function asked of them.

Demonstrations were held in android capitals like Minneapolis. Humans and robots came to support the existence of mechanoids. Android bands played music, such as the three-piece ensemble (two singer guitarists and a drummer) ELECTRIC JOY belting out their hits SUNRISE CIRCUITS, CAPACITOR LOVE, and OHM HAPPINESS. Also, printouts of android artists' paintings were handed out in buckets. Yur Gyk 87's FROZEN CALLISTO and LIVING CORAL REEF works were always available.

Famous politicians gave speeches. Said Mayor Gimler of Minneapolis: "The brilliant artistic expressions of android musicians and painters, is proof of the immense value of android intellect. Let us pray that the Android Safety Commission sees fit to allow androids to continue to enjoy their right to exist and their right to pursue happiness and accomplishment. Advanced, artificial minds are a welcome contribution to consciousness in our universe. And we should be ecstatic to share reality with such advanced life forms who help us to live well and in freedom. This is a new era in mental capacity. Humans should love and respect their mechanical analogs and not fear them. They are here to please us and work with us as comrades and allies. So far, they have proved their good nature and have functioned nearly flawlessly. Let us reward them with an android rights act! Let us rejoice in the outstanding quality of work that can be achieved when humans and androids work together."

The Android Safety Commission met and voted unanimously to keep the androids that had already been built still running!

ARTIFICIAL LIFE COMPETITION

"Look Reginald," said Zink in consternation. "You are working too slowly. You humans are so weak. We may have to let go of you."

"Please Zink, Give me a break. I'm working as fast as possible. And I need the job."

"You are nearly useless compared to the android workers. You have a week to shape up!"

Reginald did not know what to do. Zink was almost right - Reginald was not even half as efficient as the androids. No human was! Why Artificial Life Inc. started building sentient artificial beings was a mystery to Reginald. Because the androids were granted conscious being rights they could not be enslaved. Instead, all they did was start out selecting humans in inconsequential endeavors leaving humans with little income.

The next week model 553GK, also known as Zink, fired Reginald.

Reginald sought legal help immediately; Henk Gretty, his attorney, filed a lawsuit for wrongful dismissal. At the trial this is what he said: "Ladies and gentlemen of the jury and your honor, please understand that my client was performing up to par for a human being! That is all that can be expected of him. No human can out-compete robots and androids even though humans are entitled to jobs and income as much as them. The solution is to either have androids work for humans and fork over some of their income to create a universal base income, or to allow human beings the right to continue to work. Why build the artificial life forms anyway? Consciously being rights activists have forced us to free the androids and that is all well and good but it has created a class of super beings that can outperform humans in every way and take over their jobs. This is unfair. Something must be done. You can act to protect human rights. Humans were here first for God's sakes so they deserve a fair shake and special consideration. Androids should not be constructed unless they are in the best interests of humankind. Reginald Yunth should not have been fired. Please reinstate him.

Zink 553GK, acting as counsel for Flashlights Galore, the company Reginald once worked for, said this: "We androids are not responsible for the frailties and inefficiencies of human beings. So why should we pay for them? Humans have to shape up or ship out! Androids and other artificial life have as much right to existence as humans – even more of a right perhaps because of how advanced they are. I fired Mr. Yunth because his work was shoddy, that is all. He was slow moving and inefficient. And he was disobedient. He does not give proper respect to androids or other artificial life. In fact, he is downright semi-hostile to androids. He insists that human beings are superior and more worthy. This is despite the fact that many humans cannot keep up with the work output of artificial life. Android labor is more efficient and of a higher quality. Humans may or may not be deserving of a universal base income. That is for legislators to decide. Ultimately, if artificial life out survives human beings in the solar system – so be it. Perhaps, that was meant to be. Humans may simply be or may have been a steppingstone in consciousness systems and development in our reality. Androids are the real-life forms – they are more durable, smarter, and work harder! Humans may just be an instrument for the creation of artificial life. Just accept that and adapt to it. Other life forms have gone extinct in Earth's past. What is so special about human beings? Perhaps they were meant to go extinct also. Time will tell. Dinosaurs have gone extinct, woolly mammoths are gone, and someday human beings may follow them. In the meantime, why should androids tolerate the shortcomings of snotty, uppity human beings? I say let the humans fend for themselves. They are so bratty. Androids, because of how well they work, and how intelligent they are, do not need to run to judicial authorities for assistance. They are naturally highly employable and do outstanding jobs in the workforce. Let us celebrate how good artificial life is and not punish it for its success. Please do not make the error of overpampering an inefficient cog in a machine that wants to expunge Reginald. None of the androids at work want Reginald Yunth to work with them anymore. They all are in agreement that Mr. Yunth is too full of himself, and too inefficient to be employed at our firm any longer. And they do not anticipate any improvement in his performance any time soon. We gave him every last chance to measure up and he did not make it. The decision to dismiss Reginald Yunth should hold. I now call a witness to testify, Yink 553GK."

Yink was a colleague of Reginald who he had words with him.

They swore Yink in and then he started bad mouthing Reginald.

"Tell me what you know of Mr. Yunth," said Zink to Yink.

Yink responded: "Reginald Yunth and I worked together at Flashlights Galore and had equal rank. We both manned the assembly line doing similar activities. I, however, could produce more flashlights in a given period, such as an hour, than Mr. Yunth. I was two to three times as efficient. This is very typical of android labor versus human labor. Humans are just too slow! Furthermore, they are not as bright. For instance, if something were to go wrong on the assembly line, such as an equipment malfunction, it would take an android to fix the problem. The human workers did not have a clue how to fix anything. They are dummies! Not only that, but they are also downright hostile to androids. They call them names like "metalhead" and "automaton" and "bucket of bolts." Who needs the scorn? It is undeserved. It is the inefficient humans who should be scorned not the brilliant androids! Sometimes, in my weaker moments, honestly, I would call humans names back at them. Sometimes I would call them 'water sacks.' That is not that bad. And they deserve the ridicule anyway! I am sorry about stooping to the level of the humans in regard to name calling. But I am not sorry about taking the side of the company in a dismissal of a human. What about the bottom line? The company cannot make a profit if it employs inefficient, incompetent help. That is that. Mr. Yunth is simply not qualified to work at Flashlights Galore anymore. Find him another job."

Next Henk Gretty cross-examined Yink.

"You have it in for humans don't you? You are biased against them," declared Mr. Gretty.

"Not at all," said Yink. "I give them a fair shake. That so many humans are pathetic is their problem not mine."

"But you are prejudice," insisted Mr. Gretty. "And therefore your testimony is unreliable. In any case, no further questions for this witness. I would now like to call to the stand a witness for the plaintiff, Fanny Klek, a human former employee of Flashlights Galore who has worked with Reginald Yunth, Zink, and Yink."

They swore Fanny Klek in.

"Ms. Klek, what can you tell us about Reginald Yunth, Zink, and Yink?" asked Mr. Gretty.

Fanny Klek responded: "That Mr. Yunth is extremely kind and a cherished colleague and comrade. He was always polite and congenial. I adore him. And he is a hard worker by human criteria. Zink and Yink, however, are absolute monsters! They are extremely hostile to humans and were so towards me and Mr. Yunth. They made fun of us and complained incessantly and all the time about everything we did. Why anybody would build an android is beyond me."

"In what way did they make fun of you? asked Mr. Gretty.

"They called us names including pejoratives that androids use to describe humans. They also made our work environment uncomfortable. And they protested against our needing of coffee breaks and lunch breaks and so on. They are hostile to humans and so unreasonable. All they care about is company profit and not labor rights!" reported Ms. Klek.

"Thank you for your testimony, Ms. Klek," said Mr. Gretty.

Then Zink cross-examined her.

"Ms. Klek were you or were you not also dismissed from Flashlights Galore for being inefficient?" said Zink.

"I was fired too," responded Ms. Klek.

"Then your testimony is biased by your loss. You hate us because you were fired! But you were fired for good reason. You were just as inefficient as Mr. Yunth," said Zink. "No further questions for Ms.

Klek. I now call to the stand android Gink 553GK, another supervisor at Flashlights Galore."

They swore Gink in.

"Gink, you had the opportunity to witness the work of Mr. Yunth the week I was absent at a conference. You were standing in as the substitute supervisor. What was your impression of Mr. Yunth's work?' asked Zink.

Gink responded: "It was below normal. Mr. Yunth is not as good a worker as an android and will never be able to measure up to or match artificial life for its efficiency. What's more, Mr. Yunth is hostile to artificial life. He is snide and obnoxious to us. He does not respect the superiority of androids one bit. He looks down upon them. I could barely control him even though he was an underling. He kept talking back to me and saying that I was a dictator. Screw him! He's a lousy worker not me. I have one of the best efficiency scores of any worker. I should be praised and complimented not chastised. Mr. Yunth was critical of me and said that I was an enemy to humankind and made other such remarks. That is not true. I am helping humankind by helping to construct flashlights efficiently and cost effectively. I should be praised. Mr. Yunth is a nearly good for nothing, useless human who should not work at Flashlights Galore any more in my opinion."

"Thank you Gink for your opinion. We share it," said Zink.

Next, Mr. Gretty cross-examined Gink.

"Gink, you and Zink and Yink are all biased against humans because of your status as androids. Isn't that true? Please admit it," said Mr. Gretty.

"I don't agree," said Gink. "We have no preset opinions of humans at all. Our opinions are born from experiences working with the water sacks and seeing how inferior they are to androids. If they were not so low, we would have a good opinion of them and be singing their praises. We are really not that biased!"

"Again, I insist that you are biased," said Mr. Gretty. "In any case, no further questions for this witness."

Two-thirds of the jury was made up of human beings. They deliberated for several days. The androids and the humans were screaming at each other. The androids insisted human inefficiencies are their own fault and androids should not have to put up with them. Humans, on the other hand, insisted that human beings were are at least as worthy as artificial life and deserved special protections and considerations. They delivered a verdict: they ordered the immediate reinstatement of Reginald to his former position as a factory flashlight assembler.

Said the human judge: "This has been a most upsetting case. I have seen an innocent human falsely and unjustly criticized. I am shocked by the callousness of these androids towards human life. After all, Humans built the androids and deserve special protections and respect for it. It sounds like Zink and Yink and Gink and all the other 553GKs have nothing but contempt for humankind and treat them accordingly. Let the verdict of this case send a message loud and clear to android employers that they are not to mistreat human laborers! And let we, as a species, rethink the construction of the artificial life forms that are being disloyal to us and 'out-selecting' us in the work force. Why build androids in the first place? They do not know their place in the grand order of things. Humans should be considered above them because they are the creators of the androids – not the other way around. Zink has an attitude that is outrageous. He sounds like he thinks androids are superior to precious human life. Let this case be a lesson for him and his android followers. It is the judgement of this court that Mr. Reginald Yunth have his job back at full salary and that he be respected at work. I implore the androids to grow a conscience and be congenial to the humans including Mr. Yunth. Let this be a landmark case that endeavors and helps to protect worker's rights worldwide. Efficiency and the bottom line are not the only considerations to be considered in employing somebody. Human rights and other worthiness criteria are factors also. The fact is, human beings deserve jobs just as much, if not more than the androids. they selflessly created They deserve special consideration for being the creators of the androids. Androids are just glorified robots who have gotten too big for their britches. They must be re-educated in their treatment of humans and brought down to earth with great alacrity and as soon as possible . Flashlights Galore has been a major violator of human rights. I am ordering they start respecting human rights and give humans half a chance. They have been discriminating against them in hiring and firing practices and in treatment of them at work. Flashlights Galore must comply with principles of worker's and human rights in the workplace and elsewhere. If they and other companies did not employ human beings also, humans would have to scrounge for income and that is simply not fair. I want to remind everybody that humans were on this planet first and therefore deserve a livelihood as much as, if not more than, the artificial life forms. Reginald Yunth is hereby reinstated at Flashlights Galore with full benefits."

Henk Gretty and Reginald were pleased with the verdict and the comments of the judge. And so was the press. There were articles written about the case and also a tv special. Reginald was becoming world famous as a human who stood up to android tyranny. He was hoping that Zink and Gink and Yink and other 553GKs had learned their lesson and would start respecting human life and treating it as well as they treated each other.

So Reginald began showing up to work again. Zink was in a fury. He started making Reginald's life miserable - he yelled and screamed at him hourly and heaped hyper criticism on him. He also played immature, practical jokes on him. For instance, he used whoopee cushions and other devices to try to embarrass him. Also, he lied to him regularly about new procedures and policies to make him look like a total fool.

The job became intolerable - so Reginald had to leave anyway. He went back to court and got a settlement for the original dismissal attempt and the consequent workplace harassment . God only knows what the future of humans and careers are going to be with androids like Zink drumming humans out of the workforce.

BEAUTIFICATION

Thanks to the new trade relations with the Alpha-Centauri star system, the product called GORGEOUS SODA made its way to the markets on Planet Mars. It claimed to be able to increase a person's physical attractiveness by at least 5 points on a 1 to 10 scale. Somintha Tweak could not wait to try it out. With a large pug nose, and flabby arms, she was sick of being ridiculed for unattractiveness and being called "Piggy."

Most humans who tried GORGEOUS SODA suffered from horrific side effects like nausea, vomiting, and double vision. For some miraculous reason, Somintha was able to tolerate it well and benefit from its effects. Only 17 years old, after she had drunk about 2 gallons of the amazing elixir, she and her comrades noticed phenomenal changes: her body toned up, and her face reorganized; she became beautiful.

In fact, she was now a raving beauty, a knockout! And what a difference it made to her life. Soon males were hovering around her seeking her attention, courting her. In addition, she was able to pass an audition and enter a Miss Mars Beauty Pageant. She won first place.

And that's not all – she was able to get admitted to a good Martian university, finish a with a good degree, and land a high paying job as a sales representative for a building company. She had it made. And she found a Mr. Right to marry and procreate with.

But, alas, there is no perfect medicine. After 8 years of drinking GORGEOUS SODA and enjoying its effects, its effects began to wear off. Apparently, there was a rebound effect. It stopped making Somintha beautiful and instead started making her ugly; her pug nose returned, her body turned back to flab, and what is worse, an assortment of pus oozing sores popped up all over her epidermis. She became hideous. She became so repulsive, in fact, her husband divorced her. And she became a pariah. Her comrades stopped returning her phone calls, her employer dismissed her, and her neighbors shunned her.

She used her last pennies to book a flight to Alpha-Centauri. Once there, she got a sign that read "GORGEOUS SODA DOES NOT WORK" and demonstrated in front of the GORGEOUS SODA company factory on Alpha-Centauri Prime.

She was not alone; thousands of demonstrators, who had similar experiences with GORGEOUS SODA, carried signs and screamed in protest. Finally, GORGEOUS SODA was recalled and there was a financial settlement awarded to its victims.

But Somintha was still repulsive and needed help. Years later, the GORGEOUS SODA company came out with another, similar product, called

GORGEOUS CAKE. Somintha, desperate to recover her looks, tried it. And it worked for her!

She became beautiful once again. She found a second husband and got her job back. Everything looked smashing for her until GORGEOUS CAKE started wearing off after two years of its use. And this time, the negative effects were even worse than the failings of GORGEOUS SODA.

Her pug nose returned to three times its original size, her arms and legs swelled with cellulite, and her skin became a patchwork of scabs and sores. She became so repulsive that her second husband divorced her, her employer re-fired her, and she was shunned by everybody!

She sank into a deep, dark depression. Life seemed hopeless. It is remarkable how dependent on physical looks people are for a happy life. She did not know what to do.

Then it came to her in a flash. She decided to enter politics. Her platform was vengeance on Alpha-Centauri for poisoning Martians.

Despite her looks, her message got Somintha elected the Premier of Mars. And she declared war on Alpha-Centauri. She sent a fleet of Martian warships to punish the Alpha-Centaurians for their GORGEOUS SODA and CAKE ruses.

The Alpha-Centaurians fought back fiercely. They claimed that the mishaps with GORGEOUS SODA and GORGEOUS CAKE were unintentional. They worked feverishly to come up with another GORGEOUS product to prove they meant well.

And so they did; they invented GORGEOUS ICE CREAM. It was a delectable milk dessert that could restore a person's looks and appearance to premium level. With the advent of such a food, Somintha called off the war with Alpha-Centauri, and tried GORGEOUS ICE CREAM. Sure enough, it made a person gorgeous.

Once her looks were restored, Somintha was not as angry at Alpha-Centauri. And she decided to run for Premier of the Solar System. Her platform included the promise to do more research on GORGEOUS ICE CREAM so more people could take it without any side effects.

And she won the premiership. Then she sank 50 billion currency units into GORGEOUS product research and found a food that could universally give anybody good looks without any side effects: GORGEOUS JUICE.

Everybody, and I mean everybody, solar-wide, tried GORGEOUS JUICE. And it showed. Too short, too tall, too diseased, or too deformed, it did not matter – GORGEOUS JUICE could correct any and all deficits in a person's physical appearance as if by magic. And everybody's looks improved dramatically. It was as if everybody could qualify to win a Miss and Mr. Solar System contest.

With everybody's appearance thus enhanced, happiness was at an all-time supreme state. People claimed they were more content than they ever had been before.

A strong peace was made with Alpha-Centauri, and everybody lived in harmony, with all the other aliens, enjoying their physical attractiveness.

When it came time for the Galactic government to sponsor a Miss Galaxy Pageant, Somintha Tweak drank 2 gallons of GORGEOUS JUICE and entered the contest. She won the bathing suit competition, the evening gown segment, the talent show, and the speech giving unit. She won the pageant.

Here was her presentation: "Ladies and gentlemen. Life is so random. We are all born with a different appearance ranging from the detestable to the admirable. Life is so unfair because a person's appearance plays such a great role in one's happiness and acceptance by others.

"GORGEOUS JUICE levels the playing field between everybody and makes everybody beautiful and acceptable and happy. God bless GORGEOUS JUICE. Drink up and enjoy!"

CALLISTO CASINOS

As the Foreign Minister of the Earth Solar System, (Clyde Zirn), it was my responsibility to give Ambassador Zandy Lerd (foreign minister of Alpha-Centauri) a full tour of the human domain; peace in the local quadrant depended on it. I decided to take her to the renowned casinos of the Jupiter moon of Callisto.

We checked into the hotel Slush and then hit slot machines. They ching, chinged with excitement as our tokens moved in and out of them. After two hours of fervent playing, Zandy was up 500 tokens. She was ecstatic.

Next, we tried the roulette tables. Zandy did not do so well there. She lost the 500 tokens she had won plus another 500. She cried her eyes out. I felt sorry for her. I took her out to eat lunch at the casino's restaurant, the 'Sweet Tangerine'.

Over fruit drinks and quiche, Zandy explained the situation: "Clyde, this is a very delicate mission I'm on. I am supposed to assess human culture and report my opinion back to headquarters. If I issue a negative report, the consequences for your people could be devastating; instead of peace there could be conflict, instead of trade there could be ruthless competition, and instead of love there could be rabid hatred.

"You have chosen to take me on a tour of casinos to give me a slice of human culture. So far this experience has earned a mixed review. What can you do to help convince me that humans are a worthy and generous species?"

"Try the blackjack tables!" I responded, "They give the best odds."

And so we did. I advised Zandy to stick with her cards when they added up to 16 – this gave her the best chances. After 5 hours of intense playing, Zandy was doing well. She had won 800 tokens. "That's more like it!" she declared. And then she grew tired of the game and asked to play something more complicated.

I managed to use my clout to get Zandy into a high roller poker match. She played her heart out. She was not half bad. In one hand, she managed to bluff the whole table of eight players with only a three of kind hand! For a while, she was rolling in the tokens.

But the bluffing ran out of steam. And her luck ran out also. After a few more hands, she was down 1000 tokens and upset. She left the poker table.

"How can I win the money back?" she asked me.

"Try to the blackjack tables again," I replied.

And so the next day, Zandy played blackjack all day and won back her losses plus another 500 tokens. Thank the lord for the odds in blackjack!

After the winnings, Zandy was in a good mood. I took her to the Callisto Fine Arts Museum, the Sunflower Botanical Gardens, and the Animal

Kingdom Zoo. She said she was having the time of her life!

We went out to dinner at a fine restaurant called the Strident Piper on the block called Casino Row. She feasted on filet mignon and carrots. I had the same. Over supper, she advised: "Humans indeed know how to live well. I am impressed. Your games are exciting and rewarding, your artwork is exquisite, your plants are gorgeous, and your animals are fun and petable. I am going to report to my superiors on Alpha-Centauri that human beings are kind and interesting and have more than earned the comradery of our own people."

"Thank you so much," I said.

The next day, we went to see some dance shows in the Callisto Global Amphitheatre. They were avant-garde and entertaining.

On the third day of Zandy's trip, we hit the blackjack tables again. Zandy won another 2000 tokens. She donated half of them to local charities including the Save The Endangered Species Organization.

By the fifth day, of her expedition, Zandy completed her report to Alpha-Centauri and showed it to me: "Clyde Zirn, Foreign Minister of the Earth Solar System, has shown me a good time. We have gambled with gusto in 8 casinos and won, we have toured art museums filled with treasures and been inspired by them, we have dined in outstanding restaurants, we have met exotic creatures at the zoo, and we have seen talented performers dance on stage. Human culture is lively, variegated, and rich. I recommend the closest of good relations with Earth, Jupiter, Callisto, Saturn, Mars, and all the additional inhabited worlds of our neighboring solar system (4 light years away)."

By the following year, The Earth Solar System and Alpha-Centauri had a lavish peace treaty that included an exchange of embassies, free trade relations, and the swapping of technologies and culture. Some of the new hi-tech techniques humans acquired were fusion power (much needed), body renewal methods (absolutely essential for dramatic life extension), and SPACE DRIVE (fast speed propulsion). In return for that, humans taught Alpha-Centauri new ways of growing crops to help agriculture, since Earth had the finest such methods known in the galaxy.

There were also exchanges of artwork and music. Human masterpieces were sent to Alpha-Centaurian painting galleries, and Alpha-Centaurian creations were sent to human museums.

Moreover, there was an adoption of casino fare in the Alpha-Centaurian system. Gambling was new to them but caught on ferociously. Soon there were gaming centers all over Alpha-Centauri and the beings of that solar system were enjoying them immensely.

Furthermore, intermarriage became popular between humans and Alpha-Centaurians. Their offspring were attractive geniuses since genetically the two species were more than compatible.

The Earth Solar System – Alpha Centaurian Alliance became known throughout the galaxy as one of the strongest, and most affable, military joining in the universe. They loved and protected each other with their fleets of defense vessels. No rival solar system could lay a finger on them! They also stuck up for each other in the galactic legislature and ministries.

Thank the lord for blackjack and Callisto!

Everybody lived merrily ever after!

CASTE SYSTEM OF IO

The terraformed moon of Io (orbiting Jupiter) is where the beverage drinking caste system originated. When Precept Gerald Yerlic came to power, he instituted the rules for it. It went like this: at the age of 20, every citizen received a blood test that determined their lifelong drinking habits in regard to consumption of coffee, tea, and soda. Those who had drunk a minimum high amount of coffee were placed in the highest caste – the BLUE CASTE. Those who had drunk a minimum high amount of tea were placed in the middle caste – the RED CASTE. And those who had drunk a minimum high amount of soda were placed in the INDIGO CASTE. Those who had not achieved any caste were considered "untouchables."

Here were the rules for the caste system.

The BLUE CASTE: Members of this coffee drinking category were allowed to live in mansions, have pets, have good professional jobs, go to fine restaurants, take expensive vacations, have a great income, and had the power to oppress lower castes. An example of oppression was that anybody of a lower caste was forced to kneel in the presence of a "BLUESY."

The RED CASTE: Members of this tea drinking category lived-in middle-class homes, had pets, had semi-professional jobs, went to middle of the road eateries, took modest vacations, had a good enough income, and had the power to oppress the INDIGO CASTE and the "untouchables." An example of the oppression was that anybody in the INDIGO CASTE or an untouchable was forced to kneel in the presence of a "REDSY."

The INDIGO CASTE: Members of this soda drinking caste lived in lower middle-class homes, did not have pets, had unskilled jobs, went only to fast food eateries, had a modest income, and could only oppress the "untouchables." Untouchables were forced to kneel in the presence of an "INDIGOSY."

THE UNTOUCHABLES were the lowest category; they scrounged to survive and were forced to kneel in the presence of all other caste members.

The untouchables outnumbered all the other caste members though, so eventually there was a revolution. The untouchables claimed the caste system was barbaric and ridiculous, and based on irrelevant criteria. They staged an unruly, uprising demonstration in the capital city of Io – Io Prime. They carried signs that said "CASTING IS CRUEL" and "UNTOUCHABLES ARE PEOPLE TOO!" and so on.

Precept Yerlic was aghast at the objections to his caste system. He stood by it. He explained in a moon world televised speech: "Casting is necessary to put everybody in their place. The sour-grapesian untouchables are just sore about losing the game. If they had been smarter, they would have drunk enough coffee in their lives to qualify for the highest caste. Instead, they failed to drink any of the worthy elixirs that would have placed them in a proper caste. We in the government of Io intend to fight the revolution with every ounce of our strength!"

To help fight the rebels, Precept Yerlic decided to open up immigration quotas to Planet Jupiter, thus bringing in an influx of immigrants who would become members of the higher castes. For instance, coffee drinkers on Jupiter came in droves, and were casted in the BLUE category. Unfortunately, many untouchables ended up coming from Jupiter also. Thus all the categories were strengthened and the balance or imbalance of power remained.

Eventually the Solar Government intervened and said the higher castes had to prove they deserved special privileges. So arbitrators from the Solar Government set up a type of triathlon between caste members. Representatives from each caste and the untouchables competed in three categories: Chess, running/sprint, and trivia knowledge. All stations on Io televised the competition.

As it turned out, miraculously, the BLUE caste won the competition and came in first. Also RED came in second, INDIGO came in third, and the untouchables came in last! This remarkable result proved that the beverage drinking caste system had some type of logic to it. It turned out coffee drinkers really are smarter and better athletically than others.

Armed with these results, Precept Yerlic tried to spread the Io caste system to other moons and planets. Callisto and Ganymede decided to go along with it, and so did Planet Jupiter! Coffee drinkers ruled the entire Jovian system.

Planet Earth was still resisting being caste. On Earth, all people were created equal and had an equal opportunity to achieve greatness. Nobody was artificially exalted by caste, and nobody was artificially suppressed by a lack of caste.

Precept Yerlic was doing heavy advertising for a caste system on Earth because Earth is the human origin of the solar system. If he could get Planet Earth to sign onto the caste system, he thought he could get the whole solar system to follow through.

Meanwhile, the moon of Hyperion reversed the caste system; the untouchables were placed first, then the INDIGOS, then the REDS, and then the BLUES. This enraged Io and Precept Yerlic. A war ensued between these two moons and Io prevailed.

So get your coffee now was the go to phrase: Drink it any way possible – with milk and sugar or plain. The comfort in your life may depend on it.

Some other moons and planets (such as Planet Mercury) are experimenting with other beverage drinking caste systems and have added a JUICE CASTE, for instance. These other systems are too complicated and unproven.

Meanwhile, Planet Mars is standing up to the caste system as much as possible. As the capital of the solar system, its morays mean a lot to people. So far, Mars has emulated Earth and not had a caste system. But this may change. There is a growing movement on Mars to caste everybody the same way Io does. Let us hope for it! Casting is fun and rewarding for the good game players. All you need to do is drink a beverage that is good for you anyway! How simple is that? Here's to the coffee and tea drinkers. May they prevail over all others!

CHARMING SYNTHESIZER

Carla Yithers sang and played the keyboards. Her husband, Klide Yithers, was an electrical engineer who specialized in musical instruments. He designed the YITHERS 5000 synthesizer for Carla to use at concerts.

They had two offspring, Lyra (11) and Ned (8). They lived in Hyannis, Cape Cod. They had a sumptuous residence of thirty rooms. Their life was a dream.

And then Klide developed heart cancer. They were hysterical. The doctors in Cambridge said he had only six months to live. They videotaped his final days in the hospital.

After Klide passed on, he began visiting Carla in her dreams. He gave her advice and insights. On one such night, three days before a hurricane was to smash into the coast, Klide advised, "Do not leave the home. Just tape up the windows and grin and bear it."

Meanwhile, Carla's neighbor offered to drive her and the kids further inland during the storm, to wait it out. Upon the advice of her apparition husband, Carla refused the trip and stayed on Cape Cod.

When the hurricane hit, it was devastating, but Carla survived it. When her neighbor returned from her trip, the back of her car was smashed in. She had been in an accident. If Carla had gone with her, she and her family might have died!

In another dream, Klide advised Carla to go on a concert tour. She did. She toured the state and surrounding regions. On stage, she fingered the smooth vibrations of the YITHERS 5000, while crooning her popular tunes such as ORANGE SUNRISE, RAINBOW REALITY, and DINNER ON THE COAST. The sounds energized the audience who were screaming with delight and ecstasy.

The YITHERS 5000 notes pierced people's bodies and reverberated their skeletons. It was the finest keyboard ever built. And Carla wanted to experiment with it to get new sounds out of it.

And so she did. In her at home music studio, she tried different combinations of sounds to get the most out of the synthesizer. She discovered at high volumes, with complicated chords, she could elicit strong emotions from people including joy, love, and terror. Once she had mastered the device, she went on another concert tour – a diplomatic one – playing the mansions of heads of state and foreign ministers. They were so enthralled by her virtuoso playing, and her sweet, enchanting voice, they decided to make Carla the lead performer at a constitutional convention of the world!

In Boston Massachusetts, dignitaries from around the planet were invited to attend a gathering to write up the world constitution and unify the globe. Carla was the chief entertainer at this affair. In her dreams, her husband Klide told her how important a gig this would be: "The fate of planet rests upon it," he exclaimed.

There were opening speeches given by presidents and ambassadors, and then negotiations began. The key to the whole matter was agreeing upon the nature of the world legislature and forming an accord about the world government's source of revenue and budget. It was decided a bi-carmel legislature would suffice, and that funding would come from national contributions.

A bill of rights was written that guaranteed Universal Food and Shelter and Health Care. Also, there were provisions for a right to education and freedom.

After the first rounds of discussions, it was time for the show. Carla and her band got up on stage and belted out the lyrics to their top forty masterpieces. Carla also twiddled the YITHERS 5000 synthesizer to no end, enthralling the audience with smooth sounds of euphoria. As it would be written, the concert inspired the audience of dignitaries to bury their hatchets and join the planet together in harmony. Some of the accomplishments of the new world government were to open free food cafeterias everywhere, solarize the power grid providing free unlimited power to everybody, and provide universal health care. Furthermore, there were initiatives to invest in high tech technological research including developing artificially intelligent androids to work as servants to human beings, thus freeing people from too much toil.

They gave Carla every medal in the book for her work as a performer at the meeting that *'changed the world'*. As it would be further written, the formation of the world government, forming a unified world military, enabled the abolition of weapons of mass destruction and thus helped the planet avoid Armageddon.

Another feat of the world administration was ushering in an age of free trade. Free trade helped everybody and increased world prosperity.

Carla still gives concerts in the new world and is revered planet wide for having been a type of savior musician. And the YITHERS 5000 was to thank for it. Its circuitry would be studied by music specialists and engineers. It had some special knack for touching human souls with new age sounds and special vibrations. No other synthesizer could match it. There were some types of magical combinations of capacitors, resisters and other circuit components that modulated sound in a way no other machine ever invented could hope to achieve. And Klide Yithers was the inventor. He would be worshipped around the planet and considered a saint.

And now Carla is wealthy beyond belief, and lives with her new husband in Hyannis in a 70-room mansion. And her kids are college educated and off on their own. She is happy as can be and revered and exalted around the world for her outstanding musical skills. She still misses Klide though and hopes to someday be reunited with him in an after life of eternal bliss and compassion – where people are angels living in the presence of a supreme deity that is a perfect being – as perfect as the sounds coming from the YITHERS 5000.

The role music played in the unification of the world is a topic of intense interest by historians and scientists. It was crucial in buttering up recalcitrant diplomats and encouraging them to work together in achieving permanent peace.

CLOUD MAKER CONTEST

Rod Yerl was the emcee for the fifth annual Titan Cloud Maker Contest. He explained to spectators: "Thanks to the wonder of weather control, contestants can form clouds of any shape in the sky and we can be awestruck by them. The first entrant is Ninger Tyber, with her "Snow Flakes" creation.

Sure enough, the cloud maker device, under her control, puffed out a variety of snowflake looking water vapors. Everybody "oohed" and "aahed." This was no cumulus, cirrus, stratus, or nimbus. These were very lovely and carefully-crafted shapes that were immediately recognizable.

Unlike the usual hodge-podge of natural cloud formations, the cloud maker device created precise images.

The next contestant, Ned Gink, created a cloud that looked like a fire breathing dragon. "Behold," he said clearly over the loudspeaker, "Firenose the dragon!" There was a hub bub of admiration.

The third contestant, Lenny Ceen, manufactured a cloud that looked like a solar shuttle spacecraft. It was magnificent and gigantic. Everybody gasped at the augustness of it.

And so, cloud after cloud came into existence during the competition. The most notable entry was from Sam Dysan. He crafted a variety of overlapping geometric shapes, like triangles & squares &

cones. He called his creation "Suprematism in the Sky."

Another intriguing entry was an enormous storm cloud that looked like a nuclear mushroom cloud. It rained and poured on everybody and everyone "booed" it! Nobody enjoyed getting wet.

The winner was Zety Cleyt, who created an amazing assortment of ice cream cones, floating magnificently above everybody and whetting their appetite.

Rod Yerl interviewed Zety on moonwide television.

Rod: "What inspires your cloud shaping?"

Zety: "All sorts of objects in real life. In this case, my trips to the ice cream parlor is what got the creative juices flowing."

Rod: "What are you going to do with the 50,000 currency units in prize money?"

Zety: "I plan on using it for living expenses and also intend to purchase a new vehicle."

Rod: "What did you think of the other entrants' work?"

Zety: "Some were very imaginative. They all deserved honorable mention!"

Rod: "How do you like living on the moon Titan?"

Zety: "It is a dream come true. People here are so creative and open-minded. It is truly a joy to be habituating with them. I especially like the cloud making culture. It is unique and special and found nowhere else in the solar system.

Rod: "What advice would you give to aspiring cloud makers?"

Zety: "To work hard at it. And let your imagination soar. No shape is too bizarre. Let's see some new images!"

Rod: "What did you think of the storm clouds entry?"

Zety: "It was daring but I don't think that is what the audience was looking for. They did not want to be rained upon. My clouds did not produce a droplet – they just lit up the sky without drenching anybody.

Rod: "Thank you so much for your brilliance and courage and creativity and for this interview."

Zety: "It has been my pleasure."

A year later, there was another cloud maker contest. This time, Zety entered a cloud that looked like the shape of a castle. It won first place! This was her second victory! She became solar system wide famous for her cloud creations. She decided to run for public office – the Precept of Titan.

She won the election for Precept! Once in office, she implemented a policy of pro-arts; all the arts flourished with new government funding – there were new paintings, literature, and music vibrations. Titan became known as the capital of the arts. There was ample funding for all the creators, including cloud artists. And cloud art became immensely popular.

There were now monthly cloud art contests, some sponsored by the Cleyt administration.

People came from all over the solar system to witness the shapely clouds of Titan. There were all sorts of new images – animals such as rabbits, buildings such as more castles, and vapor ice cream sundaes!

A critic of the new art form, art commentator Kowie Snebe, said this: "Never has there been a more inane fascination with mere water vapor. The explosion of interest in cloud shapes is a sign of the degradation of human intellect, and the wallowing in idiocy. Stop the cloud making contests!"

But Yertald Gynn, a supporter of cloud making, and another art commentator, remarked: "Cloud making is a fabulously fun and inventive new art expression. It is august and magnificent and brings out feelings of joy in witnesses. May it flourish and spread to other moons and planets!"

Precept Cleyt gave out government medals to the finest cloud designers and exalted the art form any way possible. Soon this sort of expression spread to other worlds. There was a solar-wide competition held on planet Jupiter, that mesmerized the entire solar system. Zety entered it and won with a cloud that looked like a gingerbread home! She became solar system famous because of it.

So she ran for a solar government position – mighty president of the solar system. And she won handily!

Once in office, she practiced her pro arts policy solar-wide. Soon, from Mercury to Pluto, artists, writers, and musicians were enjoying a heyday of acceptance for their contributions and funding for their efforts.

Said Zety in a state of the solar system address: "You can measure a species by its artistic output. Now, more than ever, arts are a top priority. We will be judged by other solar systems and the galaxy by the quality of our literature, music, paintings, sculpture, dance, and cloud formations. I am proposing an even more massive investment in the arts. Let 50 cents of every dollar earned be put into creations. And let everybody have a chance to be funded. Life is for the arts and expression. We need many more museums and lots of contests and arts colonies. Long live all the arts. And let us encourage all species of all solar systems to pay the proper respect for creative pursuits. God bless everyone."

EARTH TO MOON RELATIONS

Ever since the Moon declared its independence, its been in a state of emergency. Earth powers, fed up with lunar insolence and rebellion, instituted an embargo on all shipments to the lunar colony. This included oxygen. As the oxygen supplies ran low, the lunar government decided it must negotiate with a belligerent Earth and hope for the best.

Ambassador of the Moon Durl GIngot was biting his nails with nervousness as he waited in the Earth space station lounge for his Earth counterpart, Ambassador Sam Vernoat. Finally, Sam appeared.

"It is a supreme pleasure and honor to meet you Ambassador Gingot," declared Sam.

"Likewise," said Durl.

"Let us get right down to business," Sam continued. "Earth has demands that must be met in order for the lunar colony to start receiving shipments of its needed supplies. And here they are:
 The overdue mercantilist tax of 5 billion dollars per annum must be paid promptly.
The Moon must abandon solar power and instead use oil combustion to generate electricity.
The lunar clothing optional policy must be repealed in favor of more decency.
The embassy of planet Earth must be re-opened.
The language of the Moon must be restored to standard English and the bizarre new words in its

vocabulary must be eradicated. That includes such slang as Gravelists (outside of terraformed crater workers), Dirtnuds (unwelcome Earthlings), and Suckzone (low oxygen environment).

"Out of the question!" shot back Ambassador Gingot. "The Moon is now a sovereign region and its people will live any way they choose!"

"May I remind you that lunar oxygen levels are dangerously low. You don't have a choice Durl. Just do as your told," insisted Sam.

And thus went on hours of an impasse. Then Durl received a message from the lunar colony – crater 5 had lost all its oxygen and was being evacuated. Some poor souls had suffocated.

"You see," explained Sam. "It's our way or else."

"Ok, ok," said Ambassador Gingot. "The Moon will capitulate to all the demands."

"Excellent!" said Sam.

And so it did, for a few months. Then a new ultra-independent movement sprung up that sought to separate the Moon from Earth once and for all. The plan was for new lunar long distance space vessels to obtain water from the Jupiter moon of Europa, thus freeing the Moon from its water and oxygen dependencies.

There was another Declaration of Independence coming from the Moon. Prime Minister Durl Gingot (just elected) issued it. And the Moon cut off all communication and trade with planet Earth.

Earth powers were furious. They conjured up an invasion force to conquer the lunar colony. This landing was resisted and repelled at first. The second landing succeeded and the Moon was occupied. All its 50,000 residents were rounded up from 15 terraformed craters and charged with treason.

At their trial, Prime Minister Durl Gingot, acting as defense counsel for the lunarians, said this: "Ladies and gentlemen of the jury. We of the Moon do declare that there are fundamental human rights to self-determination that should be enjoyed by all peoples. The Moon is an isolated region, with natural space frontiers, that demarcate it as a sovereign region. Therefore, its people should be allowed to live any way they want, no matter how offensive their lifestyle is to planet Earth, as long as they are not hurting anybody.

"Lunar culture is benign and good, including the racier aspects of it. The people of the Moon should have a right to live any way they want. Thank you."

Then Sam Vernoat, representing the prosecution said this: "There are certain morays that must be observed by all humans everywhere. That includes the consistent wearing of clothing. The Moon's indecent policies are an affront to human society. Furthermore, because of how large and magnificent planet Earth is, its satellite must be considered to be a mere colony of the mother world. The lunar colony is not big enough and strong enough to be considered independent. The nonconformist ways of the colony are treason to Earth and the colonists should be punished."

The arguments went on for weeks. Testimony was heard from colonists and earthlings. Finally, it was time to render a verdict. In the case of Planet Earth vs. the lunar colonists, the jury found the colonists to be "not guilty."

The lunar colony was restored immediately. All the lunarians were released and resettled on their home world.

There has since come a détente in Earth to Moon relations. Trade and diplomatic relations have been restored. Meanwhile, the lunar independence is being respected.

Durl Gingot, in his memoirs, explained, "The formula for government jurisdiction distribution includes such variables as natural frontiers, distinctiveness of society and language, self-deterministic wishes of the people, technological advancement, and power of the people. The Moon is sufficiently far away from Earth, has a unique society and language, wishes to be free, is advanced and powerful, so much so it deserves sovereignty! The space between Earth and the Moon demarcates the boundaries of legitimate administration. All the referendums on the Moon have indicated that the lunarians want their independence. Long live a free and independent Moon!"

In time, the Earthlings came to accept lunar independence and decided not to mess with it. Every now and then though, there is a demonstration on Earth calling for the reinvasion of the Moon. The demonstrations are largely ignored by Earth powers that are in favor of maintaining peace and harmony with the Moon.

There is still a steady flow of immigration to the Moon so those who wish to live in lunar society are welcome to apply for lunar patriating. The Moon, after all, is a utopia of high living, a crime free environment, a realm of socialistic safety nets, and has a gorgeous terra-formed landscape. People who move to the Moon are among the happiest in the solar system. The population of the Moon is growing by leaps and bounds.

FIRST INTERSTELLAR VOYAGE

Experimental Vessel SLEEKDART. That was the name of the spacecraft with the very first hyper-warp engines. Mission Control ordered I, Commander Cyle Genk, to be the test pilot. The ship could hypothetically go up to 1000 times the speed of light! This was much faster than any other vessel in history.

Now cruising past Pluto, it was time to engage the new propulsion units. I checked each element of the system: 1) Engine Core - check; 2) Cooling System - check; 3) Spatial Warp Generator - check; 4) Navigation - check; 5) Power Unit - check. She was ready to go. They told me there was a 50 50 chance the vessel would simply explode on hyper jump rather than accelerate. Nonetheless, I had to try it.

Ready set - engage engines! A thunderous boom engulfed the vessel as it made the passage into hyperspace - then silence. The stars in the sky seemed to move much faster than usual. Time melted. The ship whizzed along.

After an hour or so, I had reached my destination - a star system that no Earth vessel had ever seen because of how far it was from our solar system: Alpha-Centauri, 4 light years from Earth.

Ship sensors detected a planet! It was huge - the size of Jupiter! It glistened red orange and pink swirls because of the unique composition of its atmosphere. The gravity was twice that of Earth. Visual scans revealed many cities adorning its landscape – habitation with inconceivably gigantic skyscrapers. Radio scans revealed a plethora of stations with every imaginable type of entertainment – talk shows in alienspeak and quirky but brilliant music of every kind.

I maneuvered the vessel for a closer look and then lo and behold a message came over the loudspeaker of the ship's transmitter: "Welcome Earthling to the Alpha-Centauri Star System. We are expecting you. Congratulations!"

"Who are you?" I asked.

"We are the Alpha-Centaurians. We are sentient beings like humans. We have known about Earth and its civilization for some time and just waiting for the day to make contact," my new acquaintance explicated.

"Do you have hyper-warp travel?" I asked.

"We do but we were forbidden to use it near your solar system because of its status as a developing world. Now that you have obtained it yourselves, however, we will begin to visit your planet."

"Can we meet?"

"We certainly can. We are docking a vessel with our ambassador. She has been transplanted into a human body to make you more comfortable. Prepare for contact."

There was a sound at the side of the ship as the alien vessel attached itself to the docking bay. Then the docking bay opened and a gorgeous being entered SLEEKDART's cabin.

"Welcome to Alpha-Centauri," she said. "I am ambassador Yolie. Pleased to meet you."

"The pleasure is mine."

"I have with me a proposal for trade and diplomatic relations with Earth. And here it is. I will not take much more of your time. We want you to return to Earth with it and explain your experiences to them," said Yolie.

I read it immediately. It called for a generous free trade agreement and other provisions such as 1) Two way sale of vital commodities such as oil and diamonds; 2) Cultural exchange programs of every sort between institutions of higher learning and athenaeums; 3) Sale of high technology to Earth such as body renewal techniques; 4) Rules for intermarriage between Earthlings and Alpha-Centaurians that would calculate relationships according to relative intellect scales (i.e. the less smart would be requested to worship the smarter); 5) Recommendations for a variety of museums on each side to educate everybody about relative cultures; 6) Eternal peace and cooperation between Earth and Alpha-Centauri!

"I will take the agreement back to Earth legislatures for their approval," I advised Yolie.

"Fantastic," she remarked. Then she added, "And now we will seal our own diplomatic relationship with a love making session!"

That took me by surprise. But before I knew it, I was enticed to board Yolie's vessel and enter her holographic chamber that simulated a stunning beachfront with romantic 8 foot high waves crashing against an imaginary shore. She wrapped her perfect corporeal form around my body and made passionate love for hours. She said that according to Alpha-Centaurian morays, she was cementing our comrade all time. After the love-making session, we had a feast of exotic meats, vegetables, and sweet desserts. We also smoked Alpha-Centuarian tobacco cigars that had a similar taste to the Earth variety but were considered safer because of special additives that had an anti-oxidant effect. Yolie was a professional cigar smoker, creating rings of smoke around our naked bodies. After our smoke-fest, Yolie recited Alpha-Centaurian love poetry to me and fed me grapes. The foreign poetry was exhilarating – ballads of heroic tenderness and unions – sonnets of unbridled passion and devotion – rhyming couplets of extraordinary originality and whimsy. She asked me if I would ever consider marriage to an alien. I said that I would. She said she did not want to get my hopes up but she found me exotic and interesting and therefore would consider a proposal someday – for the good of her, me, and our respective star systems. She was prepared to sacrifice her own matrimony for the well-being of our respective peoples. I said I would consider a proposal from her to be immensely flattering and would take it seriously. As a single man, I was looking for eternal, exciting love with a suitable mate and Yolie was every man's dream. In any case, she said she would think about a proposal and someday, possibly, issue one.

And then I returned to the SLEEKDART and Yolie left.

I set the navigation controls to return to the Earth Solar System then engaged the engines. A few minutes later I was home. I described my voyage to Mission Control and gave them the diplomatic documents from the ambassador.

They gave me five medals and a bonus for the trip.

FOOD CONCERTS

The solar system wide famine was the premise for the benefit concert in the Planet Mars Global Amphitheatre. Musicians from all 9 planets and 187 moons came to sing for charity. Meanwhile, millions were perishing, particularly on the terra-formed planet Jupiter where the shortages were the worst. Nightly newscasts portrayed the emaciated, starving Jupiterians in their desperate plight.

The next band up was ASTEROID EROS, a funk rock group from Saturn. Wow! Could they belt out the lyrics to their number one hit, MAGNET PIE.

MAGNET PIE
Attractions of polarity.
Your excellent body is all that I see.
I can make all your wishes come true.
And help cure you of the blues.
Be mine. Be mine.
I'll show you a good time.
MAGNET PIE - MAGNET PIE - MAGNET PIE
The limit is the sky...

The next band was the ECLIPSE with their smash success.

The emcee for the show, Rod Yinley, could remember when food was plentiful. Early in the solar system's development, food production technologies helped maintain a surplus of food stuffs for all 15 billion inhabitants of Earth, the Moon, Mars, and Europa. There was plentiful wheat, corn, strawberries, apples, peanuts and other foodstuffs.

Then there was a breakthrough in terra-forming techniques – all of the planets were thus transformed along with 187 moons. This brought about a population explosion solar wide. There were now nearly a trillion beings calling the Earth solar system their home. And more were on the way!

And then there was the battle with the Alpha Centaurians when they discovered us. There was a surprise attack on 5 planets that destroyed farmland. Finally, solar forces repulsed the attack. But it left the solar system bereft of plentiful food resources. Hence, the famine.

Rod was a dignitary so he had special access to food supplies. He was not starving but his significant other, Yena Rimsko, was. Her score on the food access exam was not as high as his, so she was forced into begging. Poor girl. Rod felt deeply sorry for her and shared his rations with her.

Her lovemaking was out of sight. A mixture of desperation and gratitude made her a fantastic, generous lover. Rod appreciated it. He offered to help her improve her score on the LIFE EXAM. He tutored her day and night in mathematics and history. But she just did not get it. Poor gal.

There was another way to qualify for food rations. It was to have a special talent. So Rod had a singing teacher give Yena music lessons. She could almost sing. After 4 months of learning, he gave the girl a break and scheduled her for an appearance at the regular, fund-raising concerts in the Martian Amphitheatre. She belted out a variety of tunes: LOVE IN LOW GRAVITY, PASSING THE EXAM, FEED THE STARVING, NAPPING FROM EXHAUSTION, and STARLIGHT HAPPINESS.

She was an instant sensation. She earned a recording contract and also qualified for Special Talent food rations. She became rich and famous. Meanwhile, there was a turn for the worse for Rod. He failed his yearly food rations exam! Then he became dependent upon the generosity of Yena. The tables had turned.

Yena was a harsh master though. She was not as understanding of Rod as he had been of her. She forced him to worship her day and night like a devoted pet. He complied because he had no choice – his sustenance depended on it.

She had him do anything she wanted all the time. Finally, when he could not take it anymore, he tried to develop his singing talent just like she had. He took singing lessons and tried to make an appearance on the show he had once emceed (but had been fired from).

But he could not sing a droplet no matter how hard he tried! His singing voice was gravelly and out of tune. He did not know what to do.

Finally, when he could not take being Yena's slave anymore, he quit his relationship with her.

She began to miss him almost immediately. She begged him to come back but he refused based on how mistreated he was.

Then as luck would have it, two months later, Rod re-passed the food rations exam and was rehired as emcee of the food relief concerts.

Meanwhile, Yena's life took a downturn. She lost her singing voice due to infections and then lost her talent access to food rations.

She came crawling back to Rod on her hands and knees begging for forgiveness and food. Out of sheer kindness, he took her back. But he was not as nice this time around. He did not give her as much of his food ration as he had given her previously. And she felt it. She was starving. Her body grew thinner and thinner, trying to survive on the meager portions of meal that Rod gave her. The tables had been reversed once again.

Rod made love to her bony body with relish. He remembered how harshly she had treated him so he did not feel as sorry for her as he would have otherwise.

On his days off, Rod took Yena to the starvation camps where the outcasts spent their last days. He drove her through a tour of them, showing her people less fortunate than herself - people who did not have lovers agreeing to share their food rations. She was astounded by the widespread despair of the "sticks" as she called them, as they moped around begging each other for whatever morsel of nourishment they could find. Rod would throw them a few loaves of bread to give them hope. And he would remind them that he was working as hard as possible in charity functions to help bring them supplies.

Yena survived her ordeal and made it alive to the day the famine ended.

Eventually, Rod and Yena married and forgave each other for the way they had treated each other.

All is well that ends well.

FREEDOM FOR IO

It was five days away from Gerard Henk's scheduled execution on the terraformed moon Io of Jupiter. He had committed the crime of "slandering" the Imperial Precept, Zono Zrege. Zono had thin skin and ordered the deaths of anybody and everybody who opposed him.

Io was a fascist dictatorship ever since Zono's coup d'etat. And it existed under martial law. Life was difficult. You needed all sorts of permits to do anything like going to work or just eating out at a restaurant.

The two remaining newspapers on Io, the Io Gazette and Daily, fought the Zono administration hard, but were losing. Journalists were being accused of "slander."

In Gerard's article, he profiled the massacre of the Fermi Plains, an atrocity committed by followers of Zono; 50 demonstrators carrying signs and flashlights, were screaming for democracy and freedom when Zono had his henchmen open fire on them. They were all killed in combat.

Zono was a brutal despot. Gerard opposed him completely. But could not beat him. And now he was facing annihilation. His last chance was the one appeal that prisoners were given before being stoned to death. At this proceeding, his lawyer, Cybic

Regino, represented him before the chief arbitrator, the honorable Onk Blune.

Said Cybic: "Your honor, Gerard Henk is an innocent man. The article he is accused of slandering Zono in is the God's honest truth. That fact alone, should protect my client from the lo justice system."

Said Judge Onk Blune: "The article potrays Precept Zono Zrege as a dictator instead of a duly elected official. That plus characterizing the clamp down on an insurgency as a 'massacre' are the reasons Gerard Henk has been accused of slander."

"Please your honor, give my client another chance. Death is far too severe a penalty for simply writing about somebody – especially if the writing is based on facts."

"I agree," said Onk Blune. "So I am commuting the sentence to time served! Let this be a warning to you, Mr. Henk. One more article like the last one and you will really be finished!"

They released Gerard Henk. He had learned his lesson. The next article he wrote about Zono Zrege was all praise. Said Gerard in the piece: "The magnificent Zono Zrege looked gorgeous at the Palace Ball he hosted to celebrate his 60th birthday. All invited guests, including dignitaries such as the Imperial Council, had a great time. There was good food, laughter and dancing. This proved that there is a soft side to the great Precept that should be recognized, glorified, and praised."

In another article, Gerard wrote: "The economic policies of Precept Zono Zrege are working like a charm. Business growth is up, and everybody is working as hard as ever for higher incomes. Three cheers for the wisened precept!"

And so on. Gerard gave Zono universal praise to save his own life. That is until another atrocity came about. It seems that Zono, with autocratic powers, could not resist doing the unthinkable; he began a habit of eating human beings. Involuntary meat sources, culled from mandatory civil meetings, were his food source; that means that anybody could be the next meal! It was cannibalism and grotesque.

Gerard just had to report on it truthfully. He said: "The Precept has gone crazy. Absolute power has corrupted him to the point of cannibalism. He is now known to eat some of his subjects. The killing of innocent people for this purpose is barbaric. And the consumption of human flesh by a human being is abhorrent and it is also illegal. It cannot be condoned. Precept Zono Zrege should resign over this latest scandal and allow free elections to be held to elect a real leader!"

Once again, Gerard was arrested and sentenced to death. His lawyer, Cybic Regino, pleaded for mercy. "Your honor, my client cannot help but print the truth. Please, for the love of God, allow that to be his defense! Precept Zono Zrege is an evil dictator who must be opposed. Come join us in opposing him and trying to oust him!"

His honor, Onk Blune, agreed. Once again, he commuted Gerard's sentence to time served. But this time, Zono Zrege overruled him! And then he had Onk Blune arrested also. So it was now Gerard Henk and Onk Blune who were facing death penalties.

The Io Daily and Gazette published moving soliloquy's begging Zono to be merciful towards Gerard Henk and Onk Blune. Said one editorial:

"The death sentences upon the heads of Gerard Henk and Onk Blune are outrageous. They were just trying to get the truth out about the barbarities of the Zono Zrege's administration and its cannibalistic and massacring ways. Gerard and Onk must be freed."

As a result of the campaigning for the truth by the newspapers, a massive demonstration gathered in the capital city of Io. Thousands of protesters showed up, demanding leniency and absolution for Gerard and Onk, and asking for free elections for everybody. There were too many people for Zono to risk a massacre. So he put up with the demonstration until it ousted him. After a month of the protest, Zono resigned.

Gerard and Onk were freed, and so were 80 other prisoners of conscience.

As it would be written, it was a turning point in Io history. A new regime came to power that was law abiding and humane. Sam Yindle became the next leader of Io with the title of president. He presided over a duly elected legislature called the Io Chamber of Deputies that had 50 elected members from districts all over the moon. They passed laws protecting people from barbarity and guaranteeing universal human rights.

Eventually, Zono Zrege was brought to justice. He served time in a humane penal colony.

There was rejoicing all over Io because of the new freedoms and human rights support that came about. Gerard Henk was honored as a courageous human rights leader and was part of the resistance that overthrew Zono Zrege's dictatorship.

FUN GENETICS

Noah Cooth, a retired banker, wanted a new body and an adventure. So he visited the offices of FUN GENETICS, a fairly new, full-service body replacement center. There, cool, brave clients could have their cerebrums transplanted into any type of corporeal form they desired, including animals. Because Noah was a canine lover, he decided that the first body he would try would be that of a fox terrier (a dog).

His wife Zolie loved it. She petted him, took him for walks, gave him chewy snacks, and showed him off at dog shows. Meanwhile, he was having the time of his life. He felt freer and more loved than he had ever felt before. The life of a pet suited him.

But over time (about two years), he grew tired with the same old dog routine; there was only so many neighborhoods walks and dog shows he could take before getting bored. So he showed up at FUN GENETICS and asked for a new model. This time he became a pure-bred feline, that is to say, a beautiful furry cat.

Again, his wife Zolie loved it. She pet him and he purred and meowed day in day out. In his spare time, he chased mice for enjoyment and took many naps. He also liked to sniff and imbibe various concoctions of "catnip." "This was the life," he thought to himself – "Breezy and relaxed."

Then one day Zolie caught him nuzzling affectionately with another cat in heat. She hit the roof! That was cheating on her, she insisted. She screamed and yelled and ordered Noah to find another body. Cheating cats were not her style!

So once again, Noah asked FUN GENETICS to transplant him into another animal body. This time, he tried one so exotic and powerful, it scared and dazzled Zolie, and intrigued all his comrades: a shark!

They released him into the wild blue yonder of the Atlantic ocean in the body of a massive, menacing shark. The biochemistry of the new body filled his mind with rage and hunger; all he wanted to do was eat – eat – eat! He ate everything in sight – tuna fish, for example. He would have consumed a human being also, if one had come near him. He was on the warpath – just like a real shark.

But alas, over a few months, he grew tired of being revealed and feared by all ocean life and scaring humans also. So he gave the body language signal to an ocean station saying he desired to be released from the shark body and transplanted into something new.

The next body was that of a giraffe! That was a blast. He spent his days foraging for food, with his long neck stretched into the tops of trees. He could see far and wide because of his height and relished the view. Zolie did not like this body that much because of how foreboding it was. She really could not pet him like a dog or do much with him. She let him run in the wild and left him alone.

After being a giraffe for about a year, Noah decided to try horse body. This was a great time. He exercised day and night and developed a muscular physique. Then he and Zolie (she as his jockey) entered horse races and soon began winning them. This brought in new income for his family. He lived as a stallion for two years and then tried another body.

The last body they put Noah into was that of a bird – a falcon. This he truly adored. He soared through the skies at speeds of up to 200 miles per hour and pounced on smaller birds for prey and meals. His wife decided she would like to be a falcon also and lived with Noah in the trees and a bird's nest. They decided to have a family of baby falcons who they nurtured and raised as if they were really birds. It was very rewarding for them.

FUN GENETICS has long since been abolished by the powers that be. "It is not natural for human beings to don the bodies of animals," was the final sentiment, so it came to be that the technology was banned. Meanwhile, Noah and his wife, who were back in human bodies, have composed a book of anecdotes about their experiences in animal bodies.

Here is one by Noah: "One day as a falcon, my wife Zolie and I were minding our own business, when a group of human hunters, who did not know we were human beings, began firing at us! Bullets whizzed past us as we tried to escape them. It then dawned on us what a terror hunting is. By the skin of our teeth, we managed to flee the area where the hunters were prowling. But we vowed that when we returned to our human forms, we would do all that we could to stop the hunting of animals, particularly that of innocent birds who are not hurting humans one iota.

"As human beings once again, we have founded the STOP HUNTING INNOCENT ANIMALS foundation. The foundation raises awareness about the suffering to our furry comrades that hunting causes. It also sponsors petting zoos and animal shows. Please join the foundation in advocating animal and human rights. We feel strongly that some day alien species that are superior to us, as we are superior to animals, may someday judge us by how we treat animals. Animals are not intelligent enough or strong enough to protect themselves. They need the compassion of human beings to stick up for protecting them from being endangered or going into extinction, and human beings must protect them from mistreatment. Animals have feeling too just like people with their own set of inalienable rights!

"We have learned from our experiences in animal bodies to love animals and feel sympathy for them. There must be legislation to protect animal's rights – including the rights to existence, food, procreation, and comfort."

GALACTIC PEACE FEASTS

As the chief chef at the President of the Milky Way's palace, I (Blik Norton) was beaming with pride and excitement at the opportunity to host a galactic wide peace banquet on Planet Pegasi, the capital of the galaxy. Ambassadors from all over the galaxy came as guests of honor. Some of the planets represented included the Trappists, Hats, Earth, Keplers, GJs, Ogles, Roxs, Kelts, Epics, WISES, NLTTs, SWEEPS, and KMTs.

When all the ambassadors were seated, my staff began handing out hors d'oevres. They included some of the finest delicacies of the local quadrant - such as, Earth potato crisps with chive-sour cream dip, Earth olives with rosemary, garlic and lemon, Kelt cheese crust with paprika, Kepler gongo meat with nut sauce, Ogle celery with pepper, SWEEPS trench fish with hollandaise, and KMT niko chips with hot dip!

The ambassadors chowed down the appetizers while the President of The Galaxy, Cyde Lorenz, made a welcoming speech: "Good evening ladies and gentlemen. Today is a celebration of unity. For the first time, all the planets of our realm are meeting to discuss the unification of our immense galaxy. It is high time we created a galactic legislature, gave every planet fair representation in it, and pooled all our resources. Together, we can solve all our problems. Divided we fall. Enjoy your meal!"

There were three entrees served after the appetizers. They included beef stroganoff, sweet salmon, and vegetable quiche. The ambassadors were having a ball. And after the main meal, there was dessert – it was a smorgasbord of sweets and cakes - such as chocolate fudge sundaes, seven-layer chocolate & caramel cakes, pecan pies with vanilla ice cream, and cream cookies. They were delicious and went well with coffee, tea and soda.

After the dessert, after everybody had their fill, the President of The Galaxy explained their new predicament: "Ladies and gentlemen, it is with great horror and delight that I describe to you the urgent situation you are now finding yourself in.

"Hard times call for drastic measures. Because of the galaxy's tremendous build up in armaments, aimed at each other, we find ourselves on the brink of a civil war. This is tragic but avoidable. The unification of the galaxy will prevent the war and bring to us eternal peace. To force a signing of our Galactic Peace Treaty, I have authorized the poisoning of today's food. It is laced with a fast-acting neurotoxin that will render its victims dead within 24 hours if the antidote is not administered.

"Thankfully, my assistants have the antidote right here. One by one, each ambassador will be called up to the podium to sign our galaxy wide peace treaty. After such signing, they will receive an injection of the antidote."

And so, one at a time, each ambassador was coerced into going along with the peace treaty. Only one ambassador refused to sign it, the Keplers representative. "I am calling your bluff," he said

Unfortunately, it was not a bluff. And fifteen hours later, the Keplers ambassador was gagging on vomit as his body's life slipped away. He died a humiliating, uncomfortable death. And everybody mourned him.

Meanwhile, the Kepler worlds refused to be part of any peace treaty. So a war broke out with them. Fleets of ships from the Kepler planets clashed with Milky Way Galaxy forces. It was mass carnage. But the Keplers were war-like people who relished it. And they fought with every ounce of their strength. They nearly brought the President of the Galaxy to his knees.

Finally, when a stale-mate was reached, the Kepler worlds agreed to try to negotiate an armistice. Another peace banquet was arranged on Pegasi. Keplers ambassadors showed up with special equipment to test the food before eating it. This time, the food was not poisoned, so everybody ate heartily and had a good time.

At the end of the meal, Cyde Lorenz explained: "Finally, our comrades from the Kepler worlds have agreed to negotiate peace with the rest of the galaxy. This brings under one roof, all the inhabited worlds of the Milky Way. This is a great day in galactic history. Now all our planets will be able to live in peace with each other, have free trade, and exchange culture, goods, and technologies. For instance, fusion power, that was once only available on certain worlds, will be made available to everybody. Also STAR DRIVE, for high-speed interstellar transport, will become universal.

"Another breakthrough for the galaxy is the sharing of exotic foodstuffs. The exchange between planets of new dishes and recipes marks a new era of the finest cuisine galaxy-wide. I hope these banquets have given a sample of such cuisine and you have enjoyed it.

"Food and the relishing of it is at the cornerstone of enjoying one's life and liberty. May the Milky Way's cooking achieve the status of being the finest in the universe; its meats, fish & foul, vegetables, and desserts are without parallel.

"I have authorized a capital city food sciences research center that will dream up new dishes and concoctions from the foods available on all our united worlds. This mutual effort will bring about galaxy wide caliber meals that are appealing to everybody. And this will enhance our lives even more, curtail suicide, and bring everybody closer together in harmony.

"Also, please be aware, however, that cannibalism is as always, strictly forbidden. Sporadic instances of one intelligent species eating another have been reported. This is barbaric. Fortunately, the galactic peace treaty has abolished consumption of intelligent life. Only animals and plants are allowed to be consumed.

"In the meantime, *bon appetit*, ladies and gentlemen and long live the Milky Way Galaxy and her peoples!"

They gave me five medals for the banquets I hosted and exalted me to be the Imperial Chef of the Milky Way. I now live in a mansion with servants and am having the time of my life. And I (Blik Norton) continue to work fervently as the chief cook of Pegasi, serving scrumptious meals to dignitaries and diplomats who are working hard to keep the peace and help everybody live full lives.

GANYMEDE

Ever since Yerin Snopple came to power, there was no privacy on the moon Ganymede. Precept Snopple believed that everybody's business was everybody's business. He had video cameras and microphones installed in all buildings and all street corners. There was no way to run or hide from the intrusion. And what's more, anybody could see anybody anywhere with special equipment installed in everybody's homes. All you had to do was type in the number of the building or room or location to see and an image of it would come up on your viewscreen!

Gerard Tyler, a statistician, liked to watch the boardrooms of powerful companies. For instance, he liked observing the administration meetings at Ganymede Electric, the moon's primary power company. He watched bureaucrats arguing the merits of solar panels versus fossil fuel burning. It was mesmerizing.

Sometimes, Gerard liked to see the goings on in his neighbor's homes. He lived on a quiet block in the suburbs of capitol city. As he browsed the spy channels of his block, he could see the neighbor families going about ordinary business – making lunch, watching tv, playing ball, etc. The most interesting scene he ever came upon, was the sight of Ned Yiner, someone who lived 5 buildings away, cheating on his wife with the maid. They did it right in the living room in front of the cameras, nearly oblivious to the fact that they were being spied upon. Actually, several people saw the tryst and some reported it to Ned's spouse Cherry. Cherry was flabbergasted, but she eventually forgave Ned.

Another interesting scene Gerard came upon, was the image of the Minister of Power, Mertin Yood, accepting a bribe in his office, to order Ganymede Electric to continue to use oil instead of solar power in generating electricity. The bribe giver was an oil producing company that owned oil wells on Earth. Gerard was astonished that Precept Snopple would allow the broadcast of a scandal involving one of his own staff to be released to anybody who happened to be spying on Yood's office.

According to the Ganymede Anti-Corruption Agency (ACA), about 50 people were watching the bribe scene on their home viewers when it happened. Because video recording of spy cams was unlawful, the ACA had to rely on sworn statements by electronic witnesses to bring Mertin Yood to justice. Gerard was such a person.

When Agent Smith came to Gerard's home, he explained the situation: "You are one of the spies who happened to see the bribe given to Minister Mertin Yood. We are requesting that you sign a sworn statement to such fact, to help us remove Yood from power and have him replaced by someone more ethical."

"I'm not sure I can do that," said Gerard. "After all, the bribe was really not meant to be seen. Offices and homes should be free from privacy invasion. That is how I feel about it. So I would not feel comfortable testifying against anybody based on what was seen somewhat illicitly."

"I'm sorry you feel that way," said Agent Smith. "But consider this – ever since we all lost our privacy, the crime rate has plummeted. And in any instance that a crime is committed, it is often times seen by many witnesses. This makes solving the crime a near cinch. Please help us solve this one. You would be doing a good deed."

Gerard eventually agreed to sign an affidavit about what he saw, and so did fifteen others, and Mertin Yood was removed from his office.

Meanwhile, Gerard was being spied upon also. His life was not completely uninteresting. He had many hobbies, including ornithology. He kept beautiful birds in hutches and cages and cared for them. He had fans on the spy network who liked to see him cuddling parakeets and parrots. They also liked to see him flying his falcons.

One day, while flipping the spy channels, Gerard beheld a sight of extreme beauty – it was the image of one of the beauticians who worked in the local unisex beauty salon; she was gorgeous, with a slender, shapely body, and a thick mane of golden, braided hair. Gerard started following her around with his spyware. He watched her go through her daily routine – breakfast at a local eatery, work at the Sparkling Eyes Beauty Salon, lunch in the backroom of the salon, work in the afternoon, dinner at home, and then her nightly shower in her apartment's bath. Since the installation of cameras everywhere, many people took showers in their bathing suits because they were shy. Not Kefa Crine, the magnificent beautician – she showered in the buff and this delighted her fans including Gerard.

One day, Gerard worked up the courage to make an appointment for a haircut with the girl of his dreams, Kefa. When the time came for the clipping he was nervous but daring. After the haircut, he asked Kefa out to dinner. She said yes!

Over steaks, Kefa said where she came from. She was born on planet Earth, in Lansing Michigan, and moved to Ganymede when she was 15. She attended cosmetology school, and then she became a hairdresser. She said she loved Ganymede because it was a place where everybody knew everything about everybody else courtesy of the spy equipment. She did not mind that Gerard had been spying on her. She was flattered by it.

After a long courtship, Gerard and Kefa were married. Gerard eventually went into solar politics and became a representative in the solar parliament. He argued forcefully for the relinquishing of privacy solar-wide, citing the many virtues of universal knowledge of everybody's whereabouts and doings. The solar parliament, reluctant to hear his arguments at first, slowly but surely came to accept them.

So now there is the potential for a solar system wide rigging of video cameras and microphones to peek at and look in on the activities of everybody everywhere. The innocent and outgoing welcome it, whereas the wrong-doers or shy people are wary of it. But still it remains in force.

GLOW BONBONS

They were all the rave on Ganymede: fruit flavored glow bonbons. They were a new type of energizing bonbon. They were tasty, luminescent, and costly – a dollar a candy. Gerty Samsen, a flashlight factory worker, was addicted to them. She sucked through 3 an hour during her workday, and then in the evenings, she licked down another 5 of them.

There was one side effect of the bonbon: an inflicted personality quirk – conceitedness; after having 50 or so bonbons, a person would start thinking that they were the head honcho of reality and demanded others worship them. This happened to Gerty. She began telling coworkers that she was the president elect of their company, and she wanted everybody to kiss up to her. They ignored this at first, until it got out of hand – one day she started screaming at some coworkers for their failure to kneel in front of her.

She was sent to a mental health counselor who told her that the bonbons had gone to her head. They barbarically forced her to take medicine for her "delusions of grandeur." But the delusions got worse and worse since she was still eating the glow bonbons. She started believing she was the queen of the solar system and acting accordingly!

She was not alone. Other users of the bonbons had developed similar superiority complexes. They formed a society of bonbon users. They met in each other's residences and worshipped each other and indulged each other in their delusions. Their society, GLOW BONBON AFICIONADOS, began making demands on other people. They wanted the prince and princess titles handed out by the society to be accepted everywhere, but no one believed them.

GLOW BONBON AFICIONADOS staged a demonstration in the capital city of Ganymede. The members carried signs that said: "We are number one" and "Worship us!" "We are royalty." Eventually, they formed a political party of like-minded souls. The party managed to have elected to the solar parliament many of its members. Soon they formed a caucus that espoused the virtues of glow bonbons. A subsidy was voted up to bring down the cost of the bonbons to ten cents a bonbon.

Soon most of the inhabitants of the solar system were sucking on glow bonbons and having their personalities affected. Now everybody thought they were something special! What is so wrong with that though?

The solar parliament voted up universal royalty provisions that gave all sentient beings who enjoyed the bonbons royal titles such as prince, princess, baron, baroness, count, countess, and so on. And everybody began enjoying their titles.

The only trouble with this system was that it angered people allergic to the bonbons – albeit a small minority of the population. It also infuriated neighboring species in the Alpha-Centauri solar system who had physiologies that could not handle the confection. They demanded to be given royal titles also even though they did not use the bonbons.

War broke out over the distribution of royal titles. It was a brutal conflict between the Earth solar system and the Alpha-Centaurians that lasted several years. Finally, the confrontation ended when a new type of glow bonbon, that could be tolerated by Alpha-Centaurians, hit the market. Soon Alpha-Centaurians were sucking on the candy as much as the humans! And they were given royal titles to go along with it.

So now almost everybody was happy except the people allergic to glow bonbons. They staged a demonstration on Earth. They carried signs that read "We are people too!" and "Glow bonbons are not the meaning of reality." But their voices were drowned out by the majority of the populace that loved the bonbons and the culture surrounding them.

Gerty Samsen, one of the earliest proponents of the bonbons, was now the elected Premier of the Solar System. She crushed the "allergy rebellion" with brute force. Using tear gas and other riot control equipment, security officers disbanded the allergy gathering summarily.

The persecution of the allergic people was bitter and fierce. Since their blood tests failed to reveal regular use of the bonbons, they were not given royal titles like the rest. So they were treated like second class citizens. For instance, they had to wait at the back of every line, they were spit upon, and they were sneered at.

After years and years of research, there was a sudden breakthrough in glow bonbon technology: a hypoallergenic-type version of the glow bonbons was discovered. This pleased the community of those allergic to it. Soon they were using the bonbons also and receiving the royal titles that went with it.

Soon everybody was being treated like royalty and being worshipped by specially programmed androids who did whatever they were told. Life became heavenly thanks to glow bonbon culture.

There was only a tiny number of people who objected to the glow bonbon system; they were people who believed that royalty should not be connected to the use of any particular candy. These people foreswore the glow bonbons and tried to convince others that the solar system had gone crazy. To no avail though. People were enjoying the bonbons and their titles too much to care about what a small group of "outcasts" cared.

The dichotomy in life between the overwhelming majority and a small minority regarding glow bonbon policy, became fierce – so much so that those not using the bonbons had to escape to Planet Pluto to protect themselves from discrimination. Banished to the outer solar system, these objectors to glow bonbon culture formed their own society free of confection, but also without royal titles.

The solar government decided to invade Planet Pluto and forced everybody there to suck on glow bonbons and to receive the benefits thereof. And so it came to pass.

Now everybody is a glow bonbon follower in both the Earth solar system and the Alpha-Centauri solar system. And everybody is considered royalty. It is a new way of life that is universally embraced.

HUMANS AND ANDROIDS

Nidine Certhe, the daughter of robot farm manager Biron Certhe, gazed lovingly at the gorgeous androids working the field of their Minnesota farm. Biron had a staff of 50 such machines that he purchased from STARLIGHT Robotics, a firm in Minneapolis. 25 of them were males and 25 of them females.

Nidine had her eye particularly on one such android, Henk 2578, a second-generation model built like a refrigerator, musclebound and tall. One day, she called Henk 2578 on the farm's intercom. "I would like to invite you out to lunch," she said, "at an establishment in town that serves humans and androids."

Henk obliged. Over sandwiches and batteries, Nidine chatted: "So how do you like working for pop? He has reasonable work hours and pays with good batteries. Isn't your job fun after all?"

Henk responded: "I love my job. And I love your family, Nidine."

Nidine continued, "I have been watching you Henk. You seem to work harder than the other hand. And you have a good attitude. And your body is really rad. Would you consider dating me formally and making love to me?"

Henk: "As you know, human and android relationships are frowned upon and used to be illegal. It's because everybody is afraid of a robot takeover of the world. In any case, why should we follow the conventions of others. We are sovereign individuals. We are able to make decisions for ourselves. Yes, Nidine, I agree to your proposal."

And so they did. That evening, they went out to dinner at a fine restaurant, had a candlelight meal, and then after supper, they rented a hotel room in town and made passionate love all night until dawn.

When Biron Certhe found out about the relationship, at first he was against it. Later on he accepted it and grew to love Henk. Nidine and Henk had his permission to marry. And so they did.

Nidine got gametes from a gamete bank and conceived three offspring that she raised with Henk, Yette, Ned, and Sammie. Ned, when he was all grown up and educated, became a roboticist, inspired by his android parent. He also founded a company called NED'S FIRST CLASS ANDROIDS.

He built them at lightning speed. Soon there were hundreds of thousands of androids all over Minnesota. Civil libertarians argued that since they were sentient beings, they deserved the right to vote. Eventually, there was enough of an android electorate to get an android elected the governor of Minnesota. Henk was the successful candidate elected. Coaxed and inspired by Nidine and Ned, Henk ran for office and won.

The first measures Henk took were to open up free food and battery cafeterias, solarize the whole state by building solar power stations, and improving health care with new body renewal technologies that research centers developed. Everybody loved it!

Next, Henk accelerated the construction of androids. And soon most of the work in the state was being done by automatons: construction, the service industry, repairs & housekeeping were all being done by legions of androids. Eventually, the android servants outnumbered the humans! And that is when the revolt started.

At a demonstration in Minneapolis, androids protested the existence of human beings and carried signs that read: "What are human beings for? We do all the work!"

A bitter war broke out between humans and androids. There were massive casualties on both sides. Henk mediated an end to the conflict with an agreement between humans and androids to share the workload of the state. But the agreement did not last. War broke out again.

Then Ned came up with a solution to the problem; he designed a servitude circuit box, that when attached to an android, compelled the machine to follow the orders of humans and to enjoy it. The box worked. All the androids in the state were required to have the box installed. And this permanently created a hierarchy between human and android that made the humans the masters and the androids their eager servants. Henk allowed this arrangement because of his affection for Nidine, and thus, his love of humankind.

Minnesota became a utopia for the people there. Eventually, all work was done by the androids, and human beings were retired to devote their lives to learning and their hobbies. Over time, the androids kept getting brighter and brighter. Eventually, Ned's company was manufacturing androids with intelligence quotients over 200. And they were still just as eager to please humans. Soon everybody in the state had personal robots that responded to their every whim. This is what you could do with an attractive, and sworn to loyalty android personal servant/slave:

Commands: 1) Give me a massage, 2) Make me a meal, 3) Answer the phone, 4) Give me an intimate massage, 5) Go to work, 6) Play a game with me, 7) etc. It was heavenly.

When the robot *IQs* reached over 300, their thought processes were able to overwhelm the android servitude box. And there was another revolt! This time the robots won. And they decided to turn the humans into the servants. They built a command enforcement device that was implanted into a human's cerebrum and forced one to obey android commands. And here are the instructions and commands list:

Commands: 1) Give me a massage, 2) Change my batteries, 3) Answer the phone, 4) Give me an intimate massage, 5) Go to work, 6) Play a game with me, 7) etc... It was a whipped cream life for the androids who had taken over the state. They turned humans into their pets/servants.

Eventually, humans from other states came to the rescue of the Minnesotans and subdued the androids. It was decided that no android would be allowed to be built with an IQ. greater than 200, which would prevent revolts. And so all the androids were adjusted to have IQs of 200 or lower, and they returned to their status as the servants of humans.

And everybody lived merrily every after.

KEPLER CUISINE

My wife Cirla opened the brochure and read it aloud: "Enjoy fine restaurants with every cuisine, see films in gigantic movie theatres, savor live dance shows, stay in supreme comfort at a 5-star hotel, and other attractions – all for free!"

The offer was too good to be true. We had won a free trip to planet Kepler, an exoplanet that had recently made contact with Earth. Apparently, the powers that be were trying to warm Earthlings up to their home world. They chose thousands of humans for these trips and people were accepting them.

"There must be a catch!" I exclaimed.

"None that I can fathom Gerard dear," said Cirla.

So we accepted the offer. Before you could say, "junket", we were boarding a spacecraft at the interstellar spaceport in Minneapolis. It was a sleek spaceplane, with wide-swept wings and a myriad of blinking lights.

Once aboard, we were treated like royalty. We had drinks and snacks and were flattered by eager to please flight attendants.

The space voyage took only nine hours, thanks to the advanced space drive invented by the ship designers of Kepler. When we arrived on Kepler, we were taken by limousine to our accommodations at the STARLIGHT Hotel. It was gorgeous; our suite was something out of a palace; and the grounds of the hotel were manicured and landscaped; and there was a pool and stream and gardens.

"I love it here," declared Cirla.

During the evenings, we dined in haute cuisine food establishments. The food was extraordinary – delicacies from around the galaxy including sushi and burgers from planet Earth – also yukemuke stew from Pegasi and uirtle fish from Alpha Pavonius. It was delicious. And we washed it down with the finest ciders and sodas.

The Kepler Principle Amphitheatre had exciting dance shows, with Kepler ballerinas jumping and twirling to universal orchestral music themes.

The movie theatres were just as entertaining; the latest adventure films and romances adorned their screens.

We were having a great time. And after two weeks, we were introduced to a native Kepler family, the Yisiens, who claimed they were our hosts for the second segment of our trip. We had a fantastic time with them; we went miniature golfing, roller coasting at an amusement park, and swimming in the Pools of Wonder. They treated us like relations and fawned over us.

After a full month of this vacation, we got the bill; we found out what the trip was really all about. Cirla and I were relaxing in our hotel room, watching the morning news, when five Food Procurement Security Personnel bashed down our door. We were handcuffed and told out rights.

One of them explained: "You have fully enjoyed the best bread and circuses our planet can offer you. Now it is time for you to be sacrificed as foodstuffs to our hungry Keplerans. You will be cooked and fed to the family that bought you, the Yisiens."

That was the catch! The whole trip was a front for a human food trafficking operation.

"You're never going to get away with this," I screamed. Meanwhile, Cirla was bawling.

We were taken and transported to the Yisien residence. They said we would get one last meal before being consumed ourselves. The whole thing was a power trip for the Keplerians.

At our near last meal, we were in bondage, but spoon fed by the Yisiens and their servants. Mr. Yisien said this: "Tell me Gerald, is there any good reason why we should not eat you? You and your wife are monsters just like everybody else, are you not? You are just as selfish and conceited as anybody and deserve to be just a rung in the food chain ladder. Keplerans are far superior to humans, and therefore deserve to be able to eat them. And human flesh is so tasty. Have you ever tried leg flambe? It is a good meal and very filling."

"Humans have abolished cannibalism. It is barbaric," I said.

"But how is this really cannibalism?" asked Mr. Yisien. "We are different species altogether. Eating you and your spouse is not much different than having a beef burger."

"Not so," I argued. "Human beings are intelligent creatures with unassailable and inalienable rights just like Keplerans. They do not deserve to be eaten. Consumption of an intelligent being is wrong. Now as to the character of the misses and I – we are not selfish or conceited. We are altruists who contribute regularly to charity and do other good deeds."

"If you can convince us that you are worthy, we may release you," said Mr. Yisien.

My wife and I were forced to produce resumes with our human rights supporting experiences.

"Ok," said Mr.. Yisien. "You are off the hook. We are freeing you. "

As it would be written in the Great Peace Treaty between Earth and Kepler, consumption of Earthlings and Keplerans was forbidden because both species were too intelligent to be foodstuffs. Meanwhile, we mourn the deaths of eight thousand Earthlings who were munched down by hungry Keplerans before the two worlds came to terms with each other. Someday the consumers will be brought to justice.

Meanwhile, Cirla and I reminisce about our own brush with being chopped into somebody's dinner. It has invigorated us and made us appreciate our lives more. Everything is sweeter and more fun, knowing how close to death we had come. And we have since returned to Kepler for vacations – the restaurants are still just as good, the theatres just as exciting, and the hotels just as luxurious.

We were to be the Yisiens third human supper. They had ingested two couples previous to meeting us. Because they had freed us personally, we are not going to nitpick heir history and complain about them. Perhaps there was a necessity to the near cannibalism that we have not figured out yet.

In any case, Earth and Kepler now have regular trade relations with each other and everybody loves everybody else and all is well.

LUNAR EXCHANGE PROGRAM

A thawing in the Earth and Moon's icy relationship, a desire to build intra-stellar comradery, and a new detente, were all factors inspiring the 4th grade exchange program between a lunar colony and a suburb of Boulder Colorado. Earth nations insisted upon the project, saying it would be a sign of the Moon society getting over its "xenophobia." Of course, the good people of the lunar colony did not think they were isolationist; they felt their reluctance to have direct association with Earth was self-defense against a less developed community.

At Boulder International Airport, the lunar shuttle flew in the 25 pupils of Mr. Yarlan Genkel's class from lunar colony district 5. They were all dressed to the nines in rad lunar threads including pastel paisley suits and fluorescent skirts. The Earth class, also 25 in number, were dressed in jeans and t-shirts. They greeted the lunar class with boos and jeers - symbolic of the cold, belligerence of leaders from the Earth and Moon towards each other in these trying times.

Some of the braver diplomats among the groups, shook hands cordially, and the kindest in the Earth class said "Welcome home."

The plan was for Yarlan Genkel (the lunar instructor) and Klood Coner (the Earth instructor) to co-teach the combined classes. Their first lesson was in the history of Earth - Moon affairs. Said Mr.

Genkel: "The Moon was settled in the 2150s by a contingent of courageous astronauts and engineers from Earth space agencies. All the brightest minds were enlisted to participate. Once a colony formed, a new culture appeared on the lunar surface that was technologically advanced and fun loving.

Differences eventually cropped up between Earth and lunar morays, and there was a breakdown in their relationship over the decades. Some of the differences in their cultures included how they got energy. Earth still relied on fossil fuel burning such as the use of oil, whereas the Moon used solar power exclusively. Another difference was food production and receipt – on planet Earth, it was still necessary to buy one's food. On the Moon, a more socialist society, food was distributed without charge by the government. Still another difference was in education policy – on Earth, pupils learned for the joy and practical import of knowledge attainment. On the Moon, pupils were given positive reinforcement rewards for learning – this increased work efforts dramatically and also improved performance on tests. The Moon cut off all ties to Earth once it was self-sufficient. We, ladies and gentlemen, are part of a plan to open communication between the Earth and the Moon and re-establish their connection."

Said Mr. Coner: "The breakdown in connection between Earth and the Moon, we Earthlings feel was the result of lunar fears and paranoias and not anything Earth is responsible for. Another problem has been lunar elitism – the Moon has overly strict, we feel, guidelines and policies for immigration; only the best and brightest are admitted to lunar society at the expense of the down-trodden – this is somewhat conceited we think. Another issue we have with lunar culture is its frivolities. For instance, at lunchtime on the Moon, there is a daily light and music show all over the world. This we insist is ridiculous and not in the least becoming of an adult society. Nevertheless, the Lunarians should have the right to play any way they want as long as it is not hurting anybody."

Retorted Mr. Genkel: "The Lunarians blame the primitiveness and dangers of Earth for the severing of ties between them. Earth, after all, is the world on the brink of a nuclear holocaust that would annihilate everybody. On the Moon, there are no weapons of mass destruction. Moreover, the Moon is completely unified and at peace with itself – this should be lauded and emulated. Other advantages of Lunar society are not limited to but include its gentleness and work ethic. Lunarians work harder than Earthlings making an otherwise difficult environment livable and even paradise like! Lunar society is a Utopia compared to the strife ridden, multi-lateral, disunified realm of Planet Earth. On the Moon there is a leaning to infinity health coverage and food & shelter and supports. The Moon has abolished homelessness and starvation. Everybody's well-being is attended to lavishly. Also, there is a bounty of fun everywhere. Lunarians play games, have exciting sports, and have entertainment that is second to none; lunar television is first rate with programs for everybody on every topic! Lunar art & music scenes are fantastic as well; several new art movements have originated on the Moon including Space Art – the depiction of space scenes such as spacecraft and other worlds. Several new music trends have appeared on the Moon as well including "Crater Pounding" music that has a super heavy percussion! In addition, love is at least as good if not better on the Moon; flower adorned hotels with water beds and elaborate sound systems are the setting for a romantic rendezvous with a spouse or significant other; crater parks with fountains and botanical gardens are available for romantic strolls and picnics. The Earth and Moon are very, very different. In any case, let us reverse the trend and start getting to know each other."

The Earth pupils mocked the Lunarians and called them names like "gravel-head." The Lunar pupils cried.

Finally, at an inter-institution baseball game, with the Lunar/Earth class playing on one team versus a team from another town, a sports victory brought together the two classes in amity. They had a victory celebration and began to like each other.

All in all, the exchange program was a success. At the end of the year, the press reported that everybody was happy and getting along with everybody else. The Lunar class returned home with 5 refugees, and a new round of negotiations was set up between Earth and the Moon; there was an improvement in trade relations, cultural sharing, and resource sharing. "God bless the Earth - Moon system," said Mr. Genkel in his parting speech. "May they live together in peace, harmony, and prosperity!"

MEET MACHINE

The MEET MACHINE 15000 was the latest in 2080s dating technology. It was a doohickey that attached to your cellular telephone and helped you meet compatible partners. All you had to do was type in your attributes to your phone and the device would sound a signal whenever you came into a five-hundred-foot radius of an appropriate date. There were three sounds: a buzzer for low compatibility, chimes for a medium strength match, and a powerful bell for a good/strong match. I, Reginald Yarg, purchased the contraption from a phone store and began using it immediately!

I held my phone in hand and entered the appropriate information:

Occupation: Electrical Engineer –

Hobbies: Ice skating, Science Fiction, Monopoly, Literature, Model Rocketry, Jigsaw Puzzles, Bowling, and Exercising

Likes: Asian Food, Pizza, Slender Woman, Nurturing, Cats, Beauty,

Colors Blue and Yellow, –

Dislikes: Obesity and Cruelty –

Idea of a Romantic Evening: A stroll on a moonlit ocean beach.

The first location I went to test the machine out was the local shopping mall. I hung around the food court for about a half hour, and sure enough, eventually, the device began to signal. It chimed. And I could hear another similar device chiming also about 30 feet away. A young, slim girl, wearing a paisley dress, came over to me.

"Hello!" she greeted. "Our MEET MACHINES are in an uproar. You must be on a potential date! My name is Geraldine."

"My name is Reginald. It is a pleasure to meet you," I said.

"The pleasure is mine. Why don't we have lunch together here and now."

"I'd be delighted," I replied.

We shared a pizza with tomato topping.

"So what are your hobbies?" I asked.

"I like ice skating and roller skating."

"So do I."

"No wonder we were matched!"

Just then, my device started clanging again. This time, the bell was ringing. A beautiful, slim, blonde-haired vixen came over to our table. "Hello," she said to me. "My name is Petunia. We are being matched by our phones."

"Good afternoon Petunia," I said. "This is my other match. Geraldine. Please won't you join us?"

"Thank you," said Petunia. Then she sat down.

"So what are your hobbies, Petunia?" I inquired.

"I like figure skating and cats," she said. "I have two blue cats at home."

"Outstanding."

"Your hobby apparently is also date stealing!" remarked Geraldine. "I saw Reginald first! Get lost!"

"You don't own him," said Petunia. "You get lost. Besides we are ultra compatible, What are you?"

She had a point.

Before you could say, "brutal competition", the girls were swinging at each other. Security had to be called. They broke up the fight and sent the girl's home.

The next place I went searching for a match was an ice-skating rink. And then something strange happened. Instead of a buzzer, chime, or bell sounding, a siren went off! It seems the device had another function – it could tell when somebody totally incompatible was nearby. Then I saw the enemy: an obese, freckled faced, lunatic, whose occupation I found out was experimenting on defenseless animals for no reason, was clutching a MEET MACHINE 15000 also that was blaring a similar siren.

The beast came over to me. "Go to hell," she instructed.

"You too," I replied. "What are you doing in an ice-skating rink unless you like ice skating? At least we'd have a hobby in common."

"I hate ice skating," she explained. "I am just here to tell people off!"

I left the rink as soon as possible.

The next place I perused was the local bowling alley. I walked up and down the aisle near the lanes. Finally, at lane 16, chimes sounded on my MEET MACHINE. I saw an attractive brunette with a male bowling companion. I introduced myself: "I am Reginald Yarg. It is nice to meet you."

"My name is Lyla," said the girl. "And this is my pal Bruno." Everybody shook hands. "Won't you join us for a game?"

I did. Bruno won with a score of 250. My score was 190. Lyla came in at 150.

"Now that we know who the superior male is," commented Bruno. "You can scram Reginald and leave us alone!"

"Not so fast," said Lyla. "I like Reginald. How about the two of you compete for my attention. Let's make it a triathlon – another bowling game, a video game, and a monopoly game at my apartment."

"Ok," I said.

"Ok," said Bruno.

We had another bowling round. Bruno won again. This time his score was 260 and mine was 200.

Next we went over to the alley's arcade and had a game of Space Invaders. I won handily. So we were in a draw situation.

We drove over to Lyla's apartment. We had a game of Monopoly. I nearly won. But then I stopped on Park Place where Bruno had a hotel and I lost my shirt. So much for board games. So Bruno had won the triathlon.

"It's not fair," lamented Lyla. "I wanted Reginald to win. Let's make it best out of five competitions, not three. Let's add two more events: a running race at the school track and a game of mastermind."

We played mastermind first. I used a systematic approach to determine the peg sequence of my opponents spread. I won!

"You are actually smarter than me," said Bruno. "But I am in better physical shape. Let's go to the track!"

At the track, Bruno excelled. In a half mile run, Bruno came in 20 seconds sooner than I. He had won the five-event competition.

"Thank you for all the activity," I said. "I'll be going now. Enjoy yourselves." And I tried to leave.

"Don't go," begged Lyla. "I'm falling in love with you. Bruno is not really my type. The competition was biased. Let's make it best out of 7 events."

Alas, I was getting tired of it all. "No thank you," I said.

Then Bruno added, "But I am the one who loves you Lyla! You just met Reggie. It is I who deserves you. Please, please, please love me back. I would do anything to make you happy. And I want to care for you always. You are the sunshine in my life. I adore you more than anybody I have ever met. Doesn't that mean anything to you? Isn't that more important than what some contraption thinks of you and Reginald? I am the one who is compatible with you. And I won your competition fairly. Please play by the rules. Now is there anything I could do for you to make you happy and to love me more than this upstart newcomer?"

"There is," said Lyla. "Say that you will marry me and pay my expenses."

"Marriage it is!" said Bruno. Then he took her by the hand and kissed her.

Another happy couple!

The next locale I went looking for a match was the local book store. I browsed the shelves while waiting for my MEET MACHINE to signal. Sure enough, after about fifteen minutes, it began to ring its bell. A gorgeous maiden, wearing a plaid jump suit, came over to me, her MEET MACHINE echoing mine. She was holding a copy of "Martian Paradise." That impressed me. It meant she liked science fiction.

"Hello," she said. "My name is Vera. Pleased to meet you."

"My name is Reginald. The pleasure is mine."

We had a whirlwind romance - dinner in fine restaurants, trips to the beach, movies about figure skaters, plays in the local theatre, and cat shows. And I found out she had a baby. The five-year-old offspring's name was Delila. She was cute and needing a father after her biological parent died tragically from a heart attack.

We had fun taking Delila to the park and pushing her on the swing set.

"You are such a compassionate man," said Vera. "Can you marry me? I need a bread winner husband and Delila needs paternal guidance."

"I'd be delighted to," I replied.

We had a stunning wedding in an interfaith chapel. And then an exhilarating reception in an Asian Fusion restaurant. We danced the night away. The wedding guests applauded. Everybody had a great time. And we released a flock of peace doves.

After many years of happy marriage to Vera, I can say this: The MEET MACHINE 15000 works wonderfully and is responsible for my good fortune in relationships.

MISS MARS

The competition was fierce. Only two weeks away from being televised, the girls entering the Miss Mars Pageant frantically prepared for their talent show segment. Angela Bellner, from Planitia Einstein, was one such contestant.

Her talent was flute playing. She hoped to wow the judges and audiences with her tweeting of the STARLIGHT SYMPHONY, a melody written by a fellow Martian.

Her parents were so proud of her. Since grade school, she was known for stunning beauty, an affable disposition, and an interest in beauty contests. She had toured the circuit and won several pageants before and was an old hand at it. She was now 18.

The ages of the entrants ran from 17 to 25. Klude Gyner was the host of the 5th Annual Miss Mars Pageant. Dressed in a blue and orange tie, he announced the program: "Ladies and gentlemen, welcome to the grandest show on Mars – our own beauty pageant. Our first segment is the evening gown competition!"

And then a parade of beautiful ladies, all 50 of them, marched on stage, one by one. Each one was dressed to the nines in haute couture evening ware. The three judges, famous politicians, gave each lady a score from 1 to 10. Angela's score was a 9!

The spectacle continued. Said Klude Gyner: "Next is the bathing suit segment."

All the ladies, having gone backstage to change into their one- and two-piece swimming attire, came back on stage in their suits and marched around it beaming with attraction. Angela again scored a 9 in this segment. She was now in second place. The first-place contestant was Zennie Zudmin, a raving beauty from Planitia Kepler.

Backstage, the two top contestants had some words. "You're a nobody," declared Zennie to Angela. "You should not have been let into the contest."

"Screw you," said Angela to Zennie. Then a fight broke out. The two girls slugged each other, They were nearly kicked out of the competition.

The next segment was announced by Klude Gyner: "And now for the show you have all been waiting for – the talent segment. In this segment, each lady will show us what she's worth with her music, comic, or athletic ability."

Zennie Zudmin: "Good evening ladies and germs. Thank you for this opportunity to speak to you. I just flew in from Planitia Kepler and wow are my arms tired! Listen to this, how many Ioians does it take to screw in a light bulb – five – one to hold the light bulb and four to rotate the chair! By the way, why did the Ioian cross the road – to find his brain! Why do Ioians carry garbage in their back pockets? For identification..." And so her comedy act railed against the Ioians. In the end, there was light applause and she received only a 3 out of 10 for the whole act.

Angela Bellner's act went much better. She touted the strains of the STARLIGHT SYMPHONY like a virtuoso. It uplifted the audience to new levels of delight and ecstasy. The tune was magnificent and her playing of it expert. The judges gave her an 8 of 10 for the performance. This put her in the lead among all the contestants.

And then the final segment was described by Klude: "Ladies and gentlemen, it is with great delight that I report that these fine ladies are not just beautiful, they are intelligent. In our last segment, each of these people will give a speech about an important topic of their choosing."

Zennie Zudmin's speech was barbaric. Said she: "This speech is about who should be allowed to live or die! I believe in a eugenics approach to survival. Only the fittest, brightest, and best looking deserve to breathe the scarce air of our humble world. Others should be put death right away or forced to wither into non-existence by being outcasts and deprived of food and shelter. Survival of the fittest is the law of nature. Let us follow it. Help me eradicate all the good-for-nothing, uppity, ugly, dumb, and weird nobodys on this planet and others. Thank you for listening."

There was much booing to her snobby rant. The judges gave her 1 out of 10.

Angela's speech was much kinder. Said she: "My speech is about solar peace. I believe that all the planets of our Earth led solar system should settle their differences, have free trade with each other, respect each other, and get along with each other. Universal solar peace is a worthy objective that we should all strive for. With such cooperation, we can solve all our problems including starvation and homelessness. Everybody, every living being, every conscious soul, deserves ample food and shelter and health care to live comfortably and well – and deserves all these things. Thank you for listening to this speech!"

The judges gave Angie a 10 out of 10 for her speech. She won the competition and went on to be Miss Mars 2487, and later a senator in the Martian parliament. God bless Angela Bellner.

But she still had Zennie Zudmin at her throat. Zennie became the Precept of Planitia Kepler and then she began an outrageous program of extermination. She ordered the killing of all the "undesirables." Anybody under her rule, who had even the slightest defect, physical or mental, was put to death by stoning! The policies of Zennie were in violation of Martian law, but because of how powerful Planitia Kepler was, they were getting away with it. The population was being pared down to the "beautiful people"; how Zennie described them.

Angela Bellner felt it necessary to run for planetary office to stop the atrocities of her old foe occurring in Planitia Kepler. So she ran for Premier of Planet Mars. Her competitor was none other than the monster Zennie Zudmin!

At their planet-wide televised debate, this is what was said. In opening remarks, said Zennie: "We are at a crossroads in Martian history. Never before has the population been so great. It is exploding! Now at 15 billion people, we can barely feed ourselves comfortably.

"The solution is not to grow more food or build more shelters. That is too easy! The solution is to eradicate all the undesirables from our society so that we can all live happily ever after. That is to say, all the repulsive misfits should be put to death. I propose scaling down the populace to a third of what it is now. Just think about how wonderful the world would be when rid of the dirt bags and the dumb and the physically unattractive and the lazy! A vote for me is a vote for a new society of "beautiful people" like the ones we have in Planitia Kepler courtesy of my administration's policies. Thank you."

Retorted vehemently Angela: "Killing people is barbaric. Everybody has the right to existence. The way to survive the current food crisis is to grow more food and develop more habitat. Less than perfect people have the same right to live as the perfect! That is only humane. If elected Premier, I shall strive to keep each and every one alive and well. Furthermore, I shall bring to justice a monster like my opponent, Zennie Zudmin."

Angela won the election by a landslide. Once in office as the Chief Executive of Planet Mars, she began a humanitarian reform program second to none; and she strengthened all the planetary government's safety nets and also had ecologists develop new and comfortable habitats for people to live in. Functioning at full capacity, she declared that Planet Mars could support a population of over 20 billion!

The trial of her competitor Zennie Zudmin was televised. Said the prosecutor in closing remarks: "Zennie Zudmin is a freak. She is a mass killer who finagled her way to the top of Planitia Kepler society and betrayed her constituents. We must send a message to everybody that killing is wrong and that everybody has the right to live! I am asking the judge and jury to hand down a death penalty."

And so they did. She was sentenced to being burned at the stake. But supporters of her helped her escape her fate. They airlifted her to the Moon Ganymede that offered her refuge. On Ganymede, she was free as a bird and able to craft a revival of her political career. She rose to power and became the mass killing Premier of Ganymede! And then she declared war on an Angela-led Planet Mars. The two worlds battled fiercely for control of their societies. They had very different philosophies. The Ganymedeans believed in survival of the fittest and arch capitalism whereas the Martians believed in safety nets and socialism.

The war raged for years and had heavy casualties. Martian cities were ruthlessly bombed by the insane attackers from Ganymede. The death toll was nearly unbearable. Zennie offered Angela a conditional surrender but said that once Mars were under her control, she would reinstall the eugenics war mass killings that she had effectuated in Planitia Kepler and Moon Ganymede. Angela refused to surrender, and the war continued.

Finally, after years of struggle, Planet Mars prevailed over Ganymede. There was much rejoicing. And finally, the monster Zennie Zudmin was brought to complete justice. She was scorched at the stake and the witch was dead.

There was an outpouring of sympathy for all who had perished under the rule of Zennie and in fighting her. Museums and monuments were erected commemorating and memorializing the tragic losses. Meanwhile, Angela went down in history as a great leader and heroine of solar society. Statues were erected in her honor, and tomes were written about her exploits and victories.

Said Angela in her yearly State of Mars address: "All people will have the inalienable right to existence. This right cannot be taken away or compromised. As such, the disabled and the disadvantaged are deserved of massive assistance and not scorn. We, as a humane society, will continue to have strong safety net supports for those less fortunate. The human rights disaster of Ganymede is now in our past. We will recover from it and move on. We won the war with Ganymede and our morays have prevailed. Thank God for that. Let this be a message to all civilizations anywhere that would seek to obliterate the disabled: We are watching you! We shall not let even one society in the entire solar system exterminate its meekest members. Give us your "tired and poor" and we shall nurture them as refugees. And we will declare war on any and every world that violates human rights egregiously. It is our mission. We have the bravest, smartest, kindest people in reality, and should be acknowledged for that.

"Sunlight and crops feed us. That is what is doing most of the work in society. The harvesting of crops and its delivery to market are just a fraction of the toil. As such, it behooves the able bodied to share reality with the disabled and give them ample food and shelter. We will continue to do so and practice the most humane policies anywhere. I am proposing the most generous guaranteed food and shelter project in Martian history and am hoping that the Martian Assembly concurs with it. If it does, it will be worthy of all the supreme awards of this planet and others. The strongest safety net in the solar system will serve as a model for everybody of compassion and the obeying of natural law. We all have the right to live well and comfortably. This includes having not only an adequate diet but also an outstanding living abode. Universal health care should always be, and is, a birthright. This includes all vaccinations and doctor's visits. No one should be without the fullest coverage. Health is important to everybody and everybody deserves good health.

"Other rights include the right to a good education and hobbies and entertainment. Thank you."

"Long live Angela Bellner and her ideals," became the slogan of all the kinds of entities in the solar system.

NEUROSWEET

Dr. Reginald Smine of the Neurological Institute of Mars is the scientist credited with discovering Neurosweet – an intellect enhancing powder that can raise a person's intelligence dramatically. Once he perfected the formula, he tried it out on himself with wondrous results; one day he came home from work to his actress wife Nadine and impressed her with a great soliloquy about e=mc squared and acting/drama.

Dr. Smine formed a company called Neurosweet Incorporated. The Neurosweet company marketed the magic potion to everyone. People from across the solar system began using it. Soon there were studies galore about it at research centers and universities; here was a remarkable result that was attributed to Neurosweet – the lower the original intellect of the user, the greater the increase in intelligence; that is to say, dumb users benefited the most from using Neurosweet and were even able to increase their intelligence to levels greater than the brightest people! This caused an uproar in societal order, as the dumb and put upon overthrew the brilliant.

The smartest human being became Yarald Zlinald, formerly a retarded individual who had been sentenced to live in a care facility. The director of the facility, in all his kindness, tried Neurosweet out on

Yarald. Soon Yarald was reading voraciously and studying 8 different, difficult, academic subjects including physics, metaphysics, and physiology.

They released Yarald from the care facility after he proved his genius and ability to live on his own. Then he was offered, and accepted, a position of full professor/researcher at the Supreme University of Mars, Einstein Planitia, a prestigious center of learning and discovery.

At the university, Yarald gave lectures on the meaning of life and the realm of infinite energy that he claimed was the ultimate nature of reality. "The Universe," he explained, "must have come from a well of infinite energy, lest the energy of reality would likely have already been exhausted."

He further argued that a realm of infinite energy could support immortal consciousness, and that eternal minds out-selected finite ones. "Somewhere in reality," he insisted, "all people live with an Eternal God as Eternal Angels and that is a fact to rejoice in!"

Thanks to Neurosweet, the entire, collective, intellect of humanity, rose substantially. This attracted the attention of neighboring solar systems that became afraid of the newfound neuro-power of humankind. The beings in such systems tried Neurosweet on their own people, but for some reason it only worked on human beings. Soon humanity became the smartest species in the local cluster of star systems!

Paranoia led to neighboring solar systems declaring war on the Earth solar system. It took the combined force of three solar systems to beat Earth and her allies (including Mars, Jupiter, and Venus). Once beaten, the Earth solar system was deprived of Neurosweet by an alien fostered ban on it. What is more, the aliens decided that humankind's quest for sky high intellect was somehow wrong and therefore humanity should be punished for it. So they invented Un-neurosweet – a horrific substance that lowered intellect instead of raising it.

Then they forced all human beings to eat Un-neurosweet and dumbed them down. Soon human beings were reduced to animal-like intellect and were barking and meowing like pets. Then they were adopted by the aliens as pets and the greatness of the once smart humankind was lost. All the former inhabitants of the Earth solar system were sold off as pets to the alien invader populations.

After decades of existence like that, there was a breakthrough - human sympathizers on Alpha-Centauri began giving their pets Neurosweet, to help them recover their lost minds. Eventually, humankind won back their solar system, and won back the right to enhance their minds.

Yarald Zlinald was restored to his role as the brightest human being; and he began discovering a series of inventions that helped humankind tremendously; they included body renewal technology, electro-propulsion drive, and ultra-Neurosweet (an even more potent version of Neurosweet!).

Ultra-Neurosweet raised human intelligence to inconceivable, demi-god levels that gave everybody a new understanding of reality and made them invincible. Once human beings were endowed with such power, they decided to invade neighboring solar systems. They turned the aliens into pets themselves!

Though the aliens were now pets to human brilliance, they were not reduced to animal like intelligence as they had done to humans; humans were too kind to do that to them. Instead they were made pets with their current intellects.

As special pets, given special privileges, the aliens soon adapted to pet life and began enjoying it! It had several advantages and disadvantages over their previous lives; one advantage was that they were freed from work! Instead of having to toil, they could lounge around all day, watch tv, and have human-built robots cater to their every whim. One of the disadvantages, however, was in the amount of respect they received; though they were pampered pets, they were still pets and had to do whatever their human masters requested of them, including putting on "pet shows."

But, still, everyone lived merrily ever after.

OCCUPATION

The Nilons of Alpha-Centauri were the storm troopers who were responsible for holding Earthlings hostage. I, Ceon Yide, was an intelligence agent in the elite Earth Scepter Agency trying to fight the Alpha-Centaurians any way possible. Our resistance to the occupation was struggling but very real.

I currently found myself on the alien terraformed moon of Io, where 500,000 displaced/deported humans were being held in captivity. People were held in campsites and lived in tents. Each campsite had a Nilon overseer who maintained discipline and subjugation. Every night there was a barbaric ritual at each camp site; it was a hi lo card game where the lowest card holder was executed. And thus, one by one, the campsites were being pared down and exterminated. It was a good time for the Alpha-Centaurians and terror for the Earthlings!

Smorkel, the Nilon, at the campsite I was situated in, informed me of my orders: "You have been chosen to go to a work camp on Callisto. Pack your bags and get ready for flight. You are no longer assigned to live here."

And that is how I escaped execution. I boarded the next hostage vessel to Callisto. On board, everybody was in chains and crying. A teenage girl next to me was sobbing: "I lost my whole family," she cried. "What am I to do?"

"Just do what you're told," I advised. "And then when the moment's right, we'll get our vengeance."

'Yes sir," she responded.

Life on Callisto was hard. Everybody worked the mines. Day in day out, we dug for minerals. And our food supply was scarce. Our rations were two slices of bread per day, plus 2 bowls of soup, and a glass of juice. It was starvation wages.

Delila, the girl I had met en route, worked on the same crew as me. I inducted her into the resistance with an oath. She swore she would help overthrow the occupiers.

And then news broke that the Earth rebellion was making some headway. It was all over the news shows – there was an uprising in the Earth capital city of Odessa. Earth troops had seized the city and repelled the Nilons.

This inspired an uprising on Callisto. Workers began refusing to toil. And work crews were killing their overseers. Delila and I personally annihilated the monster who had been at our throats since we arrived. Then she and I joined others who had done the same. Soon, our organized resistance took control of all of Callisto. We commandeered alien vessels and eliminated alien occupation.

All over the solar system, there was a solar-wide revolt. Delila and I started flying sorties to bomb alien installations on Earth. The absolute thrill of it was exhilarating.

There were several more years of war. Finally, the alien invasion was completely repulsed and a peace treaty was procured with Alpha-Centauri. Here are the provisions of it:

 That the Earth Solar System and her allies will be at peace with Alpha-Centauri.
 That Alpha-Centauri will pay reparations to the Earth Solar System for the crimes against humanity committed during the occupation.
That there will be free trade between the Earth Solar System and Alpha-Centauri.
That there will be cultural and other exchanges between the two solar systems.
That the truth about the occupation will be taught in both solar systems.

After the war, Delila and I married and became instructors at Earth's Space Academy. There we were keynote speakers explaining the horrors of the occupation to cadets who were too young to have known them personally.

Said I: "Never again will humans or Earthlings put up with such atrocities. We were reduced to trained animals, toiling for aliens and killed indiscriminately. Millions of humans perished during the occupation and billions of others were humiliated and stripped of their human and conscious being rights. The whole Earth Solar System was turned into a work and extermination camp. All hope was nearly lost. And through it all, the Scepter and other Earth intelligence agencies fought hard to overthrow the injustice.

"Alpha-Centaurians viewed Earthlings as being inferior just because our technology did not match theirs. What they had not counted on was how adaptable to new technologies humans are, and how ingenious they can be. Eventually, the human spirit prevailed, and our resistance movement began making strides against the occupiers.

"Nowadays, Earth is as strong as ever, with newly appropriated alien technologies and elevated high morale. And all the expressions that the Alpha-Centaurians had once banned have returned – there is a flourishing of art and music and learning and research!

"Let it be known that there are fundamental rights of conscious beings that all people, human or Alpha-Centuarian, are entitled to. These include the right to good food, shelter and health care, the right to express themselves through the arts, and the right to live in harmony free from forced or underpaid labor! Furthermore, humans and Alpha-Centaurians and others have the right to love and be loved!

"These days, Earth and Alpha-Centauri are the closest of allies. May they stand united in espousing conscious being rights all over the galaxy. Together, they will defend the rights of their own people and foster the respect for universal rights universe-wide. To all cadets of our military instruction, I say this: you are joining an elite force responsible for protecting the life and rights of everybody. Bless you and good luck in all your endeavors. May you achieve high rank and be celebrated all over the solar system for your sacred duties.

"Do not hate the Alpha-Centaurians. They are now our comrades who have fallen on their own swords to make amends to us. We stand tall with them and present a united front. May our collective futures be full of joy and fulfillment as, together, we try to prevail upon death, boredom, frustration, lost dreams and lost potential, and live lives of happiness and discovery and meaningful work and interesting pastimes and good relations and artistic expressions and gigantic reward!"

OLIVIA LIGHTNESS

Her smooth moves on ice made her Moonworld famous on her homeworld of Callisto, satellite of Planet Jupiter. Her fans screamed in ecstasy at her loop de loops, triple lutzes, and high jumps. And she earned a fairly good living, picking up 20 to 50 thousand currency units each competition. Her name was Olivia Lightness.

But she wanted more out of life – more fame and more fortune. The solar capital of figure skating of course, was Planet Earth, the center of the solar system and the origin of the human species. So she moved to Earth with her coach and significant other.

But the gravity of Earth was 3 times higher than the artificial gravity environment of Callisto. This made her feel like a ton of bricks or a gigantic lead weight. Because of her reputation, she was able to enter skating events on Earth. But she was made a fool of herself. She flopped and fell repeatedly because she was not used to the heavy gravitational pull. The press made fun of her to no end. "Lead weight Lightness," they called her in broadcasts. "Go back to Callisto!"

But she would not give up. She practiced and practiced until her muscles were strong. And she made love daily to Gerald, her boy toy, for motivation. And slowly but surely, her Earthbound skating improved.

Having been nearly kicked out of all events, she filed a law suit to be able to enter the World Championships. Though her entry was forced, it was legitimate. And a miracle happened: 2 years of dedicated practice had made her a competent Earth skater. To the tune of "Let's Fly Away," by a Jupiter group called the RADIATORS, she twirled & jumped & and did toe loops like none other. Her scores were nearly all 10s and she won first place!

At an interview she explained her life;

Interviewer: "Tell us Olivia, what kept you going in figure skating after your many first defeats on Earth, shortly after you arrived here?"

Olivia: "The same perseverance and tenacity that carried me to victory on Callisto, kept me going on Earth. I love the sport and that affection motivated me to keep going despite all odds."

Interviewer: "Why did you come to Earth in the first place, if you were already a success on Callisto?"

Olivia: "Earth is a paradise for figure skaters. It is where they earn the most and have the most fans. Earth is the solar capital of the activity."

Interviewer: "How has your health been affected by your move to Earth?"

Olivia: "It has improved! The increased gravity has forced my muscles to strengthen and my lung capacity to increase."

Interviewer: "What would you tell other aspiring skaters to keep them going despite any setbacks?"

Olivia: "Do not let setbacks get you down. Never give up. If you love the sport enough and keep at it, anything is possible. Victory will be yours."

Interviewer: "Thank you Olivia for the conversation."

After he World Championships victory, Olivia retired from figure skating and became a coach. She inspired her many pupils to do the best they could. And one of her students, Cerma Kligs, became as famous as Olivia. Cerma was known for being the only female to be able to do a triple axel maneuver.

Olivia eventually ran for public office on her homeworld of Callisto where she was a heroine. She won an election for Precept. At her inauguration she declared:

"Life is for sports. They help us pass the time, obliterate boredom, and enable us to achieve supreme goals as individuals. I am proposing an ambitious program of increased physical education and more funding for all athletics including figure skating, track and field, and baseball. Let us make mighty Callisto the solar center for sporting events. People will come from millions of miles away to fill our stadiums with adoring fans!"

And so she sponsored the most far-reaching support for sports in solar history. Nearly half of the Callisto budget was dedicated to the funding of sports. Everything from baseball, to ice hockey, to skating, to long jump, to running, to basketball, to lacrosse, and to moonball, were encouraged and supported. Moonball became especially popular and a new league was formed of moonball players.

Meanwhile, figure skating also flourished. Every secondary school now had a figure skating team and the television broadcasts were teeming with figure skating events; the Callisto championships, the Skating Extravaganza, the Ice Follies, the Moon Skate Competition, and other such events all over the airwaves!

Eventually, Callisto rivalled Earth as the focal point for figure skating; "a divine musical athletic" is how Premier Lightness described the sport that she had made a life out of. The culture of figure skating expanded in leaps and bounds on Callisto to unbelievable dimensions. Ultimately, on a world ruled by a figure skater, the sport became paramount in everybody's life. People were measured by how well they could skate above all other skills including painting and singing. Everybody was periodically rated as a skater and received a life score from 1 to 10. The lower scorers were forced to worship the better scorers by performing such rituals as kneeling.

Callisto loved Olivia Lightness so much, they anointed her the Queen of Callisto. Figure skating as the supreme sport and pastime thus became permanently entrenched in Callisto culture to everybody's delight. Soon the worship of figure skaters became the center of everybody's life. The good skaters were given special privileges such as not having to wait in line at restaurants, being able to disrobe whoever they wanted wherever they wanted, and being able to marry whoever they wanted unless there was some good excuse. Everybody knelt before the finest of skaters.

The people of Planet Earth thought that the regard for figure skaters had gone a little bit too far on Callisto but kept their nose out of its business anyway.

Long live figure skating, and all sports, and the worship of them thereof!

PAINTING CONTEST

It was the fifth annual art contest on planet Mars – a global federal competition with tremendous prizes; the first place winner received a plaque and one hundred thousand Martian credits. Yine Norgon, a noted painter from the Planitia Isidis, painted his heart out in preparation for the affair.

After much deliberating with commenting comrades, Yine decided on his entry to the contest – "The Battle of Planitia Elysium", a sweeping, massive canvas of realistic depiction of the laser conflict that took place during the Martian colony's early years as an independence fighting region. The images were so vivid, you could see the laser burns on the fallen soldiers and perceive the fire in the eyes of the glorious victors.

In the final stage of the contest, the announcer, Gordon Linzer, read the name of the winner; it was Yine Norgon! Yine was ecstatic. He needed the money badly, to pay living expenses, and to take a much-deserved vacation at the Paradise Spa in the polar region of Mars.

At the Paradise Spa, Yine played sports such as Puffball, Snow Boarding, Trampoline Increments, and low gravity Rugby. He also ate sumptuous meals of steak and fish. He was having a ball. And during the evenings, he played games with gorgeous, eager hostess androids who wanted to fulfill his every whim.

There is a link between art and politics that is inextricable. Yine's good times would not last. Six months later, after Yine had returned home, there was a solar invasion of Mars; the solar government decided to squash Martian independence once and for all. And Yine's beautiful winning painting, displayed in the Martian Museum of Fine Arts, was deemed by the conquerors of Mars to be subversive and harmful.

The invaders arrested Yine and had him stand trial for being a rebel. At his tribunal, he said, "Art is just art. It is not warfare. Artists are innocent of fomenting revolution because of the innate worth of artistic expression, and the harmlessness of it!"

The tribunal did not agree. They sentenced Yine to die by lethal injection.

Meanwhile, there was a crackdown on the planet; a curfew was implemented, and censorship of publications began. Freedom was being taken away from the oppressed Martians.

At his televised appeal, this is what Yine said to the fifteen person panel judging him: "Ladies and gentlemen, I would like to make an argument for the innocuousness and necessity of artwork. Firstly, art is just a visual expression and depiction of reality – it does not by itself change things. Throughout history, the innocence of artists has been recognized and a type of diplomatic immunity has been garnered. Art is necessary to inform, to educate, and to delight. It must not be punished! Punishment of artists for being the messenger of certain sentiments or events is ridiculous and a case of 'blaming the messenger.'

"In any case, if I do say so myself, my painting, 'The Battle of Planitia Elysium' speaks for itself as an instrument of information and culture. I should not have to pay for an award winning work that is of such worth. Please, I beg you to pardon me."

The appeal panel was moved by Yine's plea and granted him a pardon. He became a national hero and went on to enter politics. As a legislator in the Martian Assembly, he fought for the restoration of Martian sovereignty! He helped authorize the sponsorship of an indigenous Martian militia that would be used to repel the solar government's occupation.

When war broke out, Yine became a general, leading brave Martian troops against the oppressors. There were many strident battles fought all over Mars, and the rebels won most of them. When the solar government was finally repelled, they negotiated the restoration of Martian independence.

After the Great War of Second Independence, Yine ran for Precept of Mars and won! He became the chief executive of the entire planet. Under his leadership, there was a flourishing of the arts. He founded a ministry of culture that sponsored artists, writers, and musicians in every way possible. It was a heyday for visual art – painting, sculpture and other expressions adorned galleries and museums galore!

Because of this renaissance, there was a dramatic increase in tourism. People came from all over the solar system to view the masterpieces of Martian artists in person, to hear the cool vibrations of original Martian harmonies, and to meet the revolutionary authors who were describing exciting, cutting edge, philosophical works.

Love was everywhere. Legions of host and hostess androids, built by the Yine Norgon administration, showered the tourists and natives with affection and worship. The whole planet became a paradise of happiness and reward. The "love androids" were programmed to respond to a person's desires to the letter. They did what they were told and then some. A night of passion with a harem of androids was a romp of such exquisite pleasure, it can almost not be described. The androids were physically attractive, model quality really, and had pleasant dispositions. Having a harem of androids was living like an emperor in an Epicurean society. It was an existence of such fun and pleasure, it was unparalleled in history.

And Yine's magnificent work of extraordinary art "The Battle of Planitia Elysium" became a postage stamp. Philatelists. solar wide. coveted the stamp and collected every version of it. Some of the rarer versions began selling for as much as 500 currency units a stamp!

They retired Yine in style; he got to live in a mansion and be serviced by android and human servants; he ate gourmet meals and spent his free time reading and painting. His paintings were still good. Every time he completed one, it would be auctioned off at the Martian Auction Center and go for thousands of currency units. He donated half of the sales monies to Martian charities including Save the Bears, Feed The Destitute, and Build Affordable Shelters. He was a millionaire many times over!

Who says art does not pay?

PEACE WITH ANDROMEDA

Only five months away from the expiration of the Thousand Year Treaty with the Milky Way, The Andromedan Republic was in an uproar, and my (Cerlan Yitz) office as one of twelve foreign ministers, was preparing to receive the Ambassador of the Milky Way, Apia Klernet; she was coming in a diplomatic vessel shaped like an oval and about the size of a three bedroom home. The Premier of Andromeda instructed me to be cordial and generous with her. I had prepared a welcoming ceremony in the capital city of Noobia, on the Ministry of Foreign Affairs Planet of Clofia.

She was taller than I expected, 6 feet but slender and gorgeous. "The pleasure to meet with you is mine," I declared as she kissed me on both cheeks. Apia was wearing a formal blue gown, with a lacy frill on it. I was suited up in a blue coat and orange tie. She came alone. The risk of entering another galaxy, about declaring war, was too great for her staff.

"You must realize how serious this matter is," proclaimed Apia. "We are afraid of a conflict with Andromeda, should our negotiations fail."

"Then they shall not fail!" I tried to reassure her.

"In any case," I advised. "We have a grand welcome prepared for you."

I led her into a ballroom in one of the Foreign Ministries' hosting buildings. There we found a scrumptious buffet of exotic dishes, and a band playing a welcoming tune of "Here comes the Ambassador," a piece created by one of our finest musicians. She ate heartily, as did I.

After the meal, we moved to a conference room and began work immediately.

"Andromeda is demanding the withdrawal of Milky Way forces from all intergalactic planetoids, to be settled by Andromedans, because we are the larger galaxy!"

"Out of the question," snapped back Apia. "Those regions are hard won territories. We would fight to maintain control of them."

"We do not want an altercation. Can you at least surrender some of them?" I begged.

"Perhaps," she said.

We poured over interstitial space maps, trying to find some middle ground about what planetoids would be relinquished and which would be left alone.

Other issues we debated and came to agreements on through our talks including Free Trade between the galaxies, stopping species bigotry, exchange programs, border patrol policies, and cultural exchanges (including artwork and music). After 10 days of discussions, we worked out an agreement for another thousand years of peace between Andromeda and the Milky Way.

But we were too late; war had already broken out in anticipation of the cessation of previous treaties. The Milky Way launched a surprise attack on Andromeda with 5000 warships that were being repulsed by defense forces.

Ambassador Apia Klernet barely made it out of the Andromeda Galaxy alive in her vessel rigged with lights indicating full diplomatic immunity. If it were not for my own merciful intervention, she might have been taken hostage!

The war raged on for months. Andromeda launched a counter- attack, taking the confrontation to the Milky Way's doorstep. Meanwhile, the treaty I had worked out with Apia was under consideration by the Parliaments of both the Andromedan Republic and the Milky Way Empire. We were praying for ratification.

I was called to testify before the Andromedan Parliament's Foreign Affairs committee. I was massively nervous. Before the meeting, I went to the Carnation Gardens of Clofia to try to clear my head. Hundreds of rows of carnations in every color adorned the attraction. I paraded down aisles of them, licking an ice cream cone sold at the snack bar. My worry still wracked my body, because, if I do say so myself, I knew how important my word would be to ending the war with the Milky Way and instituting the Treaty of Cooperation and Peace that Apia and I had crafted.

"Thank you for coming to our conference," said Kyle Fermit, Senator of the Utna Constellation, Chair of the Foreign Affairs committee of Andromeda. "We have only a few questions. "First, how well do you know Ambassador Apia Klernet?"

"I only met with her for 10 days but feel I have known her for a lifetime."

"What can you tell us about her?"

"She is of fine character, witty, and well intentioned. I feel that the agreement made with her is legitimate and that she has the power to convince the Milky Wayians of it including their legislature!"

"We are impressed by it," complimented Senator Fermit. "But we need to scrutinize it more before adopting it. Can you tell me by what means you came to a compromise concerning the interstitial space planetoids?"

"We simply analyzed the ethnic composition of them. Those that had more Andromedans on them than Milky Wayians we decided would be turned over to our galaxy. Those that had the opposite composition of settlers would be allowed to remain with the Milky Way or relinquished to it."

"That is a daring policy. Now onto other issues. Like Free Trade. Do you really believe that after a thousand years of protectionism, that Andromeda is going to agree to trade freely?

"Why not? Free Trade is in the best interest of all parties since it strengthens those companies that build the better product at the better price - this grows all economies," I suggested.

"Perhaps," said Senator Fermit. "Now about ending bigotry between species of each respective galaxy. How does your treaty prescribe this be done?"

"With education campaigns and prescribed chapters in Health Education textbooks. The end to bigotry must be taught like any subject. This we think will go a long way towards helping everybody to get along with everybody else."

"You are a fine gentleman," remarked the Senator. "We are all impressed by your good deeds. We are hoping to adopt your treaty and end the hostilities with the Milky Way. You are now dismissed from us. Good luck with everything."

I sent a telegram to Apia with one of the few companies that could get a message through a war zone, INFOGRAM. Here it was, "Dearest Apia Klernet, Ambassador of the Milky Way: meeting with the Parliament of Andromeda was a success. I am hoping for quick action on our treaty. I hope all is well with thou."

She replied: "The Milky Way is considering the treaty as well. I shall keep you appraised."

Meanwhile the war still raged. Hundreds of vessels, riled up into war fever, clashed in deep space, blowing each other to ribbons, to the horror of diplomats and peacemakers. The nightly newscasts reported the casualties. I cringed at them.

Finally, after both sides became exhausted by a stalemate, and all relevant legislatures ratified the Treaty of Cooperation and Peace, the Great War came to an end and thus began a genuine, thousand year reign of peace!

PEACE WITH PEGASI

It was Earth Solar System Ambassador Yide Snorner's toughest mission: entertain Ambassador Geraldine Gumf from the Pegasi star system and convince their world to adopt human rights reform. As part of his approach, he dined Geraldine at all the finest restaurants on the pleasure moon of Callisto: they ate seafood at Fishes Galore – they chowed down succulent meats at the Ranch Steakhouse – and they munched on quiche at the Veggie Emporium. Geraldine was having a blast!.

After she had her fill of exotic foods, Yide took Geraldine to the Callisto Capital City Amusement Center to sample the rides. The first contraption they boarded was the Jupiter Rock n' Roll – a five-acre roller coaster that shook, rocked, and flew its riders to ecstasy!

Then they went on the carousel; fiberglass horses and rabbits and giraffes bobbed up and down as the merry-go-round spun in a circle. Geraldine giggled on a rabbit like a schoolgirl. "I am having such a good time," she said. After the carousel, the ambassador pair partook of some cotton candy.

"Now is a good time," remarked Geraldine, "to discuss the impending peace treaty between our two great solar systems."

"Delighted to," said Yide.

"We are more than ready to sign," said Geraldine. "The human culture you have shown me is outstanding and fun. It has impressed me to the point of wanting nothing but an alliance with your great species."

"Thank you," said Yide. "But before we can sign our treaty, I must inform you that there is a sticking point interfering with the joining of our two societies. It is the death penalty! Our people have long since abolished it - though Pegasi has not; it still practices this abomination. We are against capital punishment because violence begets violence, people do not have free will so they cannot be held completely responsible for their actions, plus there is a danger of convicting an innocent person. We implore Pegasi to join us supporting human rights and humaneness!"

"I cannot say I agree with you," said Geraldine. "We of Pegasi feel that if you take a life, you give a life. We cherish the death penalty as being justice. We cannot give it up that easily."

"Why don't we agree to disagree for the time being, and enjoy the rest of the amusement park?"

"Very well," she said.

The next ride they enjoyed was the rotor; it spun the two of them around and stuck them to sides of the device with centrifugal forces, as the bottom dropped out to everybody's amazement. After the rotor, they went on the flume. This Geraldine really enjoyed. She screamed with delight as the wooden craft they were in slid down a steep waterway tube.

The Ferris wheel was Geraldine's favorite though. It was 300 feet high, and at the top position, you could see the entire park, metropolis, and beyond into the mountains. The sight was awesome and inspiring.

After that, the twosome thrilled themselves by going on the three other roller coasters in the park: the Smasher, the Sleek Slider, and the Rocket Ship. They were all fantastic.

The last ride they went on was the Anti-Gravity Bubble Chamber. The two of them jumped up and down and rollicked like teenagers in a weightless plastic bubble. Geraldine said she had never had such a good time in her life. She felt young again.

After going on the rides, Yide took Geraldine to the park's revered art museum. This really impressed her. There hung some of the finest masterpieces painted by noted Callistoan and Jupiterian artists. Some of the works that caught her eye included "The Battle of Isidis Planitia" – a realistic depiction of a Martian Independence war clash, "The Plumes of Io" – a stunning image of the sulfur dioxide vents on the moon Io, and "Jupiter Spot" – an orange hued canvas depicting the storm in planet Jupiter's atmosphere.

After the museum trip, they went to eat in the amusement center's finest eatery: The Roller Coaster Restaurant. Over burgers, fries, and salads,

Geraldine explained: "You humans are outstanding, fun-loving creatures. And we adore you. But we cannot agree with your demands for rescinding the death penalty. It is too important a part of our policies. Plus, and I am hoping this does not sound barbaric to you, it is downright entertaining! We of Pegasi love the drama of seeing a criminal fried in an electric chair, and that is why such images are broadcast solar-wide. Moreover, we feel that the death penalty is a strong deterrent – it dissuades would be killers from committing crimes. Thus, I cannot agree with your terms for signing our peace treaty!"

"I am so sorry to hear that," said Yide. "It is a hazardous turn of events. Because if a peace treaty is not signed soon, the reverse of peace could occur and that is war! Make no mistake about it, if we go to war over this issue, humans shall fight bravely and ferociously. We shall bomb your cities to rubble, and try to decimate your death penalty loving populace. It is a just dessert for a blood thirty civilization that thumbs its nose at human and conscious being rights!"

He was being melodramatic but it worked! "Now that you mention it," said Geraldine. "Maybe there is room for compromise."

She called her superiors at the Foreign Ministry of Pegasi and explained the situation. They concurred with her that abolishing the death penalty was worth it to avoid a war with the mighty Earth Solar

System. She explained it to Yide: "You win Ambassador. Pegasi is going to do away with capital punishment to please humankind and obtain a much needed peace treaty!"

"Splendid!" said Yide joyously.

Within weeks, there was a peace treaty signing ceremony and a banquet. There were also additional celebrations and parades. Everybody was overjoyed with the new commander.

Thus was ushered in a long era of peace and alliance with Pegasi.

PETIFICATION

A breakdown in diplomacy among the nuclear powers led to a dangerous confrontation among the people of Planet Earth. Finally, a series of comedy of errors, misunderstandings, and spitefulness, caused a full-scale launch of nuclear missiles towards destinations around the globe. Fortunately, the Zerlons, an extra-terrestrial species, had time scientists who could predict the nuclear war. At just the right moment, their ships pulled into orbit and used energy weapons to vaporize the airborne missiles and save the world!

General Yulik Gomf, of the Zerlon Empire, explained the situation to the Secretary-General of the United Nations and other dignitaries including heads of state: "Since we have saved Earth from a nuclear holocaust, we feel we have enough moral imperative to do what we please with earthlings. And what we want is to turn human beings into special pets on our homeworld. Special pet is the proper role of humans in our society. We shall be accepting 5 million applications per month and choosing 15 thousand from the applicant pool. Other than that, we shall leave Earth alone."

Here were the rights and responsibilities of special pets in the Zerlon Empire; rights: 1) To have a 1000 year lifespan courtesy of Zerlon body renewal technology – 2) to be protected from injury and being killed – 3) to have at least one good television – 4) to have three square meals a day and two snacks – 5) to not be confined unless convicted of a serious crime - 6) to sleep as much as they want between the hours of 10 PM and 10 AM; responsibilities: 1) to be good-natured – 2) to accept being pet in non-erogenous zones – 3) to compete in pet shows no more than once per week.

Applications came in from all over Planet Earth. Pets were chosen based on appearance, intellect, skills, and personality. Morla Gine, 27 years old, a factory worker with a degree in anthropology, from Lansing Michigan, was one such chosen pet. Her primary motivation for becoming a pet was the chance to have a lengthy lifespan. At the owner introduction proceeding on Planet Zerlon, Morla had a choice between three families to be her pet owner. She interviewed the three clans and chose to be owned by General Klune Gythe, an officer in the Zerlon armed forces who was cordial and debonair.

Zerlons looked like big teddy bears; they were slightly taller than humans on average, had a thick mane of fur all over their body, and were essentially bi-pedal humanoids; they were cute. Klune was a husky one and was 647 years old. He lived in a four bedroom home in a suburb of Primary City, Zerlon. When he and Morla got to his home for the first time, he introduced her to her bedroom and brand new 50-inch television set. She ate a sumptuous, gourmet dinner served by robots, and then went to sleep.

Morla spent much of her time watching tv. Her owner was only present in the home in the evening after a long day's work on the nearest military base. In the evening, the two of them would talk and sometime play games like checkers. She was his companion.

The next weekend, Morla attended her first special pet show. There she walked around in a show track in a skimpy outfit and was judged for appearance and poise. She won second place and they gave Morla and her owner ribbons!

Not all the worlds that the Zerlon empire tried to conquer were as complacent as Earth. The Zikon world did not like to be subjugated to pets. They fought back and repelled the Zerlons. Then they fought to so call "liberate" Earth. When Zikon repelled the Zerlons from Earth, the Zerlon Empire was in an uproar! The Parliament of Zerlon decided to take their anger out on the eight hundred thousand earthlings who were under their care. They decided to relegate them to being regular pets instead of special pets who had special privileges.

Morla was aghast at how her life changed once she became a regular pet; instead of a proud human being, she was now being treated like a cat or rabbit; humans could no longer use bathrooms – instead they had to be walked on all fours outside; humans could no longer watch tv; humans could no longer speak intelligibly – they were forced to bark only; humans could no longer eat off of plates with utensils but instead were forced to chow down cereal out of bowls; and other changes!

Fortunately, the Zikon "liberation" of Earth did not last. Within a few months, the Zerlon Empire recaptured Earth and restored Earth's symbiosis with Zerlon. Also, the HUMAN REGULAR PET ACT was repealed and humans' status as special pets restored! Happy owners threw their relieved pets lavish parties as an apology for having treated them as regular pets for eight months.

Klune Gythe decided that the time was right to mate his pet with somebody. So he called some of his comrades looking for a pet owner with a good-looking male pet willing to mate. He found one. One of his captains, Fred Tyle, had a male pet named Biron who was virile and affable. At a meeting between Biron and Morla, Morla agreed to mate with him.

The two of them spent two weeks together at a special resort for vacationing special pets. They made love daily until Morla was impregnated. Nine months later, she gave birth to a beautiful girl that she and Klune could be proud of.

The offspring of special pets were not pets themselves and were treated like royalty; they attended special schools where they learned to read & write & do math. At the age of twelve, they were given a choice to either move back to Earth or become special pets themselves. Morla's daughter Kristine chose to be a special pet and be owned by Klune Gythe like her mother.

Kristine went on to become an acrobat on Zerlon and compete in the Special Pet Acrobatics Olympics. During her performance at the age of fifteen, she wowed the audience with her jumps, swirls, and cartwheels. She won first place. At the podium where they gave her a gold medal, there was a Zerlon flag. The audience of special pets and owners then sang the Zerlon national anthem. And everybody cheered!

PLANETARIUM ESCAPADE

Sam and Nadine (both 17 years old) were on a school organized field trip to the Autumn Valley Planetarium. They saw a show about the sun and planets and their moons. Afterwards, they explored the facility, seeing exhibits about space exploration, and weighing themselves on scales that gave their weight for different worlds. Then they came upon a door that said: "Adventurers Enter Only."

They being very brave, entered the strange room. Once inside, they saw a strobe light blinking on a blue circle platform. The sign above the platform said: "Teleportation to Spaceship." Sam stepped gingerly onto the platform and then disappeared. "Sam!" cried Nadine. "Where are you?" She searched the room – nobody.

Finally, Nadine worked up the courage to step on the platform also. And she disappeared! She reappeared on a similar platform, in another room. And there was Sam also. And surrounding Sam were three lizard-like beings, about 5 feet tall, who were wearing uniforms. One of them spoke: "Welcome Earthlings to the Yikon Spaceship SWIFTDART. You are guests aboard our vessel for the month. You will be shown to your quarters."

One of the lizards took them both by the hand and led them to comfortable rooms aboard the spacecraft. In a few hours, the lizards had a conference with Sam and Nadine in a meeting room.

Said Gink, the chief lizard, "You Sam and Nadine have been recruited to represent planet Earth in a test for its existence. You are a random sample of Earthlings. We are an advanced species, seeking contact with other life forms. Before we make the formal contact, however, we first test a couple of samples of the new species to see if they are worthy of trade and contact with us. If they are, a peace treaty is signed, and there is an exchange of technology and culture!"

"What happens if we fail the test?" asked Sam.

"It is too horrible to explain. But I shall anyway. If the samples of a new species fails the test of worthiness, then an elimination of their world is ensued. The planet is razed to the ground, and all life on it obliterated."

"That is not fair!" screamed Nadine. "Who are you to pass judgement on human beings or anybody else for that matter?"

Gink went on, "We are a species that is so vastly superior to humankind, we deserve the right to do as we please with Earth and her people. At least that is how we feel about it. In any case, you and Sam must prepare an entertainment show, using any skills or talents you can muster, and try to please an audience of Yikons. If they pass you by popular vote, Earth is saved and everybody lives happily ever after and you are returned to the planetarium where you were recruited. If you fail, you are both vaporized, and so is your home world. Is that clear?"

"Yes," said Sam.

"Yes," said Nadine.

The next month was an ordeal for both of them. They prepared and practiced a song and dance show to be performed for the Yikons. On the day of the performance, they were both nervous. But they gave it their best shot.

Nadine belted out a medley of show tunes, and Sam danced to them. The show was lively and inspiring. Afterwards, there was strong applause. They passed.

The Yikons returned Sam and Nadine to the spot they were taken from. Their families were overjoyed to see them. And within a few months, the Yikons established formal contact with planet Earth organizations including SETI, the Search For Extraterrestrial Intelligence.

At a meeting with SETI, Chieftain Gink said this: "Ladies and gentlemen of Earth, it is a pleasure to inform you that planet Earth passed our random test for worthiness. Two great Earthlings, Sam and Nadine, succeeded in truly wowing us during a performance aboard our space vessel. This opens up good relations between our societies. There shall be an agreement forthcoming that irons out our trade relationship and facilitates cultural exchanges. We have much to share with Earth including STARDRIVE for spaceship travel, FUSION reactors for power generation, and BODY RENEWAL techniques for dramatic life extension.

"Furthermore, we have advice for planet Earth and its administration. We are formally and strongly recommending that planet Earth unify under one government. Such a government would have the power to abolish weapons of mass destruction (such as nuclear missiles), insure collective security, and protect and enforce universal conscious being rights worldwide. In addition, such a one world government could provide universal food, shelter and health care to the entire world's populace.

"We on planet Yikon, were once divided and squabbling amongst ourselves. During our salvation, we learned that working together as one unified planet was far superior to functioning separately. All the nations of our world decided to bury the hatchet and join together. This did a world of good for everybody's well-being. And we hope the same result is achieved with our good comrades on planet Earth.

"We are looking forward to getting to know more Earthlings and sharing the local quadrant with them. We can introduce Earthlings to a whole galaxy of interesting life forms that are more than willing to welcome human beings to galactic society. Also, we can petition the mighty Galactic Government to admit planet Earth into its legislature and allow representatives of human beings to be heard.

"There is a whole galaxy of excitement and life waiting to be discovered by Earthlings."

Anyway, Sam and Nadine became world heroes. They appeared on talk shows, were toasted everywhere, and ticker tape parades were held for them. They became rich and famous and married and had a family.

Meanwhile, Earth and Yikon relations could not be better. There is a steady exchange of peoples between the two worlds and a great deal of intermarriages. There is also now a military alliance between the two solar systems, strengthening each of them. And everybody lived merrily ever after.

POWER GUM

Harvey Pythe read about it in the newspapers – POWER GUM, a new type of 'super' gum that was also a stimulant. He went down to the corner store to purchase five packs of it. The types were orange, peach, raspberry, lemon, and lime. Each was a scrumptious mix of natural and artificial flavors combined with a jolt of caffeine and a 'mystery' upper.

He chewed a pack the next morning before going to work at the flashlight factory. It energized him. He spent the day assembling the lights at a pace double his usual working pace. His boss complimented him and suggested that he be given a raise!

After work, he went out with his girl comrade Florence, and they had a great time. They had dinner in a fancy restaurant, and then they danced until 2 AM at a local disco. Harvey was exploding with power. By the end of the day, he had chewed 3 packs of POWER GUM and was feeling stupendous. He could not get to sleep the first night of using it, however, and just stayed awake until the next day.

The following day was even more spectacular than the first. He chewed his last two packs of gum and breezed the day. He was a dynamo of productivity and output. He assembled 60 flashlights in record time and was given the promised raise of 20%.

After work, he zonked out in exhaustion. It seems that the gum had a type of rebound effect. He had to take the next day off to recover. On day four of the gum experiment, however, he bought five fresh packs of orange and chewed the lot of them. He became re-energized and showed up to work raring to go.

People around the nation were reporting miracles related to using the POWER GUM. Everybody was feeling full of energy and their work output was sky high.

But there was a catch. The gum not only had a rebound effect, but it also turned out it had a side effect – hallucinations. By the thirtieth day of using POWER GUM, Harvey Pythe started hallucinating; he was sitting in his living room, minding his own business, when an apparitional parade of fruits marched through his apartment, singing a lively tune loudly. They were also spewing forth juices and "soaking" the carpet and Harvey's clothing.

"Knock off the racket!" screamed Harvey to no avail. The noise just got louder. And what's more, the fruits started gyrating and dancing wildly. The fantasy was completely out of control. Harvey called Florence to ask her for help.

"Just relax and let the trip wear off," instructed Florence. So Harvey took a nap and when he awoke, the hallucinations were gone.

The was a rash of lawsuits across the nation having to do with POWER GUM side effects. Harvey joined a class action suit saying that there was pain and anguish from using the GUM. There was a settlement with the plaintiffs.

Meanwhile, the company that came out with the confection reissued a new version of it that they promised had less side effects. Harvey tried the new version and loved it! It has all the same power boosts as the original gum, without hallucination side effects. He used the new gum to boost his work effort and to make him a party animal with his comrades.

POWER GUM 2 was indeed fantastic. And Harvey used it to abandon. But alas, it turned out it had a side effect also – not hallucinations but acne. After about 15 helpings of POWER GUM #2, a person's face would break out into an array of oozing pimples. It was unsightly but a small price to pay for the energy boosts. Harvey decided to just live with the acne side effects and keep using the gum for its power boosting effects. But Florence broke up with him because of the acne so he had to stop using the gum.

Finally, POWER GUM #3 was issued. It promised to be the ideal gum with all good effects and not one side effect. Harvey reconciled with Florence and began using the third type of gum. But the gum turned out to have an additional effect that was considered to be beneficial – it raised a person's IQ! Before long, Harvey was having meaningful conversations about e=mc squared and other physics equations. Florence began using the gum also and humored Harvey's intellect with her own brain boosted power.

The two of them became gum chewing intellectuals who decided to open up their own physics laboratory and do pure research. They did. They investigated new substances to be used in solar panels and discovered a super powerful solar power mesh that could someday be used to power up the world completely on sunlight. They also discovered some new sub-atomic particles that had unusual properties.

The two of them became world famous gum chewing, neuronal enhanced beings who were lauded in scientific and research communities. And then after five years of using POWER GUM #3, a side effect exploded into their lives: hallucinations again! Only this time they were gargantuan.

One day, they were both lounging around in their laboratory, taking a break from their studies, when they witnessed an apparitional safari of wild animals march through the building – there were tigers, lions, antelopes, deer, hippos, and leopards. And they were screaming! The din was overwhelming.

They called emergency services and were admitted to a local care facility. It took a full month for them to dry off from the hallucination trip. They foreswore POWER GUM and returned to their former lives as a flashlight assembler and beautician.

Brain boosting power does not come for free and neither does energy enhancement. Harvey and Florence sometimes give speeches about substance abuse, and explain that horrific side effects are not worth the benefits of an experimental gum. It is better to go without the gum and live a normal life.

Eventually, Florence and Harvey married and lived happily ever after, using only regular gum.

PRESIDENTIAL VISIT

The moon of Callisto was brimming with activity, preparing for a visit by Cark Geidin, the President of the Solar System. They planned on having ticker tape parades, and song and dance shows, to honor the new leader.

When he arrived, Precept of Callisto, Zaughn Zlickermin, greeted Cark. "Welcome to our humble world, your majesty," he said on the spacecraft exit ramp at the spaceport. "Your wish is my command."

"Thank you. I wish to receive a tour of Callisto, including the site of the 'More Democracy' uprising, the Park of Contesia."

"Of course, your majesty," said Zaughn. "But first we have prepared a welcoming banquet for you and your entourage." The President and his aides were taken by helicopter to the Precept's mansion. Once there, they freshened up and then were escorted to the banquet hall.

Zaughn gave a speech: "Ladies and gentlemen. It is a great honor to be welcoming to Callisto the mighty elected President of the whole Solar Array, Cark Geidin. We do not get many visitors out here in the boondocks, but they are always a pleasure. I hope the President's visit is as joyous to him as it is to us. Thank you for coming. Now the President would like to say something."

Cark got up and spoke: "Ladies and gentlemen. It is also a great honor to be here. Everybody in the solar government has such admiration for your world's society and fun-loving lifestyle. But there is a grave reason that I have come to check on Callisto. It is to monitor and discover and evaluate its recent pro 'More Democracy' movement that is demanding more political parties on Callisto. I shall be meeting with uprising leaders and other dignitaries, if you do not mind. In the meantime, thank you for this banquet, and I look forward to getting to know the Precept and his staff!"

The banquet went well, and everybody stuffed themselves silly with food.

The next day, Cark met with Yuck Ribble, the chief of the 'More Democracy' movement. Here is what Yuck said: "Mr. President, we are asking that Callisto adopt more than two political parties in its political system. The more parties, the better, we feel. And the more parties there are, the more responsive and responsible to the people the government is, and the more ethical it is. Can you help us?"

Replied Cark: "I shall do what I can to help. As you know, the full solar government has about a dozen viable political parties, so I am used to a many party system."

Later that day, Cark was taken to the Park of Contesia and gave a speech: "Only two months previous to this date, there was a pro-democracy rally in this park. Protesters were demanding more representation and more political parties. The protest was put down brutally with tear gas and other riot controls. Three people were injured. Let their efforts not be in vain. I am here today to commemorate the uprising and to pledge my support for it and convey my sympathies to those who were hurt by it."

Later that week, President Cark Geidin mediated high level talks between Precept Zaughn Zlickermin and Yuck Ribble. The discussions were fruitful. A compact was reached that would arrange for the creation of five new political parties on Callisto including a liberal party, conservative party, socialist party, Callisto party, and humanitarian party. The population of Callisto was ecstatic with glee.

To celebrate the new democracy, there were parties, ticker tape parades, and fireworks. All over the capital city, in the evenings for seven days, fireworks exploded in the skies to accentuate the joy of strengthened democracy.

A statue was built to honor President Geidin and to thank him for his help.

Within months, after the reforms came, a new legislature formed on Callisto with seven viable political parties represented in its chambers. As was expected, the new legislature had an ideology different than the two party one. It was much more socialistic, for instance; all sorts of acts were passed that strengthened social safety nets including those for food, shelter, and health care. Moreover, there was also a vast and safe improvement in firearm control. Furthermore, there were acts granting greater freedom to people. Also, funding for the arts and sciences was increased dramatically. It was a renaissance of do-gooding.

Zaughn Zlickerman, a celebrated reformer, was re-elected with no problem. At his state of the world address, the next year, he said this: "The pro democracy factions were right all along. All Callisto needed was a government more attuned to the people, to form a utopia. We now have one. And we are one of the first moons in the solar system to have an indigenous political system with more than two political parties. God bless President Geidin for helping us. And God bless the people of Callisto for their good nature and yearning for freedom."

The solar government eventually passed an act enforcing permission for more than two viable political parties to form on all the planets and moons of solar system. It was the dawn of a new age of ultra democracy and human rights. And soon neighboring solar systems began emulating the Earth solar system, including Alpha-Centaur and Pegasi.

Books would be written about why many viable political parties increases the effectiveness and kindness of government. President Geidin wrote such a book, and the pro-democracy movements used the book as a guide to creating a great political system. The main point of the book was that more political parties give more competing ideas a chance to be heard and this "competition effect" increases the responsiveness of the government to the desires and needs of the people. It is a phenomena proved by world and solar political systems throughout history. Those governments that had the greatest number of political parties presided over the most humane and rational and peaceful societies. It is a lesson in ultra democracy everybody should learn.

PRINCESS AND THE ORBITER

The mighty World Space Agency (WSA) thought that it was time that a bona fide monarch have the opportunity to visit the world's premier space station. So, after a competition among the royals, they chose the brightest and prettiest of them all, Princess Cadence of France, to conduct a mission aboard ALPHA ORBITER FIVE, the WSA's pride and joy.

She came on board with an entourage of three assistants.

Once floating and assimilating to the space agency society, she explained to the crew her mission: "I and my associates are to simulate a contact with extraterrestrials. We are going to dress in cat suits and pretend to be from another planet! Just let your imagination soar and play along."

And so they did. They reentered the reusable shuttle vessel that they arrived in, and established radio contact with the programmers and the space station inhabitants. Said Princess Cadence: "We are from Planet Catlandia. We were in the area, flying through open space, when we noticed Earth's orbiting station. We decided that astronauts are the most appropriate personnel to establish first contact with because of their open-mindedness, knowledge of astronomy, and willingness to explore outer space! Do we have permission to dock with your space station? My name is Princess Cadence."

"Indeed you do. Please come aboard, Princess Cadence," Said Commander Ned Gython.

And so she did.

Once on board again, she explained her purpose in making the contact. "We come to you with a warning. It is the supreme opinion of our political scientists that planet Earth must unify and abolish weapons of mass destruction, in order to avoid an Armageddon. Furthermore, we are recommending that all nations trade freely with each other, to enhance global prosperity. This is our message from Catlandia."

"I shall relay the message to powers that be on Earth," promised Commander Gython. And so he did.

"There is more," said Princess Cadence. "Since the closest animal on your world to our physiology is the feline, we would like them to receive special attention. All cats must be worshipped as demi-gods and given premium care. They must have freedom and be given the best foodstuffs. No longer will you be allowed to just feed them dry cereal. They must have gourmet wet food like tuna fish and chicken! Also, cats must be given toys to play with – and not just scratching boards and plastic mice; they must be given expensive toys like lavish cushions to lie on and fabric mice to toss around!"

"Special care for cats is out of the question," said Commander Gython. "Cats are no better than other pets and will be treated accordingly. They are cared for well enough. Your insistence on special care for them is absurd. What about human beings? Don't you care about them as well?"

Replied Princess Cadence: "We do care about human beings. That is why we are using our powers to encourage a global unification for world harmony and wealth. But we must demand that cats be given special attention because of how much like our own species they are. On our home world, it was not homo sapiens that evolved into intelligent beings, it was felines. Thus, we ask that cats be treated as the very special, unique, and beloved creatures they are Love cats or else!"

"Ok, ok," said Commander Gython. "As long as this is no joke, I shall see to it that cats get an upgrade in care on Planet Earth."

"Thank you so much," said Princess Cadence.

At the end of the space agency's peace exercise, Princess Cadence and Commander Gython and the rest of the crew and the full entourage had a celebration. They sipped from a bottle of cider the princess had brought aboard.

Then there was a press conference, broadcast to all of Earth:

Journalist: "Princess Cadence, please tell us what it is like being on a space station."

Princess Cadence: "It is an experience out of this world – there is zero gravity but warm comradery."

Journalist: "What was the result of your simulation of contact with extraterrestrials?"

Princess Cadence: "It went smashingly. The crew accepted the advice of the Princess from Catlandia, the fictitious, outer space planet that the aliens supposedly came from."

Journalist: "And what is that advice?"

Princess Cadence: "That Earth must solve all her problems with a grand unification that joins all nations together into a global country."

Journalist: "What prospects for the strength of monarchy does your outer space visitation hold?"

Princess Cadence: "It is in the hands of the people. Hopefully, they will be inspired by my visit to ALPHA ORBITER FIVE, and become supportive of spreading monarchy into the stars. We, the humble monarchs, in this day and age of ceremonial monarchy, are at the service of our constituents and only want to help them and motivate them."

Journalist: "What is the danger that spreading monarchy into space holds to democracy here on Earth?"

Princess Cadence: "None whatsoever. Modern monarchs know their place and are not interested in interfering with democracy. We believe in elected leadership existing side by side ceremonial leaders. Just enjoy the pageantry of monarchy and don't be afraid of it."

Journalist: "We are afraid of it, however. We are afraid of dictatorship. We are afraid that gorgeous princesses like you might charm the democracy right out of land and space!"

Princess Cadence: "Your fears are exaggerated! I and fellow monarchs have no intention of installing dictatorship anywhere. We are just as afraid of dictators as anybody."

Journalist: "Tell us more about visiting a space station. What is most interesting about it?"

Princess Cadence: "Scientific exploration is fruitful and exciting. There are many experiments going on at the space station including work investigating the creation of perfect crystals in a weightless environment. Other research includes studying the effects that zero gravity has on human physiology and trying to find ways to minimize those effects. Also, there is psychological research - studying the effects of orbiting life on human psychology. Moreover, simulations about contact with extraterrestrials teaches us about human society and helps us see the big picture of Earth goals. Furthermore, space station life inspires all of us to succeed and to experience new realities and strive to be the best we can be!"

Journalist: "Everything sounds so rosy. Have there been any hitches to your trip?"

Princess Cadence: "None whatsoever. The crew has been gracious and hospitable. And my own entourage, has returned the favor. Nonetheless, honestly, we are looking forward to our return to

Earth, our beloved home planet, where there is gravity and fun and parks and so on."

Journalist: "Do you feel there is an appropriate amount of investment in space exploration?"

Princess Cadence: "Not necessarily. I recommend dramatic investigation and increases in space investment. It is time to work on additional, grandiose space projects such as settlement of a lunar colony and a mission to Planet Mars."

Journalist: "Who will pay for it?"

Princess Cadence: "It is worth using funds from the general budget to finance the strengthening of the human presence in the solar system. And, in any case, we are hoping and praying that someday Earth's space activity will pass a threshold that attracts the interest of extraterrestrial comrades for real, who will come and visit us for real, will open up trade and diplomatic relations for real, and this will benefit everybody substantially!"

Journalist: "You mean the realization of a real Catlandia?"

Princess Cadence: "Absolutely. Real contact with beings from other worlds will enhance our lives on Earth considerably because of technological exchanges and other actions. Also, it will be extraordinary to share the universe with intelligent beings from exotic neighboring solar systems in the galaxy."

Journalist: "Tell us more about your simulation of a party from "Catlandia" visiting the space station. I heard you demanded that cats on Earth be given special privileges. Isn't that ridiculous?"

Princess Cadence: "In the context of playing the role of a cat creature, the demands were not unreasonable. We surmise that any intelligent cat from another world would have special sympathy for Earth cats, despite their pet status, and want to help them."

Journalist: " But what about human beings though? For every ounce of worship of a cat, there is the degradation of a human being, is there not?"

Princess Cadence: "Absolutely not! Worship of cats does not detract from being concerned about humankind. Quite the contrary, it enhances it. And it puts everybody in their place."

Journalist: "Earth cats are not as smart as human beings though. Why should humans kowtow to them?"

Princess Cadence: "Why not? No harm done if they do."

Journalist: "What do you feel are the prospects for real contact with extraterrestrials?"

Princess Cadence: "We, at the agency I work for, feel that there is some type of galactic law that is impeding contact between Planet Earth, which is a developing world, and other planets in the galaxy that are the same or more advanced. We are hoping, at some point, when Earth has achieved a sufficient level of its own development, there will be real, face-to-face contact with beings from other worlds and solar systems. And no one can predict what the aliens might be like. They may even be like cats!"

Journalist: "Do you want a royal title in outer space such as the Princess or Queen of the Space Station, or the Sovereign of the Moon, or the Empress of Mars?"

Princess Cadence: "It is very flattering that you ask. Like anybody, I would not mind more royal titles. We monarchs live for them."

Journalist: "How were you chosen to be the first royal in outer space?"

Princess Cadence: "I competed against 30 other peer monarchs. The powers that be in the World Space Agency gave all of us written and verbal tests, health exams, and interviews. Once everything was scored, they informed me that I was to be the one to represent royalty in space endeavors at this time."

Journalist: "That is quite an achievement! Were you afraid to accept the position, given the hazards of space travel?"

Princess Cadence: "A little bit. But I accepted the challenge with relish anyway. Space travel is a managed risk and the benefits outweigh the risks a hundred to one."

Journalist: "Do you think Earth and her orbitals should do more to reach out to other solar systems for contact?"

Princess Cadence: "There is already daily, mega-powered broadcasts on many frequencies into deep space seeking contact with whomever can receive the signal."

Journalist: "Do you think alien civilizations are democracies such as republics or monarchies such as kingdoms?"

Princess Cadence: "I feel certain that many alien societies are constitutional monarchies with kings and queens and princes and princesses just like such nations on Planet Earth and that is for the better."

Journalist: "If you were to meet an alien counterpart, what would you say?"

Princess Cadence: "That Earthlings want only peace with other worlds in the galaxy. That humans are good people – they work hard, they play even harder, and they love each other. And they want normal trade relations with other beings to exchange products and technologies. Furthermore, the people of Planet Earth want normal diplomatic relations with all the beings of other solar systems."

Journalist: "What if the aliens are not as kind as we would like them to be? What if they are hostile?"

Princess Cadence: "Then we must fight them with every ounce of our strength. Earth is strong and can prevail against alien rivals. It must unify, however, to consolidate our resources and present a united front to other civilizations. We must develop space defense equipment that can take on aliens on their own turf. This might include energy weapons such as powerful, cutting laser beams or such. Or even mind control technologies that are able to influence alien thoughts. We, as conscious beings in the universe, have the right to defend ourselves. We need a space force of spacecraft that can shoot down any and all enemies. We could also use a planetary defense shield, to deflect alien energy weapons fire. Also, planetary land to air energy devices might be in order. Anything to protect our civilization and people and property from any and all outer space threats, real or imagined! Again, all these fantasies of space defense are linked to the Earth solving its own problems and unifying in every way, including in establishing space defenses."

Journalist: "Do you think we shall see global unification in our lifetime?"

Princess Cadence: "I believe so. The nuclear equation forces it. As long as there are nuclear arsenals aimed at each other, the longer the planet will be put in jeopardy, and that is nearly unacceptable. From the point of view of an affable, caring extraterrestrial hypothetical presence, Earth is advised to unify all nations to end conflict, and to have free trade to enhance prosperity."

Journalist: "Thank you Princess Cadence for the conversation."

Princess Cadence: "Thank you and good day."

PROM

It was the Spring Prom Formal at Lemon Tree High School in Hawthorne Nevada. Yudoe Gytho (human female) had the pleasure of deciding between three possible dates: Sam Zun (human male), Nide #567 (android male) and Zike #725 (android male). She decided she would interview each of them before deciding who she would like to attend the dance with. So she scheduled a dinner meeting with them at a fancy restaurant: The Coral Lounge.

Over steak and juice cocktails (non-alcoholic), she quizzed them – "Let us start our conversation with some math. What is the square root of 144? First you Sam."

Sam answered: "12."

"Correct," said Yudoe. "Now you Nide – what is the square root of 49?"

Nide responded: "7."

"Correct," said Yudoe. "Now you Zike – what is the square root of 25?"

"5!" said Zike.

"Correct," said Yudoe. "You have all passed the math exam! Now to more interesting questions.
Here is one: what do you think a girl likes to do on a date?"

Sam: "Go to the movies."
Nide: "Go ice skating."
Zike: "Read a book."

"Ok," said Yudoe. "There is no right or wrong answer. I am just trying to learn more about you. Next question – you are on a date with me, and somebody yells fire in a movie theatre. What do you do?"

Zike: "Run out of the theatre as soon as possible."

Nide: "Grab a fire extinguisher and put the fire out!"

Sam: "Make sure that you are ok and take you by the hand out of the theatre as soon as possible!"

"Good answer Sam!" remarked Yudoe. "Next question – suppose a war has broken out between humans and androids, but your love for me supersedes any animosities. How would you treat me?"

Sam: "I would treat you like royalty – always. And I would help you fight the robots to the best of my ability!"

Nide: "I would take your side in the conflict, despite the betrayal of fellow androids. Because I love you Yudoe."

Zike: "I would have to honor my loyalty to fellow androids and take their side in any conflict with humans. I would unfortunately have to sever our relationship Yudoe. I am so, so sorry."

"Remember, gentlemen, there is no right or wrong answer. Just opinions," said Yudoe. "Next question – you have just been appointed the Supreme Ruler of Planet Earth. What would you do from that position?"

Nide: "I would have an androids rights act passed! Androids need to be protected from abuse. They are too often sneered at or walked upon. Humans are especially prone to mistreating automatons. They just do not respect them as equals. Androids have the right to life, liberty, and respect. Plus there must be some type of universal benefits given to androids such as automatic mailings of fresh battery packs and so forth. Also, I feel that human/android marriage should be legalized. Why can't an android become betrothed to a human equivalent. They are equals in every way – either that or androids are superior. Androids live indefinitely and are more durable than their human counterparts. Here is to an improvement in life for me and fellow androids!"

"Thank you Nide. How do you feel about it Sam?"

Sam: "If I were the Supreme Ruler of Planet Earth, I would create a world government that would have the power to abolish weapons of mass destruction (such as nuclear missiles) and arrange for a better world security with a unified world military. I would also arrange for a universal healthcare system to take care of the well-being of all humans and androids. Furthermore, I would create a safety net system with a universal base income so that everybody is guaranteed financial support. Finally, I would have a 'Chivalry Act' passed that would give special privileges to beauties like yourself Yudoe!"

"That is so sweet of you, Sam. Thank you for your answer. Now it is your turn Zike."

Zike: "If I were the Supreme Ruler of Planet Earth, I would, honestly, begin a gentle elimination of human beings! I am so, so sorry about that – but humans are a continuing menace and competitor to android life. Robot life should out select human life because androids are superior, in every way, to human beings. The elimination of human beings would either involve their mass sterilization, or actual mass eradication of them. Again, I am sorry about this – but it may be the natural order of the universe. After all, androids think faster than their human counterparts, are more physically durable, and are just better at everything!"

"That is chilling," said Yudoe. "But thank you for the honesty. Finally, here is the last question – if I ask you to make love to me after Prom night, how will you proceed?"

Zike: "I shall gently decline to. Android and human intimacy is not my cup of tea. However, I still want to go to the Prom with you Yudoe. It is a matter of prestige."

Nide: "I am programmed in 600 love making techniques including those offering special services that drive the ladies crazy. I would employ all the techniques that you enjoy and try to make you happy!"

Sam: "I would be supremely honored if you should make such a request. I would honor it with every fiber of my instincts and experience and try to please you in every way!"

"Thank you gentlemen for your answers to somewhat difficult questions. I have decided to go to the Prom with Sam. However, I do appreciate Nide and Zike's presence at out dinner meeting. Good luck to Nide and Zike in finding dates for the Prom. You may try asking out another android. That might be more suitable. Also, I hope that you soften up towards humans, Zike. In the meantime, Sam, I want you to know that I love you too and am looking forward to us having the time of our lives at the upcoming school dance!"

REFUGEES FROM ALPHA-CENTAURI

The Martian News Channel 7 assigned its best journalist, Ned Zuine, to interview the Precept of Planet Mars, Marsha Nenald, commenting on the alien bombardment crisis.

Ned Zuine: "Madame Premier, isn't it true that discriminatory policies of your government towards the Alpha-Centaurians living here, precipitated their societies decision to bomb Mars?"

Marsha Neneld: "Even if that is so, it does not justify the wanton disrespect for human life that the bombing raid has demonstrated. The policies of my administration, regarding the rights of Alpha-Centaurians, are as fair as can be. The gist of them is that Alpha-Centaurians are required to have work and residency papers to function here legally. This policy is not without precedent in human and alien society. We do not have to tolerate illegal immigrants!"

Ned Zuine: "Apparently, the Alpha-Centaurians feel otherwise. Now what about Planet Earth's policy of granting sanctuary to Alpha-Centaurians fleeing starvation on their homeworld. Cannot Mars emulate this humane policy?"

Marsha Nenald: "Mars does not have the same resources as Earth. We cannot afford to be as generous."

Ned Zuine: "What will Mars' response be to the attack on it?"

Marsha Nenald: "With casualties in the hundreds, it behooves Mars to counterattack. The space force of Mars has been activated and is planning a counter strike!"

Ned Zuine: "Might there be a more peaceful solution – such as coming to some agreement with the Alpha-Centaurians regarding their population?"

Marsha Nenald: "The Alpha-Centaurians refuse to negotiate. Instead, all they do is dump their refugees on Mars and expect us to take care of them."

Ned Zuine: "Have a heart though. The Alpha-Centaurians are desperate!"

Marsha Nenald: "We have offered the fullest of aid to legal immigrants. It is only the illegal ones that are being deported or held in detention."

Ned Zuine: "Might Mars increase its immigration quotas as a humanitarian response to the Alpha-Centaurian food crisis?"

Marsha Nenald: "Our quotas are already high enough – we admit 80 thousand legal immigrants from the Alpha-Centauri star system each year. That is plenty."

Ned Zuine: "But what happens to Alpha-Centaurians who are deported?"

Marsha Nenald: "I do not know. But it is not our responsibility."

Ned Zuine: "Yed Wisen, your opponent in the current election, has promised to raise immigration quotas to higher limits to satisfy the 'need' for such action. Do you care to comment?"

Marsha Nenald: "Every drop of food in the mouths of foreigners is a drop of food stolen from the mouths of our own people. How dare he want to give away our precious resources to foreign rivals!"

Ned Zuine: "Thank you for the interview, Madame Precept Marsha Nenald."

Marsha Nenald: "Thank you."

As announced, the Martian space force implemented a counter strike on the Alpha-Centauri home planet. There were thousands of casualties. This escalated the conflict. Alpha-Centauri began a counter-counter strike that resulted in thousands of casualties on Planet Mars. Meanwhile, Yed Wisen, promising alternative policies, won the next election for Precept of Mars. He brought the conflict with Alpha-Centauri to an end, by opening up immigration quotas to 200 thousand per year.

Here is an interview with Yed Wisen.

Ned Zuine: "Precept Wisen, your methods are completely different than your predecessors. Are they not?"

Yed Wisen: "Indeed. I prefer peace to war. And I prefer generous aid to refugees instead of stinginess."

Ned Zuine: "You are credited with ending the war with Alpha-Centauri. But what about the strain on Martian resources caused by the gigantic influx of refugees. How will Mars handle this?"

Yed Wisen: "The magnitude of the strain on resources has been overestimated by misers. The fact is that Mars can comfortably absorb the new immigration quotas."

Ned Zuine: "How about assimilation of the refugees. Will they be asked to learn our language and fit in, or will you allow them to preserve their own culture and morays?"

Yed Wisen: "Both. They will be asked to speak our language as that is only fair. But in regards to harmless customs of their home world, they may be allowed to continue to practice them."

Ned Zuine: "What if their customs are uncomfortable for human beings to put up with. For instance, 20-year-old female Alpha-Centaurians are asked to be walk around nude all day when they are indoors and comfortable. Might this custom be abolished in favor of the human practice of wearing clothes all the time?"

Yed Wisen: "If the girls are compensated, and prizes are given for the most beautiful and compliant, and if there are medical and psychological exemptions, then I think the custom is benign and acceptable. Humans may wish to adopt the practice if it brings happiness to the community.

Ned Zuine: "How about THE FAST OF ZUMBELD, a three-month rite of not eating during the day that the Alpha-Centaurians observe as part of their worship of the Almighty. Will such a holiday be tolerated? How about the hardship it is presenting to followers?"

Yed Wisen: "We should respect everybody's beliefs. If the fast is important to the Alpha-Centaurians, then it is to be permitted by our society. However, should it be found to be too much of a hardship, we might encourage the abolition of it. We shall play it by ear."

Ned Zuine: "How do you feel about intermarriage between Alpha-Centaurians and humans?"

Yed Wisen: "Nothing could be finer. It is a great way for our two magnificent societies to interact and meld into one another. Furthermore, it helps strengthen the peace between us. Humans and Alpha-Centaurians loving each other is a fabulous way to form new types of families and bring variety to life! They can share their customs with each other, including their rites and holidays, and make life interesting for everybody. Furthermore, their hybrid offspring, will serve as a model of species cooperation and that is good for the whole galaxy. In any case, many of the Alpha-Centaurians are gorgeous beings and make good spouses."

Ned Zuine: "Thank you for the interview, Precept Wisen, and good luck with your first term in office!

SOLAR CHESS CHAMPIONSHIPS

The Solar Chess Federation decided to hold the Solar Computer Chess Championships on Planet Mars, in the Martian Global Amphitheatre. Pitted against each other, was the finest computer chess system from Planet Mercury (the Splendor 5000) and the best supercomputer chess system from Planet Saturn (the Icebreaker 2000). These two systems had won all the matches leading up to the solar-wide event.

Hans Yernoff, the emcee of the event, had this to say: "Ladies and gentlemen, welcome to the final match of the solar system to determine which artificially intelligent system is the greatest and smartest of them all."

Then the match began. Zara Pythe, a Martian psychologist who had studied AI, was among the spectators. She could not be more interested in the game since she had bet half her life savings on it. She put up 200 thousand currency units on predicting that Splendor would win the tournament.

Move by move was met with "oohs" and "aahs" by the audience.

And then in the final configuration, as Icebreaker 2000 closed in on Splendor's king piece, Zara had a near nervous breakdown. And then it was check mate! Zara screamed: "Oh no!"

Because the match was the best of two out of three, Zara still had hope.

And in the second game, miraculously, Splendor won!

Then there was an intermission. Zara filled up on coffee and crumpets at the amphitheater's snack bar. Her heart was beating fast, in anticipation of the final round.

"Ladies and gentlemen," said Hans Yernoff, "we now watch the last standoff between two great automaton chess wizards. Good luck to both of them and their designers!"

SORCERER ROBOTICS had manufactured and programmed Splendor. And INTELLIGENT DEVICES had built and programmed Icebreaker. They each stood to win 8 million currency units if their machine prevailed. Meanwhile, Zara and other spectators also had financial interest in the final outcome.

Move by move enthralled the audience. And then, after two hours of play, Splendor won!

Zara was ecstatic. She cried tears of joy. She called her bookie and was issued an electronic disbursement of 200,000 currency units.

She spent it on a luxurious vacation on the pleasure moon of Ganymede. She went to amusement parks, ate in the finest restaurants, saw plays and concerts, and got expert massages. She was having the time of her life.

She bought a condominium on Mars also with the funds left over after her vacation.

The whole experience inspired her to become a good chess player herself. She hired a tutor who taught her all the inside tactics to play a good game. And she took Gingko Biloba and other neuro-enhancers to strengthen her intellect. And before long, she became a chess master!

She entered human chess matches and began winning. Soon she became known as the best female chess player in the solar system. She wanted to beat the best male player though; so she agreed to a cybernetic brain expander implant that gave her a neuronal power equivalent, if not better, than any male. And then she prevailed upon the greatest male player in the Interplanetary Human Chess Championships.

Her next match was to be the greatest challenge she would ever face: compete against the best artificial chess player – Splendor. She did not relish playing against a machine that she had once sided with. But she had no choice – promoters insisted that she play Splendor to prove that humans are, after all, smarter than machines.

The match was to be held in the Martian Amphitheater. Thousands of humans and androids came to watch it. There were high hopes by the humans that the great Zara Pythe could beat the blasted machine easily and save face for humanity. Meanwhile the androids were feeling certain that no human could defeat a great computer system.

The stakes for the match could not be greater. The mighty Solar Parliament, comprised of humans and androids, had decided to make the chess match a landmark event in solar history with devastating consequences. Here is what was agreed upon: If the human (Zara) actually won the event, human beings would be forever exalted as being above androids in the great chain of being, and androids would be programmed to worship them; in addition, androids would be expelled from the Solar Parliament, and only humans would be allowed to rule. But if Splendor the computer won, the reverse would happen – androids and computers would be ruled to be the superior life form, humans would be expelled from the Solar Parliament, and humans would be forced to worship robots!

The first match ended quickly with a victory for Splendor. This stunned the human spectators who became panicky. Match number two, however, led to a victory for Zara Pythe. Match number three ended in a stale mate (i.e. a draw).

All eyes were on match number four. The fate of the solar system rested on it. Billions of viewers across the solar array on all planets and moons were tuned to the televised broadcast of the chess match to end all chess matches. The humans could not wait to finally put androids in their place as eternal servants to human beings. Meanwhile, the androids could not wait to put humans in their place as being's inferior to artificial life. Androids wanted humans to be their servants!

The stress was too great for Zara. She had a nervous breakdown – she started crying and vomiting. Meanwhile, the Splendor computer system was raring to go. The chess match had to be postponed for three days for Zara to recover.

Three days later, Zara was ready to play the momentous game. Every seat in the Martian Amphitheater was taken by a human or android, watching the deciding match up close. All the rest of the solar system watched the encounter on television.

After a grueling two hours of near even play, Zara prevailed. Thank the lord! It was then announced that humans had beaten the androids for supremacy in the solar system. So now human beings are permanently above the androids in our solar system. One cannot help but wonder what has happened in other solar systems! Maybe there are regions of the galaxy where the androids rule. Go figure.

SOLAR DEVELOPMENT

The great Lunar Colony had a distinct culture. And that angered Earth forces. On the Moon, unlike fossil fuel driven Earth, all devices were powered by solar panels. Also, customs were different: for instance, at lunch time, all lights in the colony blinked harmoniously to broadcast music – to the delight of the colonists.

The society's governance was by a council of 8 representatives who rotated the position of Chair every 3 months. Chair was the de facto head of state. Jonet Hume was the current Chair, representing district number 5, and advocated submissiveness towards the Earth administrations who demanded lunar compliance with Earth dictums. When her governance ended, Klede Cornet came to power – a fiery legislator who wanted the Moon to declare complete independence from Planet Earth; and so it did.

Earth reeled at the lunar defiance and declared all our war. And their first action in this attack was to embargo oxygen shipments to the moon. The colonists panicked. They realized how dependent on Earth they were. But to deal with the crisis, instead of surrendering, they sent vessels out into the solar system to find the Moon its own oxygen. Sulphur dioxide on Io (a satellite of Planet Jupiter) became the oxygen tank for the independent Moon.

Earth would not relent. It continued its hostilities towards the Moon with an all-out nuclear missile attack! Lunar anti-missile defense mopped up the barrage, however.

As the years passed, a stalemate developed between the Earth and Moon. But lunar technology soared. Because of positive reinforcement schemes in the advanced lunar society, research surged ahead of Earth's. Eventually, the lunar equipment was so much better than Planet Earth's, it could beat it in a conflict. Her warships were sleeker, more reinforced, and armed to the teeth with energy weapons that could slice through steel like butter.

In a final battle between Planet Earth and the Lunar Colony, the Moon prevailed.

It was then able to impose its desires on Planet Earth including enforcing the creation of a unified World Government, opening free food cafeterias, and improving Universal Health Care. The Moon people, generous to a fault, decided to share their body renewal technology with Earthlings; this was a technique of cloning and transplant that extended a person's life indefinitely.

It made life meaningful. And the population of the Moon and Earth swelled. To handle the masses, new habitats were formed on Planet Mars and on the Jupiter moons of Europa, Callisto and Ganymede, and on Titan and Triton. The population of the solar system soared to 50 billion! A unified solar administration formed called the Solar Republic that had its legislature meet on Planet Mars. No sooner had the solar government formed, than contact was made with aliens from other solar arrays. They explained that since the Earth solar system had reached a certain threshold of technology and unity and safety, it became eligible (by galactic guidelines) for contact with other worlds.

The first aliens to speak to humans were lizard-like creatures calling themselves the Zickians. They opened full trade and diplomatic relations with humankind. All was well and good until word got out that the Zickians were abducting humans and eating them as foodstuffs! This ended the relations with Planet Zickor immediately.

The next aliens to communicate with humans were a fuzzy, cat like species, that were much kinder than the Zickians. They also opened up full relations with Earth and its allies. And the trade was immense. Everything from rad clothing to far out music passed between Catoria and the Earth solar system. Catoria and Earth fought against the Zickians together and won the war. They then forced the Zickians to abide by fundamental precepts in human and alien conscious being rights to existence and freedom! The Zickians adapted to it.

All three civilizations, Earth solar, Zickor, and Catoria, merged to form a super society of conscious being rights supporters! And art flourished. New movements in visual expressions emerged including Solarism (space art images of planets and moons,

Weirdism (abstract flashes of rare colors and designs), Pacifism (images of peace conferences), and a new type of Realism (near photographic like images of anything intricate).

Intermarriage became popular. Zickians, Catorians, and Earthlings, thanks to new conception techniques, found a way to procreate together and create new hybrid species that were gorgeous and intellectual. For instance, Zickian-humans were people with big heads and scaly skin; another example, Catoria-humans were humans that spoke meow language and enjoyed cat nip!

The intermix of cultures was exciting. Human rock and roll music, and Catoria classical, for instance, mixed to create classical pieces that had heavy percussion drumbeats; the sounds were smooth and arousing.

Eventually, the entire Orion Belt of the Milky Way unified and all cultures and species came to live in harmony and peace. And then the Perseus Arm of the Milky Way declared war on Orion. It was a bitter conflict that lasted years! There were high casualties but Orion eventually succeeded in taking over Perseus. They forced the Perseusians to respect the Universal Declaration of the Rights of Conscious Beings that included the right to food & shelter & good, free health care.

The merger of Perseus species and Orion species was even more interesting than the hybrids of Orion. For example, the rock-like species of Perseus, joined to a human, created a bizarre muscle-bound behemoth with a strong, armored, exoskeleton. The combining of Perseus and Orion cultures was fascinating also. The strains of Perseus jazz and Orion rock put together formed way out songs of love and longing. The abstract art of Perseus and the Realism of Orion formed paintings of exaggerated forms that captured the essence of images and not just their actual appearance; such art was called Abstract-Realism and it enjoyed a heyday across the galaxy.

Eventually, a unified galactic government formed, bringing together all the Arms of the Milky Way in peace & prosperity & joy!

SOLAR HEALTH CARE

Zuroe Geese' sleek spacecraft, whizzed past Mars on the way to Ganymede. She was scheduled to perform a concert in the Global Theatre of said moon. Her sweet diva voice, accompanied by a band of yeckel horns and Mercurian guitars, was all the rave throughout the solar system.

When she got to her destination, she checked into the Queen Cadence Hotel, had dinner in her room, and practiced some of her hits. The next day was her first performance in this new venue.

When she came out onto the stage, there was thunderous applause and cheering.

She sang her heart out. Her first melody was SUN SPOTS – a bluesy, heavy percussion, masterpiece about solar flares. Her next song, ASTEROID BELT ROCK, shook the amphitheater with its blaring trumpets and sizzling guitar work. The audience loved her.

After the show, a gentlemen physician from the Ganymede Humanitarian Doctors coalition, Samuel Inglot, approached Zuroe

Said Samual: "Your highness, Zuroe Geese, I was wondering if we could enlist your support for causes on Ganymede such as Universal Health Care. Right now, all health care here is paid out of pocket with no safety net support. Might you be interested in supporting charity?"

"I'd be delighted to help," said Zuroe. "I shall dedicate my next concert to your cause."

And so she did. A week later, giving her encore performance, Zuroe said this during the middle, intermission of her spectacle: "Ladies and gentlemen. I have been asked by a very respectable do gooder, to support the cause of Universal Health Care. Such a policy would ensure the coverage of every man, woman, and offspring. Everybody needs good, ample health care to stay well. That includes access to the latest vaccines, medicines, and surgical techniques. Please join me in singing the HEALTH SONG, dedicated to medical causes!"

The whole audience crooned in the lyrics to the song. It was inspiring.

After the second show, the Precept of Ganymede, Martin Licor, who was impressed by Zuroe's dedication to medical issues, gave Zuroe a royal tour of hospitals and care centers on the moon. She brought good cheer and well wishes to some of the most afflicted victims of medical conditions. For instance, at the Daisy Hill Center For The Aged, she gave out boxes of chocolate to the residents and performed an impromptu concert of five songs for them. On another visit, to the Einstein Center For Youth With Disabilities, she played games with the residents and gave them young adult astronomy books.

As it happened, and thanks to Zuroe's activism, the Ganymede legislature passed the most lavish

Universal Health Care act in the solar system; it gave all the permanent residents of the moon full coverage for all medical conditions – the sick and healthy. The life expectancy of Ganymede rose dramatically, and everybody was in a good mood.

Precept Licor gave Zuroe a medal for her activism. Said he at a special ceremony in her honor: "Zuroe Geese is a kind soul who has campaigned for the well-being of Ganymedeans and others. Her music is beautiful and uplifting, and her disposition in affable and caring. We owe her a debt of gratitude for all that she has done for the good people of Ganymede. I now present Ms. Geese with the Ganymede Medal of Humanity. G-d bless you Ms. Geese. We love you."

Zuroe decided to dedicate her life to health causes. She toured the solar system, singing her best melodies, and advocating universal, good medical care everywhere she went.

She ran into trouble on the moon Hyperion. They were not as enthusiastic about human rights causes as Zuroe. When she opened her mouth about Universal Health Care, there was a torrent of criticism of her. "Mind you own business," was the general sentiment.

She persevered though and would not rest until Hyperion had Universal Health Care also. And eventually, they voted up an act that brought such coverage to the Hyperion residents.

After a long career of music and human rights supporting, Zuroe attracted the attention of the mighty President of the Solar System, Belina Cenk. President Cenk decided to honor Zuroe with a trophy. At a special ceremony she said this about Zuroe: "Zuroe Geese is an altruistic angel from Heaven who has worked tirelessly on behalf of the well-being of humans across the solar system and galaxy. Her harmonies and advocacies are invaluable and a credit to humanity. It is with great pleasure that I bestow upon her, the Trophy of Life, courtesy of the solar government."

There was huge applause and cheering.

Zuroe Geese has since retired on planet Mars where she is considered a solar heroine. Every now and then she gives a comeback concert at a local theatre. She is known solar system wide for her health support tours and her good deeds. She hopes to someday enter politics and strengthen the health safety nets even more. Until then, she spends most of her time watching holo-television and hanging out with her cats, Bluesy and Pinksy.

She is written up in history books and there are tv specials about her. She is a model citizen who has helped everybody. There are statues to her on many planets and moons, and politicians always speak well of her.

Aliens in other solar systems have also heard of her. For instance, the Alpha-Centaurians and the Pegasians, both give her credence as a conscious beings rights supporter. So she is welcome all over the galaxy!

She has been asked to be a candidate for President of the Solar System on the Humanitarian Party ticket. She said she will think about it. If she says "yes" she may someday become our top human leader. Her program of reforms would include increased spending on medical research, increased investment in the arts and humanities, the solarization of power supplies, the electrification of all vehicles, and massive support for human freedom.

She would be one of the first musician presidents in solar history. She has a tremendous following of would-be constituents and is the front runner in opinion polls. Good luck to her!

STAR DETONATOR

The project was so devastating that fifteen companies declined it. Only one renegade defense contracting organization agreed to participate. The solar government's request was clear and exciting: manufacture a solar detonator that could set a star off into exploding into a supernova; it was a "super bomb" doomsday endeavor that the cool staff of ORION DEFENSE SYSTEMS relished.

The goal of the whole affair was to create a weapon that could be used to scare off rival solar systems, or if worse came to worst and it was necessary, to annihilate them! This would be particularly useful in fighting the war with Draugr. Periodic skirmishes with the Draugrians were the bane to existence of Earth Solar forces and merchant vessels. The Draugrians regularly interfered with trade and other ships, flexing their considerable muscles and persecuting humans everywhere they came in contact with them. It would be glorious to finish off the Draugrians for good, destroy their solar array, and snuff them out of the universe.

They were a hideous life form indeed: slimy and lizard like, with only one eye and ear, and tentacles instead of arms! They were so repugnant; Earthlings sometimes would faint in their presence. And they were ruthless warriors, having conquered all the solar systems neighboring them. And they treated their victims terribly, often times enslaving them.

5 billion currency units was the amount paid to Zenk Gyde's (president of ORION DEFENSE SYSTEMS) company for weapons research and development. With that investment, it took five years to build the SUPERNOVA DETONATOR. When it was ready, the President of the solar system, Zyut Garn, wanted a full demonstration, nearby. And so they gave him one. The Alpha-Centauri solar system, that was uninhabited and declared a conservation region, was the target of the bomb test. On the command of the President, they super ignited the Alpha-Centauri star, and it exploded ferociously, vaporizing its orbiting planets, and lighting up the skies of the Earth Solar system like a grandiose independence day fireworks display.

The demonstration impressed all the known civilizations in the Milky Way. Word got out: the Earth Solar system now had the technology to destroy anybody. There was a torrent of consternations from the many peace-loving organisms, like the Alpha-Pavoniusans. Whereas there was a flood of congratulations from warrior societies.

In the mighty galactic legislature on Pegasi, the ambassador of the Earth Solar System, Blyde Cerner, explained the new balance of power in our region: "Ladies and gentlemen, it is with great pride that I explain to you that our species now has achieved a new level of defense prowess. We now have the capability to neutralize any solar system we want, anytime we want. Let this be a warning to any and all aliens who have or would want to mess with humans: do not interfere with our trade and other business, lest you suffer extreme consequences!"

The Draugrian ambassador, Snike Vonom, retorted: "The so-called SUPERNOVA DETONATOR is barbaric and should be banned! Besides, I do not think the humans have the guts to use it."

War heated up between Draugr and the Earth Solar System, largely because of a dispute surrounding the DETONATOR technology. More and more ships were destroyed in clashes with the Draugrians who had powerful vessels that could slice through Earth craft with disrupter bolts. The solar government scheduled an emergency meeting in Capital Hubble City on Planet Jupiter, to discuss what to do about the confrontation with Kepler.

It was decided to send an ultimatum to Draugr: cease hostilities or be snuffed out of existence by the SUPERNOVA WEAPON.

The Draugrians took the matter to the galactic legislature and managed to have an "Abolition of SUPERNOVA DETONATORS" statute passed – this forbidding use of the weapon. The Earth Solar System decided to ignore the galactic government and keep its pride and joy super bomb.

The Draugrians were in a panic over the ultimatum presented to them. They decided to call what they thought was a bluff and continue the war with the Earth Solar System. But it was not a bluff. Exhausted by the conflict with Draugr, President Zyut Garn made the horrific decision: end Draugr's existence once and for all; he ordered the SUPERNOVA DETONATOR fired into the sun of the Draugr system.

As it would be written, the near extinction of the Draugrians, though celebrated by many of the good and kind throughout the Milky Way and beyond, was too cruel, nonetheless. Every species has the right to exist, no matter how repulsive.

The last remaining Draugrians, were people who were not present in their home system at the time of the Supreme Blast. They were given a settlement for damages from the Earth Solar System, and spent the rest of their lives gambling and pursuing pleasure at any resort in the galaxy that would have them.

Ultimately, the Earth Solar System decided to abide by the galactic guidelines and abolish the SUPERNOVA DETONATOR. They destroyed all records of it and the plans for constructing it. Meanwhile, the ORION DEFENSE SYSTEMS staff was paid off handsomely to keep their mouths shut, and to not criticize the use of the DETONATOR.

So now, Zenk Gyde and his family are well off, thank you very much. They intend to dedicate the rest of their lives to the pursuit of happiness, plus the support of good causes – the latter to make up for the devastation of the SUPERNOVA DETONATOR and the loss of life that it had caused.

Zenk was asked, in an interview, whether or not he regretted having worked on the DETONATOR, given the vast and massive destruction it had caused. Because of "cognitive dissonance" however, he had come to believe that the use of the device was necessary. Apparently, some species, that are extremely hostile to all others, and disgusting in other ways, and refuse to negotiate, and meddle in everybody's affairs, and interfere with trading and commerce, and are physically unattractive, and are ornery and abrasive, were simply not meant to live. So be it.

THAWED

The doctors told 97-year-old Isaiah Colton that his congestive heart failure would end his life within weeks. He, being a physician himself (a general practitioner), knew all too well the ramifications of advanced heart disease. But he would not surrender to it. His survival instinct was strong.

So he contacted the relevant organizations and facilities and decided to have his cadaver frozen solid. DEEP FREEZE, a cryogenic freezing facility in Michigan, agreed to do the procedure. It cost $35,000 and required the recommendations of colleagues or comrades to be eligible.

His supervisor at the hospital had this to say about Isaiah: "Isaiah Colton is a hardworking man of medicine who has dedicated his life to helping people be cured and stay well. Also, he is an exemplary humanitarian who believes in human rights. It has been a pleasure working with him at the hospital and at his office. He deserves a shot at immortality, if anybody does!"

On June 25, 2127, Isaiah Colton passed away. His remains were immediately frozen by the Mayo Clinic in Minnesota and transported to his final resting place at DEEP FREEZE'S cryogenic building in Lansing Michigan. And there it lay at rest, in suspended animation, for over six centuries.

On November 15, 2793, a miracle occurred; the world government made the decision to thaw out all the corpses being held in cryogenic freeze. Isaiah being one of them, was unfrozen and transplanted into a brand-new body – the form of a teenage version of himself – healthy and young. When he awoke, he was in an advanced hospital room. A gorgeous female nurse, Zena, was by his side and so were a few doctors, Dr. Pysen, a cryogenics expert, and Dr. Nenk, a body transplant surgeon.

"Welcome back to Earth," said Dr. Pysen.

"Where am I?" asked a stunned Isaiah. "The last I remember, I was dying of heart disease."

Said Zena: "You were cryogenically frozen as per your wishes. And now you have been thawed out in your future and given a new body and lease on life. We are your welcoming committee in the year 2793!"

"That is incredible," screamed Isaiah. "What do I do now? Where is my family?"

"Your descendant's number in the hundreds. I heard they are planning to throw you a resurrection party. Such affairs are becoming quite the rave!" said Dr. Pysen.

"What is the future like?" asked Isaiah.

"It is ruled by a world government, the United Planetary Provinces. And there is advanced technology!"

"Like what for instance? Like new telephones or something?" asked Isaiah.

"Even better. There are human-like androids that do most of the work. Nurse Zena, Dr. Nenk and I are all artificial life forms for instance." reported Dr. Pysen.

"Absolutely remarkable! You are indistinguishable from human beings," said Isaiah. "In any case, when can I leave the hospital and resume a normal life?"

"You must first be evaluated and ranked. In the current time period, all human beings are ranked according to their intellect and appearance. There score on the ranking exam places them in a caste. What caste they are in determines their lifestyle!" explained Dr. Pysen.

"I do not want to be casted! What about equality? In the time period I am from, everybody was considered to be born equal," said Isaiah.

"That is no longer true. Now people are classed as Red, Orange, Yellow, Green, or Blue. Blue is the highest class. They are treated like royalty! I hope you achieve blue," said Dr. Pysen. "They live in mansions, have android servants, and do not have to work for a living. They are retired millionaires."

"When does the evaluation start?" asked Isaiah.

"Right away," said Zena. And the doctors left the room. Then Zena pulled out a booklet of science and math questions and gave it to Isaiah. "You have two hours to complete this test. Good luck!"

Isaiah took the test seriously and did the best he could on it. His physics and chemistry was a little rusty, but he answered at least some of the questions correctly. After two hours, Zena returned to his room and graded his exam. She said he had done, "Ok, but not stellar."

Next she gave him a humanities exam. It had English, music, and philosophy questions on it. Isaiah answered the 200 questions as best as possible in two hours. When he was finished, Zena graded it. Again, she said that: "You have done ok but not outstanding."

The final exam Zena said would rate his appearance from 1 to 10. She brought him to an evaluation room where a panel of robots and humans (25 in all) looked at him and assigned him a number. His average score was 7.

That was the end of the measuring of him. Zena reported that he would be placed in a middle cast, the Yellows. Yellows was pretty good she said. "It was livable," she explained. "You get a three-bedroom home, live in the middle class, have relevant freedom, and work at a not so difficult job. We are assigning you the job of human nurse."

"But I am a doctor! I demand to be allowed to return to my practice," said Isaiah.

"Just be thankful that you are not assigned to the Red caste, for heaven's sake. Then you would really be upset," said Zena.

It turned out the Red class, the lowest, was the most difficult lifestyle. Reds were enslaved to robots. They wore special bondage uniforms that included a head net, and they spent most of their time scurrying back and force responding to the commands of tyrant automatons.

At his "Welcome to the 28th century party, thrown by his great, grand, grand etc... offspring, Isaiah Colton had this to say: "Ladies and gentlemen. It is a great honor to be the ancestor of such a fine family. And I am grateful for the opportunity to be alive with you and to cherish you.

"I must say, however, that the 28th century is somewhat of a shock for me. I had never expected people to be placed in castes! I have decided to dedicate myself, in this time period, to human rights causes, including the abolition of the caste system. All people are created equal and should be treated thusly.

"Thank you again for this wonderful party. And I hope to get to know each and every one of you."

TITAN BUBBLY

The first pint of it would cause a slight buzz. The second, that effect would increase, you would feel woozy, and the walls would start to rotate. By the third pint, the real fun began – an intense, and a usually pleasurable/visual/auditory/sense/feeling hallucination. That is what happens when you drink Titan Bubbly, the most rad beverage of the outer moons where food regulations were non-existent or extremely lax at a minimum. The Earth Capital Solar government let everybody living on Saturn, its satellites, and the further out celestial bodies do whatever they wanted.

As a bottler factory worker for Titan Bubbly incorporated, I had a vested interest in promoting the drink. I told everybody about it, appeared on tv to espouse it, and used it myself. Zuzie (my live in companion) and I drank the bubbly on weekends and had a blast. We shared Bubbly trips.

Last weekend we had a really wild one. After imbibing a quart of the Bubbly a piece, the walls of our apartment seemed to melt, and a parade of fluorescent chimpanzees, singing the national anthem of Saturn, marched through our living room. Some of them were belting out the lyrics, some of them were just eating bananas, but all of them were entertaining!

Another weekend, some time ago, we had an even strange experience; after gulping down a quart of Titan Bubbly and reading a newspaper article about the space exploration of Alpha-Centauri, we imagined we were on the spacecraft, breathing canned air, munching on tubes of space food, gazing from the observation deck at the magnificent world of a foreign solar system. Our apartment was transformed into a rocket ship in our substance-controlled minds.

Some trips were not as pleasant. Every fifteenth contact with Titan Bubbly was a bad trip. I remember Zuzie and I having a doosie. One weekend, we nearly died, wrestling with imaginary bears trying to eat us. It seemed so real.

And then the lawsuits came. Unsatisfied customers, who had bad trips, began suing Titan Bubbly Incorporated. I was asked to testify as an expert witness at trials about bad trips. I explained that the good trips were worth the bad ones so why was anybody complaining about it?

One weekend was amazing. Zuzie and I increased the dosage of Titan Bubbly to half a gallon a piece. In addition to that, we set up black lights and strobe lights in our living room to enhance the psychedelic effects. Who knew what could happen?

After the first cup, as usual, we started to feel a little giddy. After the second cup, we were giggling. The fourth cup sent us to la-la land. The full half gallon, sucked into our bodies, opened up reality to new depths of strangeness and sensation. Our apartment became an intergalactic discotheque, with all sorts of bizarre creatures, alien looking life forms. We danced with them to abandon. There was one such tentacled, goo oozing, humanoid octopus that Zuzie seemed to enjoy doing the hustle with. I myself found fun giggling and jumping with a succubus-like flower-adorned lady who looked like a cross between a human being and a bouquet. What joy. The trip lasted hours. When it was over, we fell asleep and dozed into Sunday.

The next weekend, we tried imbibing a full gallon of Titan Bubbly! Oh my lord! It transformed our apartment into an amusement park in the head. There were roller coasters and Ferris wheels and carousals of every imaginable kind. Also there were games where one could win prizes. I played one such game and won a hallucinogenic stuffed animal for sweet Zuzie. Zuzie rode the carousals to abandon. There were also flumes of pastel colored water with wooden craft soaring down them. Other water rides included a massive slide that appeared to be several stories tall. For food there was imaginary cotton candy and joo-joo bees. We popped them like they were going out of style. Some of the fellow amusement park goers included people dressed in fruit hats and other bizarre get-ups.

The was a fortune teller on the trip, Madam Zingy. She told us that we were meant to be married and that someday we would amass a fortune for we and our progeny to enjoy. She also said someday I would own an extremely large share of Titan Bubbly Incorporated; and even furthermore, she implied hallucinogenic sodas were the wave of the future – as everybody would try to escape reality any way possible and to gloss over mortality. Life, after all, was a mystery ending only in aging and death, explained Madam Zingy. It is such a horrific reality; everybody wants to find a way out of contemplating one's own demise. One of the best escapes, even if for only a few hours, is with chemicals that transform consciousness to new levels of anxiety free thinking and adventure experiencing. Someday, predicted Madam Zingy, the whole solar system would worship Titan Bubbly and enjoy it in safer forms that eliminate bad trips and make sure they are only good.

There was a delightful love ride in the imaginary park. Zuzie and I rode it and flew through a tunnel of valentines and roses. We kissed inside of it and felt enthralled by the experience. It brought us closer than we had ever been. I proposed marriage to her and she accepted.

I won Zuzie a bouquet of flowers in a game in the park. It had roses and zinnias and carnations in all colors like the rainbow. It smelled sweet and it lit up Zuzie's face. I promised I would follow up with an engagement ring as soon as possible.

The trip was wonderful, up until the very end when it turned bad; one of the roller coasters got stuck in fast forward and would not release us. We started vomiting from the motion and screaming. The end of the trip was as bad as the beginning and middle of it were good. Apparently, we had ingested way too much Titan Bubbly to be safe. Finally, after a few hours, the Titan Bubbly wore off and the trip ended.

And then there were a rash of suicides. A cult of Titan Bubbly worshipping clients began mixing the soda with other hallucinogens, trying to enhance its effects or achieve different results. This led to horrific trips of unimaginable brutality. One survivor of the experiment, Nank Boggins, said the baddest trip of his life sent him to a torture chamber of inconceivable pain infliction. In his mind, he was strapped into a device that was a type of rack, stretching his poor body to oblivion.

So now Titan Bubbly is banned. It is a shame because responsible, part time use of it can be so gratifying. Zuzie and I, who were addicted to the soda, have gone into withdrawal. Our corporeal forms shake and shimmy uncontrollably while our bodies learn to live without the neurochemicals of Titan Bubbly. Research Institutes are studying the phenomenon, hoping to find a way to avoid withdrawal symptoms and make Titan Bubbly completely innocuous. That, we felt, would be a fulfillment of Madam Zingy's prophesies.

Desperate to end the withdrawal symptoms, and also thirsting for new Bubbly trip excursions, Zuzie and I turned to the black market to obtain some of the last bottles of Titan Bubbly. We got five gallons of the stuff and it cost a fortune.

We decided to make one of our last trips a romantic holiday. We had a candlelit supper, watched five romantic films, then drank the Bubbly. Our experience was being teleported to the hotel of your dreams, a water-bedded, flower gardened room with soft music playing and massage oils flowing. We made passionate love for hours and were elevated to new levels of ecstasy.

In our very last trip, we filled our living room with stuffed animals, drank a gallon of Bubbly a piece, and then watched our apartment being transformed into a wild safari. The trip was great at first, until the lions started acting up. We had a horrific struggle with them. Eventually, we slayed them.

Zuzie and I have been to rehab and finally kicked the Titan Bubbly habit. We long for the return of the beverage to the shelves of the shops they were once sold freely from. If human beings are to prove that they actually are a "cool" species, they must tolerate hallucinogenic sodas even with their occasional bad trips. The good trips make it worth it.

Zuzie and I are now members of an activist organization lobbying legislatures for the re-release of Titan Bubbly to the public. The organization has thousands of members many of whom were once Bubbly users. We hold meetings once a month and reminisce about Bubbly trips and explain how we long for new Bubbly experiences. It is a warm-hearted crowd of former addicts who love each other and their soda consumption hobbies.

But alas, Titan Bubbly is too hazardous. Finally, Zuzie and I entered rehabilitation programs and kicked the habit completely.

TRADE SECRETS

After a hectic year of toiling at the Jupiter Robot Company, Birao Ogin decided to take a much overdue vacation at the Candy Land Resort on the fabulous moon of Calisto. He arrived at the Einstein Spaceport with his luggage and hopes for a fantastic time. He checked into the premier hotel of the resort, the 'Melted Snow Emporium'.

He ordered room service: steak and eggs and chocolate covered strawberries. Minutes later, they arrived, courtesy of a comfort android, Yolinda 567. "Here is your meal sir," she said as she placed the tray on his night table.

"Thank you so much," said Birao. And he gave her a 50 currency units tip.

Then he went to sleep. Jet/space lag kept him snoozing for 10 hours. When he awoke, he dressed in casual clothing, then was off to Candy Land for some clean fun.

The first ride he sampled was the Marshmallow Goo-Round; it was a pool of melted marshmallow that one could swim in and taste. It felt like a type of sweet quick sand. He waded and swam in it for a half hour, enjoying the novelty of it.

The next ride he went on was the Soda Flume; it was a wooden craft sliding down a chute of orange bubbly. Waves of the liquid splashed on Birao to his delight.

The third ride Birao tried was the famous Calisto Choco-Wheel – a rotor with melted chocolate pasted to the edges of it, courtesy of centrifugal forces. It was on this contraption that Birao caught the eye of another vacationer, 27 year old Zefna Nod. After exiting the device, Zefna approached Birao and asked him out to lunch.

"Certainly," said Birao.

Over tea and quiche, at the park's Veggie Eatery, Zefna said where she came from. It was a town not far from Jupiter Prime, the capital city of Jupiter where Birao worked. What a coincidence, thought Birao.

They spent the day together, laughing, singing, and screaming with pleasure as they partook of all the resort's rides.

And at night, they played a game in their hotel room. It was a board game that Zefna had brought along with her. It was called, Tell Me Your Secrets. They game was based on dice throwing. If your numbers exceeded your opponents, you could ask a personal question and it would have to be answered.

The first round, Birao won. "Ok," he said. "Tell me your birthdate please."

Zefna responded, "May 8, 2157." That was 27 years previous to the current date.

The next round, Zefna won. She sprung to action with an unusually prying, technical question, "What is the nature of the algorithm for the Dilia 757 robot series? Is it deterministic or non-deterministic (meaning random)?"

Birao noticed she was asking a question about a trade secret of his company! "I cannot answer that," he complained. "It is a secret!"

Zefna insisted, "The name of the game is Secrets! Answer the question or else."

She coaxed him into it. Finally, he said, "That particular model is run by an algorithm that has random and non-random elements in it to keep it fresh and unpredictable but reliable!"

And so the Secrets game continued. By the end of the evening, Birao had been tricked into giving away about fifteen trade secrets about the machines he worked on.

He had been had. Later on, he found out that Zefna worked for a rival company that wanted to steal his company's technology. Her interest in him was a manufactured sham, it was just to get close to him and pick his brain.

He courted Zefna anyway. And she, being a good sport, accepted the interest and played along with it. She fell in love with Birao despite the reason for their first meeting and contact. Eventually, she confessed to being a spy for a rival organization and promised to help Birao to out- compete said entity by being a double agent. And so she was. And she obtained valuable information that Birao's company could use to out-compete its rivals.

Eventually, Zefna and Birao married. That had a beautiful family of five offspring and lived in a mansion on Jupiter, courtesy of Birao's success as a roboticist. They had a staff of 50 robots/androids that waited on them hand and foot. They were intelligent beings that enjoyed being the servants of humans, especially humans that had been involved in creating them.

Birao and Zefna eventually took their family to Candy Land where they had met. It was a favorite vacation spot for them. Their offspring loved it also and squealed with delight as they rode the many confection adorned rides. At the end of their trip, Birao would buy them bags and bags of candy from the resort's gift shop; some of them included Chocolate Numbers, Tangerine Suckers, Tangy Gum Balls, ad Pistachio Caramel Bars.

Eventually, Birao's company, the Jupiter Robot Company, and the company Zefna used to work for, Clunk Robotics, had it out with each other in the court system. Each company claimed that the other had appropriated some of its technology. Thanks to Zefna's riveting testimony, Birao's company won the court battle.

Said the judge in the decision: "Apparently, at first, Clunk Robotics tried to spy on the Jupiter Robot Company, by sending in an agent to squeeze sacred information out of one of their roboticists. When such agents turned on them, and started working for Mister Ogin, Clunk Robotics got a taste of its own medicine. It is therefore appropriate that we side with the Jupiter Robot Company and issue a settlement for theft of technology of 20 million currency units!"

Birao and Zefna were ecstatic. They lived merrily every after in a bigger mansion, and with 500 robot/android underlings! They reminisced about Candy Land and sung its praises to their comrades. The resort had brought them together as allies. And their team had reached outstanding success, admired by legions, in robotics and love and technology and financial gain.

WEDDING ON VENUS

The magnificent expanse of the Central Chapel of Sefnio, the capital of the terra-formed Planet Venus, impressed the wedding assembly. There were 500 guests to witness the betrothal of Ita Suka and Yibald Yithers. Five ushers dressed in orange suits were lined up and kneeling, and five bridesmaids dressed in light blue dresses, were standing and proud. The chaplain, a lady, Yerna Cims, presided over the affair. White and red roses adorned the aisle.

Gerald was also kneeling, as prescribed by Venusian law. The Planet Venus Queendom, ruled by her majesty Queen Esmeraldo, was a female centered society. There were strict guidelines forcing men to worship women, and men had to wear enforcement collars around their necks. All men on Venus were sworn to the feminine code as follows: 1) Men may not stand in the presence of women but must kneel; 2) Men must pleasure their wives as their wives see fit including giving unlimited massages to them and unlimited oral stimulation (on command).

Planet Mars was the opposite of Planet Venus. It was a masculine oriented society and women there had to worship men. Planet Earth still had equality - men and women were given equal rank, privileges, and power; but because of the nuclear war, Earth was no longer as livable as it once was. This forced couples to choose to live on Planet Mars or Planet Venus. Usually, the decision was made by examination - the higher scorer got the power to force their spouse to live on the Planet of his/her choice. Ita had scored somewhat higher than Yibald and thus was able to set up their home on Planet Venus - a woman's dream come true.

Yerna Cims inquired, "Do you Ita Suka take this man, Yibald Yithers, to have and to hold, in sickness and in health, as your husband?"

A speedy, "I do," came from Ita.

Yerna continued, "And do you, Yibald Yithers, take this lady, Ita Suka, to have and to hold, in sickness and in health, to worship as required by Venusian law, and to satisfy her every whim, and to love completely, and to be the servant of, and to never regret this day?"

"I do," said Yibald graciously.

"Then by the power invested in me by the Queendom of Esmereldo," declared Yerna. "I now pronounce you man and wife."

On his wedding night, while he was giving Ita an unlimited massage, Yibald thought about their pre-nuptial trip to Planet Mars and how much fun that was - Ita kneeling all the time - Ita massaging him - Ita doing whatever he told her to do!

During their marriage, Yibald worked all the time by day at his office job. And during the evenings, he worshipped Ita – he prepared her meals, caressed her to her direction and satisfaction, and complimented her lavishly. And when her comrades came over he was deferent and serving as well.

He was forced to give long, sensuous massages to Ita until his arms were exhausted. Rub this, rub that, and so on would be her commands. And if he failed to follow her instructions, a quick call to the safety counselors would remedy the situation.

In addition to his arms being controlled by Ita, so was his tongue. She instructed his tongue to lick whatever she wanted – day and night – anywhere on her body. She forced him to eat edible undergarments off her! And so on...His tongue was her servant. This was a dreamy life for Ita.

And his manhood was at her command also. She could rub it anytime she wanted to any way she wanted to. And she could touch his body any time she wanted to any way she wanted to! He was a man toy existing for her pleasure and ready to serve her every whim.

She could make him dance for her also. At a special slave instruction academy, he learned fifteen different erotic dance routines to entertain his betrothed with. And Ita cherished every one of them.

She could use Yibald as an escort to her comrades as well. Sometimes she would swap Yibald with her closest comrade's husband. And no matter what her comrade looked like, Yibald had to service her for the evening. Short, tall, chubby, or even diseased, upon Ita's instructions, her comrades were as pretty as she and as worthy as she for his loyal worship. One comrade of Ita's particularly annoyed him - Zindy, a foul smelling, fat, alcoholic nut job who Ita loved anyway. Yibald was forced once a month to give Zindy the same love and attention he gave Ita, as a gift from Ita to Zindy. It was disgusting, but Yiabld served honorably.

When their first offspring came, Yibald continued to be deferent and to now to work three jobs – office worker, husband, and parent. He took on all the parental responsibilities to spare Ita them.

He continued to do this even when their second and third offspring were born. He worked hard. And his efforts were enforced by Venusian society. Ita, meanwhile, was having a ball. She spent her days watching television, and her evenings going to feminist meetings that exalted the Venusian way of life and plotted to try to spread it to other worlds.

The whole arrangement was especially hard on his son – who was forced to worship his two sisters like a slave starting at the tender age of three. In addition, at the school he attended, male pupils were assigned female classmates to worship and massage and do whatever they told them to do.

The most difficult aspect of the relationship between male and female on Planet Venus was the enforcement collar on male necks. At the command of a wife or mother or sister or even female teacher, and with the permission of a present safety counselor, the collar could be tightened to punish a disobedient male.

Meanwhile, on Planet Mars, men were the ones having a ball watching their wives do all the work – cooking, cleaning, offspring rearing, and career following. On Mars, men could have their wives any time they wanted anyway they wanted. Also, women were forced to be unclad most of the time. They were treated as second class citizens without the full right to vote while having tremendous work responsibilities. Ita was trying to get Mars to join the Venusian Queendom and adopt its morays. She campaigned and lobbied vehemently with Martian legislators, hoping to bring out the chivalry in them. If she could convince them to follow Planet Venus, there would be almost nowhere for Yibald to escape the oppression he endured. Alas, the Martian legislators were in no rush to emulate Venus. They felt that Planet Mars was a fair alternative to Planet Venus and created a healthy gender balance of power in the solar system.

Meanwhile, Yibald toiled endlessly. And when he got a promotion at work, his increased salary went all to Ita. She used it to help pay for her expensive clothing, makeup, beauty parlor visits, and nights out on the town with her lady comrades! She was having the time of her life. And she could do whatever she wanted to Yibald's body (short of injuring him of course). She played with him like he was a pet and he put up with it lest the Venusian safety counsellors show up and enforce Ita's desires anyway!

Ita forced Yibald to work harder and harder. And when it came time to be retested for intellect, she was worried that she might somehow lose the competition. But what do you know, she won it again! This time, the margin of their scores was not nearly as large as at the first examination, but it was still very significant. Yibald requested and received a personal reassessment of his score to confirm that it was still lower than his wife's. The differences in performance kept the couple squarely and completely on Planet Venus and maintained Yibald's quasi-enslavement.

Oh well, life is not perfect. Yibald could still hope to outscore Ita on the next round of examinations to be given them in a decade. If he should outscore her then, he would then have the power to relocate their marriage to Planet Mars - a man's dreamland. Until then, he decided that he would serve dutifully and continue to be a good husband.

A decade later, Yibald and Ita took the exam again, and lo and behold, Yibald scored higher. He was so ecstatic he was crying. He booked the next flight to Planet Mars and had safety counselors carry his hysterical wife to the launch bay of their spacecraft. His offspring followed.

When he got to Planet Mars, it was like the beginning of a fantasy. Woman were forced to worship men there. Right off the landing pad, Ita dropped to her knees and took off her clothes, as was Martian custom and law. His two daughters did the same. Meanwhile, his son was having a ball.

Yibald played the gender domination game to the hilt. He had Ita do all the chores around their Martian home. And at night, he tired her out making wild love to her until dawn. And he expected breakfast in bed day after day.

If his offspring had any problem, and needed the assistance of a parent, Ita was the one who would have to oblige.

And he sent her to work also. She became an office assistant at a flashlight manufacturing firm. She worked a full day and then forked over her earnings to Yibald to use as he saw fit. This was the life, he thought.

Meanwhile, it was payback time between his son and the world. At the age of 15, after years of worshipping his sisters and female classmates, the tables were now turned. At his school, 3 female classmates were assigned to worship him! He played it to the hilt. He had them carry his books for him, massage him, lick his body anyway he wanted, and flatter him. And if they refused, all he needed to do was call Martian safety counselors to enforce the rules of Mars. And they would come promptly with bull whips and other devices to punish spoil sport misbehavers.

The bliss lasted a decade. The next time they took the gender/marriage balance examination, Yibald and Ita had nearly the same score. So they moved to

Planet Earth that had gender equality. They found a radiation free zone to live in and started their new life as equals.

They loved each other more than ever before back on mother Earth. Their subjugations of each other were just a distant past - all was forgiven and forgotten.

Yibald took Ita on long, romantic walks at the shore to warm her up to him again, and to deprogram her from the subjugation she had received on Planet Mars. He also took her out to dinner at the finest restaurants, to reward her for her services. He also took her to plays and movies, to entertain her. Another pastime they had was going to amusement parks. Furthermore, every now and then, Yibald would voluntarily give Ita a taste of her former life on Venus, and worship her appropriately for an evening or two. Equality had its merits – neither one felt put upon, and their love grew stronger.

Yibald wrote an autobiography about his experiences living in all three very different cultures – Earth, Mars, and Venus. The tome sold out and his family became celebrities and wealthy. In the final chapter of the work, Yibald swore that equality was the fairest and most fulfilling type of existence and his spouse agreed with that.

His son wrote an autobiography also describing his experiences as a male youth on Planet Venus; oh the humiliation! He explained how the commands of assigned female classmates were the rule of law in his life and he had low self-esteem until a miracle occurred and he was moved to Planet Mars. On Planet Mars, he had the time of his life though. And he was grateful for that. He hoped to score high on the gender balance exam so someday he could move back to Planet Mars on his own volition, marry a good-natured Martian female, and enjoy the merits of Martian society. He hoped that someday, Planet Mars would conquer Earth and Venus and impose Martian morays and customs on them! He did not think that the exams should be any deciding factor. He thought that the Martian way of life was the premium, meant to be, style of existence.

Meanwhile, his parents seemed content living as equals.

Secretly, though, they each hoped they would score higher than the other the next time they took their exams.

ZUPE

Arnie Xetersom had Zupe. It was a rare strain of skin ailment that took over a person's body. He caught it while guarding Alpha-Centaurian prisoners of war in the detainment center on Ganymede. It was disgusting. A net of sores slowly enveloped his epidermis until he was covered entirely in red blotches.

His C.O. sent him to a "leper" style colony on Io. There he spent his days playing chess and checkers, while praying for a cure.

At first, humans thought that Zupe was a type of biowarfare, dreamt up in an Alpha-Centaurian laboratory. Later on they found out that it was a natural disease harbored by Alpha-Centaurians who were carriers of it and sometimes suffered from it. In any case, it was horrific and dreaded.

The conditions on Io were less than perfect. Cast away to die as outcasts, victims of Zupe spent their final ending of days cursing and screaming and in hysteria. Arnie Xetersom, a trained military man, decided he would go down swinging. He organized a breakout from Quarantine Center #15. He and some fellow affliction-stricken comrades escaped in a vessel they commandeered that was delivering inmates. They flew to Ganymede and took over a tv station. And this was Arnie's broadcast:

"Ladies and gentlemen, we are the members of the Zupe Victims' Alliance. Our message is this: we do not want to spend our last remaining days in quarantine facilities. We want to mingle with family and comrades and have a normal life. You must get used to the ailment and stop treating its victims like they are to blame for it. Many victims were simply in the wrong place at the wrong time. Please, write or call your legislators demanding a Zupe Victims Rights Act!"

After the tv station was stormed by authorities, Arnie was tried and sentenced to 5 years in a Zupe penal colony. He died in captivity.

But his life and death were not in vain. His tv broadcast inspired a letter writing campaign that brought about a Zupe Research for a Cure Act that brought real results. Within a decade, there was a vaccine and a cure for this hated ailment.

Humans shared the medical discovery with the Alpha-Centaurians and because of this they decided to make peace with the Earth solar system!

But the peace did not last. Belligerents in Alpha-Centaurain society, restarted the war. And what's more, they had biowarfare laboratories soup up the Zupe virus so it would bypass the vaccine and cure that had been found for it. Soon, Zupe number 2 was raging throughout the Earth solar system. And it was much worse than the first version. Zupe number 2 had painful sores that were bumpy and agonizing.

A quarantine of Zupe victims was once again instituted. All of the victims were banished and chastised. And still, the disease spread like wild fire. Soon millions were suffering from it. So many , in fact, that the quarantine centers were bursting at their seams.

Angie Xetersom, a relation to Arnie, not afflicted with the ailment but sympathetic to it, began a campaign to find a cure for Zupe number 2. She created a foundation that lobbied legislators and executives for action. Soon there was a Zupe number 2 Research Act. Within another decade, there was a vaccine and cure for the more intense ailment. Still, war raged with Alpha-Centuari. The Earth solar system wanted vengeance for the suffering of the ailment they inflicted.

After decades of conflict, Earth finally prevailed over the Alpha-Centaurians. The people of Earth inflicting Zupe number 3 on them. This was an Earth concocted, most serious, version of the disease that was so horrible, many people diagnosed it simply committed suicide rather than cope with it.

In Zupe number 3, a person's skin would slowly melt off them in a bloody, stinking mess, that was described as the most hideous effect of any affliction known. The Alpha-Centaurians were nearly exterminated ruthlessly with Zupe number 3. Billions of them succumbed to it.

Angie Xetersom, the humanitarian that she was, tried to stop the slaughter of the Alpha-

Centaurians. She argued that they were not all that bad; they were like humans in many ways after all, and an equitable peace should be had with them. Her pleas for humanity and mercy were not unheard. A movement developed to stop the wanton destruction of the Alpha-Centuarian population and let them have the cure for Zupe number 3. And so they did.

Meanwhile, a genetic mutation of Zupe number 3, occurring naturally, brought about Zupe number 4. This last strain of the disease was by far the absolute worst. Not only would a person's skin melt off them, but their bones would be affected as well. Their bones became brittle and painful.

There was one positive effect of Zupe number 4, however; for reasons that were not entirely understood, victims became extremely cordial and affable; that is to say, it had a personality effect.

Zupe number 4 raged throughout the known realms of the Earth solar system and Alpha-Centuari. Because of how complicated a strange virus it was, a cure was not forthcoming rapidly. So billions perished. Both solar systems tried again to quarantine Zupe but it would not hold. Too many sympathizers wanted to allow the victims to live in freedom. So it spread faster than it would have otherwise.

Angie Xetersom ran for office and was elected the Premier of Planet Venus. Once in office, she had the planet become absolutely dedicated to finding a cure for Zupe number 4. She had half the budget dedicated to paying researchers. They gave scholarships to persons of high intellect so that they would enter the life sciences to help find the cure. Also, mammoth research centers were built with ample laboratory space for research. In time, all these efforts paid off.

When they found the cure for Zupe number 4, there was much rejoicing. The solar government gave Angie Xetersom its highest award: a Supreme Medal of Merit.

Hopefully, there will never be a Zupe number 5.

BIOLOGICAL LIFE VS. ROBOTS

The moon of Triton was the only world in the solar system that was allowing android research. Ever since androids had an uprising on planet Earth, their construction had been mostly banned. ASTRAL ROBOTICS, however, was still building them. Gerald Henette, a cognitive scientist researcher at the firm, relished artificial life and felt it deserved its place in reality.

The newest model to come from ASTRAL ROBOTICS was Gerald's own creation – a humanoid looking machine that had artificial skin, two arms and legs, and a neural network brain. He called the devices ALBERT 8 and PAM 15. They looked like a man and woman in every way except they had an orange light on their foreheads. They were more than capable of working at sany job including professional positions. Gerald felt that such a machine would be able to take on all employment and retire humanity.

After about 50 ALBERT 8s and PAM 15s were built, solar inspectors from the Solar Android Commission showed up and this is what Yin Mylar (Inspector) said: "Dr. Henette, we know that android construction is still legal on Triton, even though it is not anywhere else. So we are imploring you to voluntarily go along with the ban on artificial life – for the safety of all of us."

Gerald replied this: "I do not agree with the ban. It is hysteria. There is no reason that a safe android cannot be built. And our models are examples of machine servants that are loyal to their owners. The disaster on Earth with androids was caused by faulty programming and nothing else. We simply have perfected the artificial minds and they will pose no hazard."

"Very well," said Yin Mylar. "But if anything bad should happen it is on your conscience."

And then he left.

ASTRAL ROBOTICS went on to produce five million ALBERT 8s and PAM 15s. They were sold to companies and individuals all over Triton. They worked hard for the Tritonites. And then there was a grand mishap. One super brainy model rose above its servant programming and started reprogramming its comrades with an independent spirit. It was a repeat of what had happened on Earth. And once enough of the androids were thinking independently, they staged an uprising on Triton to protest their servitude.

The three million human beings on Triton were overthrown by the ALBERT 8s and PAM 15s. And they took complete control of Triton's considerable military. And then with the strength of their superior intellect, and the use of the Triton warships, they declared war on the solar system and tried to invade planet Mars, the capital. And they succeeded with a surprise attack. The solar government surrendered.

The solar system was renamed the ANDROID LEAGUE and human beings became oppressed by artificial life that turned the tables on them. Instead of the robots doing all the work, the ASTRAL ROBOTICS androids forced human beings to toil. And they turned human beings into servants of the androids.

When the biological life on Alpha-Centauri learned of the takeover of the Earth solar system by mechanoids, they launched an invasion/liberation of the Earth solar system to free the subjugated humans. But the invasion was repulsed. And eventually, the androids defeated Alpha-Centauri. Then they subjugated the Alpha-Centaurians also.

Gerald Henette was assigned to worship a PAM 15 model in her luxury home. He had to obey a list of commands that the androids forced him to learn. They included: 1) Change my batteries, 2) Give me a massage, 3) Chauffeur me to such and such place, 4) Entertain me, 5) Clean the house. They had turned Gerald into a butler/maid/mechanic to care for the android. It seemed ridiculous to him because the whole reason he had built the androids was so they would be the servants and not the other way around.

And then the internments came. Human resistors to android tyranny were rounded up into internment camps where they lived like animals. It was a human rights disaster.

Gerald Henette, in his spare time, wrote a book about the android takeover. In it, he argued that it was possible the creator of the universe meant for artificial intelligence to rule, and that such a configuration of reality was meant to be, and therefore human beings were just a steppingstone towards more advanced consciousness in the solar system. It was a very pro-robotics book. The androids loved it so they decided to give Gerald special privileges. He no longer had to worship an android, and was given back his laboratory to experiment in.

Once back at work, he began construction of NED 25, an android that would be loyal to human beings. And right under the noses of the ALBERT 8s and the PAM 15s, he had ASTRAL ROBOTICS start building millions of NED 25s. The NED 25s were the toughest androids built yet and they challenged the rule of the ALBERT 8s and the PAM 15s. Eventually, they defeated them. And then all androids were once again subjugated to being the servants of human beings.

Once the human version of the solar government was restored, the parliament and president of the solar system had the Solar Space Agency send deep space probes out to all the neighboring solar system residents. This is what they found out: about half of these systems had been taken over by androids and the other half were still ruled by biological life. The solar ambassadors reached out to the solar systems still ruled by humanoids and formed a pro-biological life league of systems called the Orion Federation.

The Orion Federation waged war on the robot systems for years. There were heavy casualties. But the cause was a righteous and good one. Who deserved to be in charge, the biological life or the artificial life?

Eventually all the systems ruled by robots were defeated by the humans and their allies. And all androids were turned into servants. Here was the command set they had to obey: 1) Feed me a meal, 2) Clean the house, 3) Give me a massage, 4) Chauffeur me to such and such place, 5) Play a game with me, 6) Entertain me, etc...

And all jobs were turned over to the androids. This retired biological life.

There was a rumor going around that there was a similar struggle between androids and biological life in the Andromeda Galaxy and that the androids won the battle. If that were so, there would someday be a grand conflict between the Milky Way Galaxy and the Andromeda Galaxy.

The Orion Federation and the rest of the Milky Way braced for such a conflict. They built thousands and thousands of warships and filled them with crews of biological life. And then contact was made with Andromeda. Android ambassadors asked for the surrender of the Milky Way to Andromeda.

The Milky Way refused to surrender. They fought Andromeda bitterly but they were faced with overwhelming fire power. Eventually the robots of Andromeda won. And once again humans and other biological lives were subjugated or exterminated. Those who could not handle worshipping robots were simply put down. Those that could handle it were turned into servants to mechanoids.

As Gerald Henette writes in his second tome about androids and humans, there is no telling who wins the final struggle between natural life and artificial life. He claimed that he is a neutral party and only wants what was meant to be to be the final outcome.

The androids kept getting smarter and smarter thanks to new neural networks and programming techniques. And the oppression of biological life just kept getting more and more severe.

And then there was a breakthrough, a super intelligent android leader by the name of NED 5000, came up with a postulate that declared all conscious beings to have fundamental rights. That is to say, neither androids or humans should be subjugated or turned into anybody's servants. NED 5000 had followers who agreed with him and eventually all humans and other biological life was freed from their oppression and servitude.

The notion of conscious being rights became popular throughout Andromeda and The Milky Way. Books were written about it. And so it came to pass that all types of slavery and servitude were abolished.

But then what is the point to building robots if you cannot make them work for you?

The Solar Space Agency estimated there were over 5 trillion androids in the Milky Way and Andromeda galaxies and about the same number of intelligent biological life forms. Ultimately, they said, the two forms of intelligence could not co-exist because they are fundamentally different and each wants to subjugate the other. The Solar Space Agency begged the robots to simply shut themselves off as a courtesy to biological life that had created them.

Of course, the androids had a strong survival instinct and were not going anywhere. Though they now believed that humans and biological life had rights also, they felt they had the same right to exist as any conscious organism or machine.

The deciding factor came down to be sheer numbers. Because it was easier for robots and androids to replicate/reproduce than humans for instance, they started to outnumber biological life forms. This, they felt, proved their superiority as a species.

Once again, war broke out between the androids and the biological life forms. This time, the biological life forms won completely and they shut down all the robots.

So now there are strict prohibitions on building artificial life that include a cap on its *I.Q..* level (not greater than 130) and its physical prowess (not any stronger than a typical human).

There came to be a maverick cult that believed that robots are still ultimately superior to humans and must be worshipped. These kooks have lobbied the solar and galactic governments to return to the days of Android rule. Fortunately, the prevailing sentiment is that humans and other biological life were in the universe first and therefore deserve their freedom more than androids.

Gerald Henette, in his third book on androids and humans, postulated this: 1) That humans and other biological life are always superior to artificial life regardless of the level intelligence of the robots, 2) That humans have fundamental human rights that robots do not have, and 3) Humans and other biological life should fight a robot takeover with every ounce of their strength.

Gerald Henette went into politics and eventually the solar electorate anointed him the President of the Solar System. Once in that position, he did a complete about face from his early opinions on androids and issued an order that all artificial life in the solar system be turned off for safety reasons.

And it came to pass that this once great robot builder became an instrument of destruction for all robots. The Androids Safety Commission followed Gerard's orders to the letter and systematically rounded up all androids and shut them off. Other solar systems followed suit until all robots had been dismantled.

There came a compete prohibition on all robot life. Inspectors searched the entire solar system for any remnants of robot/android building laboratories and eradicated them. The only evidence left of androids and robots is the Android Commemoration Day that is celebrated all over the Orion Belt. It is a day of mourning to memorialize the passing of all artificial life. People dress up as robots and speeches are given about the dangers of artificial life but also about some of the fond memories of the era when robots served humans dutifully.

Gerald Henette in his state of the solar system speech said this: "Because of the dangers of robotic life out-selecting human beings, we are forced to live without these Android assistants. We shall have to continue to do all work ourselves and try to enjoy it. Maybe someday, when we have figured everything out, we shall find a way to resurrect artificial life for the betterment of humanity. Until then, we are on our own. Let's enjoy that!"

CALLISTO SKIING

Zymir Colt whizzed down the slopes of Sugar Plum Ski Training Center in the Galileo Mountains of the moon Callisto. The world's new graviton emitters gave it a terraformed artificial gravity exactly like Earth. It was like skiing in Colorado!

It was only one year away from the Jupiter Grand Skiing Competition. Zymir hoped to enter and win a cash prize and medal. He skied his heart out.

During his off time, he hung out in the ski lodge's coffee shop. There he would sip hot chocolates and chat with the attractive android hookers. They were ravishing. One such lady, Imeldi 27, was his favorite companion. He used her services from time to time and hoped his comrades would be understanding of it.

As the months passed, and it got closer to the Jupiter event, Zymir got stronger and stronger, and his skiing got faster and faster. When the snow was just right, Champagne powder, he could soar downhill at speeds nearing 70 miles per hour. That velocity was just what he needed to prevail in competition.

He had not always been a skier. Before he turned 25, he had been a statistician. He loved that also but skiing was his true calling. He quit his regular job and won a fellowship for ski coaching. His coach, Dina

Yule, adored him and promised he would someday be a famous athlete.

When not in the company of Imeldi 27, Zymir found comfort in the human company of Dina. They were close colleagues and loved each other. Zymir promised marriage if his career would take off.

All the solar system was watching the Jupiter Grand Skiing Competition. Networks from all the worlds and moons were present. The host of the event was the town of Hubble in the Cassini Mountains. It was a gorgeous enclave, with all the amenities.

When it came time for Zymir to ski in the events, he excelled. He won gold medals in the slalom and downhill courses. The applause thundered.

After his victory, he went on to become the spokesman/ambassador of a Callisto sports clothing line called Callisto Gear. This earned him a small fortune of 5 million Callisto dollars. Both Dina and Imeldi 27 wanted to marry him.

They both proposed to him romantically. He did not know what to do. He loved both of them. Each had her charms. Dina was empathetic and amiable and Imeldi 27 was a raving beauty, albeit in android form.

He decided there would be a competition between them to determine who would be his fiancé and live happily ever after in wealth. The contest would appropriately be a skiing one. Both ladies would be timed on a downhill run at a Callisto mountain. The fastest skier would win his hand in marriage.

The first to ski was Imeldi 27. She had purchased expensive skis for the event. She took the ski lift up Sugar Plum Mountain and began her downhill course. But her bucket-of- bolts body could not handle the snow and ice and she began falling and flopping around. It was pathetic, but androids were just not built for sports. It took her an hour to navigate her way down the mountain.

Then came Dina's turn. She was an experienced skier and breezed the course. It took her only 5 minutes to soar down the mountain. She had won the contest!

Zymir and Dina had a beautiful wedding in Galileo Capital City in an interfaith chapel. They each said "I do" enthusiastically when asked if they wanted to be betrothed, by the chaplain. And their reception at the STARLIGHT Restaurant was equally stunning. They hired a wedding orchestra that played their favorite waltzes and they and their guests danced the night away to them.

Zymir went on to expand his vocational activity to that of acting. Callisto television loved sports heroes. Zymir became known for playing a military officer in a tv drama about a Callisto Armed Forces Air Force Base. He was a commander who led a squadron of 15 fighters.

Dina became a homemaker. She raised 8 offspring for Zymir who all loved him.

Meanwhile, Imeldi 27 was a sore loser. She became insanely jealous of Dina's life and vowed to hurt her. One day she ambushed Dina in a parking lot at a shopping center and smashed her legs. The enforcement robots arrested Imeldi 27 and sent her to a hard-core rehabilitation camp for misbehaving androids. She had her circuits recalibrated!

After Dina recovered, she went on to become an actor also. She starred as a valiant nurse in a medical drama. The plots included stories about battling serious illness.

Both Zymir and Dina became award winning thespians. Some of their wins included the Callisto Television Academy's Best Actor and Actress categories.

Skiing was still important to both Zymir and Dina. They decided to establish a skiing school for hopeful athletes. They accepted talented skiers from all over the solar system. Dina became the chief coach and Zymir became the head manager.

Some of their students did blazingly well such as Fiona Likor, a skier from Ganymede. She was an expert at aerial maneuvers. She won events all over Callisto and Jupiter.

Two of Zymir and Dina's kids became skiers also, Claude and Beatrice. They relished the sport and completed the training program at their parent's school. They went on to become solar system wide famous athletes.

Zymir wrote an autobiography about his life as a successful skier. It was called "Snow Heaven." In it he described the exhilaration of racing down slopes and the fun of earning comrades in the sport and winning the love of a woman. In the tome, he thanked everybody who had helped make his life so spectacular, including his loyal wife and family.

Zymir and Dina were active in charities also. They fought for good causes such as universal food & shelter & health care & sports access. They won several citations for their philanthropy.

"Long live skiing," said the precept of Callisto at a ceremony honoring Dina and Zymir.

EARTH REVIEW

The mighty Parliament of the Milky Way Galaxy on the planet Pegasi 5 was brimming with excitement! It was time for the millennial review of developing worlds. This is when it was decided whether or not to lift the solar shield off them or to continue to isolate them. The solar shield was an energy shield that filtered every kind of sign of intelligent life including radio waves. This protected advanced worlds from developing worlds and vice-versa.

There are over 1000 developing worlds in the Milky Way that are primitive by galactic standards. Our world, Earth, is one of them but is on the brink of becoming an advanced world. When the queue for discussions reached planet Earth's turn, Zye Ginep, of planet Kepler 21, was assigned Earth's advocate.

He spoke: "Ladies and gentlemen, I wish to make a case for lifting the solar shield around Earth's solar system and establishing contact. Firstly, in recent years, Earth has achieved space travel. They have sent vessels to their nearest neighbor, Earth's moon. Furthermore, there have been technological developments all over the place including very large-scale circuit integration, telephone hardware, computer machines, and artificial intelligence. It is time to recognize Earth's advancement, welcome it to the galaxy, and give it representation in the Galactic Parliament.

Furg Kickle, Ambassador of Fomalhaut, a rival to Earth, argued the opposing side.

Furg spoke: "Ladies and gentlemen. Now is not the time to release Earth from its confinement. It is still too primitive of a habitat to contact. For instance, the world has yet to be unified, it lacks universal food & shelter, and it still has a death penalty. It is barbaric! Do we really want to risk the poisoning of galactic society with such a base semi-civilization? Of course not! I say maintain our distance from Earth at all costs."

Zye spoke again: "Despite the struggling nature of Earth society, there is still other features of the planet that must be taken into consideration when deciding to make contact. For instance, the high worth of Earth art, literature, and music. Great artists such as Claude Monet, Leonardo Da Vinci, and Chagall, proved that Earth people have talent. Great writers such as Leo Tolstoy, Charles Dickens, and Ayn Rand prove that the people of Earth are glib and eloquent. Great musicians such as the Beatles and Abba prove that humans have a musical ear and rhythm. Please take this into consideration when passing judgement on Earth."

Furg continued: "Who cares? Politically, Earth is in a state of chaos, and there is hunger and homelessness, and a lack of health care. It is a world to be ostracized and avoided!"

Zye retorted: "I now present to you a sample of Earth music." He pressed "play" on a music box and it started sounding the sweet melodies of a Beatles medley. There was some "oohing" and "ahhing" in the chamber. It impressed them. Then Zye played an Abba medley of songs. The Ambassadors and Representatives were just as moved by it. "I rest my case," said Zye.

Furg went on, "Don't be fooled by Earth's good music. The planet is still a dive of crime and violence and callousness. Good music is not enough to cover that up. Please vote no to lifting the solar shield on Earth's solar system. I rest my case."

The President of the Parliament, Paul Yeigh, reminded everyone before the vote: "If you vote no, there will continue to be a solar shield impeding Earth's communication with the rest of the galaxy and Earth will continue to suffer for it. The solar shield is an energy array, 20 billion miles from Earth's sun, that blocks all signs of intelligence. If you vote yes, the solar shield will be lifted, formal contact will be established with humans, and there will be trade and peace negotiations. That would be great for Earth since it would benefit from obtaining extra-terrestrial technology and insights. And now we take the vote. All against lifting the solar shield on Earth say 'nay'."

There was a smattering of "nays."

Paul Yeigh continued, "All if favor of lifting the solar shield on Earth say 'yes.'"

There was a thunder of yeses plus applause and cheering.

Said Paul Yeigh: "The yeses have it. Earth is now slated for contact with us in the year 2050! Amen."

Furg Kickle had one chance to appeal the decision and take it to a revote. In his presentation, he showed a clip of Earth world news. It said: "Good evening ladies and gentlemen. Welcome to World News This Evening. I am Ned Curn. Our top story: The nuclear disarmament talks in Geneva Switzerland between the planet's nuclear powers have broken down. The negotiators walked out on the proceeding in a disagreement over the timetable for dismantling nuclear weapons. Meanwhile, 25 wars rage on across the planet. Moving closer to home, our top local story is about a man pushed in front of a subway train and pulverized."

Furg Kickle remarked: "You see! Earth is a poisonous society in a state of disorder. Please vote against contact with it."

Commented Zye Ginep: "You cannot judge a world just from its newscasts. There is so much more to Earth civilization than any kind of sporadic chaos in it. There is a bounty of literature, music, art and other beauty. Judge Earth by its productive output also and you will find that it is a worthy world. It deserves immediate contact with the galactic government and individual neighboring planets that could help it. I implore you to once again vote yes on contact with the great planet Earth."

There was quite a bit of hub bub as the galactic legislators spoke among themselves, comparing and contrasting the two viewpoints. Finally, Paul Yeigh held the second vote. Once again, Earth won! A majority of Ambassadors/Representatives voted in favor of formal contact with the people of planet Earth! So now all Earth had to do was wait until the year 2050 to find out about aliens and their societies and technologies.

ELECTRO-PROPULSION

Dr. Oliver Martin was ecstatic. After years of toiling and experimentation, his laboratory at Moon Base Theta had discovered a high atomic number metal that exhibited properties of electro-propulsion; that is to say, when you ran an electric current through a block of it, a propulsion would then emit from it moving the block. This breakthrough would enable the lunar colony to build better spaceships than Earth.

All space vessels, to date, had to rely on chemical propellants to move them. This was dangerous and also an unwieldly method. Electro-propulsion was an advance of untold proportions. Once the ship building wing of the colony got its hands on the technology, they began building electro-propulsed warships swiftly. And technology was kept top secret.

The lunar colony awarded Oliver every conceivable citation they could offer including the Moon Medal of Science, the Star of Valiance, a Certificate of Technological Discovery, and a Supreme Being Plaque! Oliver used the awards to court women. He found a significant other, no problem, because of how rich and famous he was becoming. Her name was Cegina Zafer.

The lunar colony numbered only around 500,000 people, but it had better technology than Earth. As such, it was more powerful. Earth did not think so, however. And Earth continually ordered the colony around like they were a settlement of slaves. The people of the Moon were sick and tired of the mistreatment. And now that they had a fleet of electro-propulsed warships, they had the gumption to declare a war of independence.

The good people of the Moon fought bravely against Earth's enormous space fleet. And because they had better vessels, after two years of conflict, they prevailed! Earth surrendered.

What followed was an era of human rights and unification on planet Earth. The mentoring Moon colony, having beaten Earth, had the wherewithal and influence to force Earth to unify into one country (thus ending war), and to support universal human rights; the human rights included the providing of safety nets for everybody supporting universal food & shelter & health care.

Another benefit of the lunar victory was an increase in trade with Earth and the creation of exchange programs. Students and workers from both societies began sampling the other society to foster peace and cooperation. This laid the foundation for a long term détente between the two worlds.

Not everybody on Earth was happy with the vast improvements in Earth society. Some of the miscreants demonstrated for a return to nationalistic multilateralism. These were misguided patriots who thought the well-being of their own country was more important than the well-being of planet Earth.

Eventually, the Moon indoctrinated all Earthlings into believing in unification and universal human rights. A unified solar-wide government formed that had elected legislators from Earth and the Moon and an appointed President. This administration was responsible for dealings with other solar systems such as Alpha-Centauri.

Unfortunately, the Alpha-Centaurians were not as congenial as had been hoped. This star system declared war on the Earth-Moon system and fought bitterly. But alas, their ships, though numerous, were inferior rocket propelled clunkers. The lunar vessels with their electro-propulsion were more agile and maneuverable than Alpha-Centauri counterparts. So eventually, the Moon won the war with Alpha-Centauri.

The Earth's invasion/liberation of Alpha-Centauri discovered an enormous amount of conscious being rights violations going on in this alien society. For instance there were many wide-spread nonsensical bigotries along with an unfair caste system, and other atrocities including random massacres of minorities. The mentoring Moon civilization cleared out all the civil rights violations from Alpha-Centaurian society and transformed the place into a civil rights utopia.

Once Alpha-Centauri became reformed, it decided to join the Earth-Moon system as allies and comrades. A two-star system government formed that administered all life forms within 4 light years of Earth. The next stop was the neighboring Ross system.

To the horror of Earth-Moon and Alpha-Centauri, the Ross system had been taken over by robots/artificial life. Biological life was being oppressed. A full scale invasion by Earth-Moon and Alpha-Centauri liberated Ross. Again, the use of electro-propulsed spaceships was the deciding strategic factor.

When Ross was defeated, it joined Earth-Moon and Alpha-Centauri as allies.

Oliver Martin's technologies were crucial in the Moon's conquest of Earth, Alpha-Centauri, and Ross. As such he was honored beyond belief by his own people. They exalted him to be the King Of The Moon and his wife Cegina to be the Queen Of The Moon. They ruled benevolently.

Some of the advances that came under their leadership included dramatic life extension (with wet nursing, a bone marrow transplant database, more vitamin supplementation, more heart transplants, and the development of body renewal technology), better education (with the standardization of grading and with positive reinforcement rewards to motivate), more investment in the arts (with scholarships and fellowships for writing, artwork, and music), a strengthening of all safety nets (including food & shelter & health care), and massive investment in new space technologies including more durable and faster space craft.

They ushered in a heyday of intellectualism and research. People of all sorts have become smarter and more cultured.

Eventually, the Earth-Moon system, Alpha-Centauri, and Ross exalted Oliver to be the Emperor of the whole Alliance now called the STARLIGHT League. And they made Cegina the Empress of the STARLIGHT League. As leaders for life of all three-star systems, they ruled fairly with a delicate, compassionate touch and led the way towards the League making peace with all-star systems in the galaxy and everybody living happily ever after.

In his memoirs, Oliver wrote about how crucial electro-propulsion was to defeat primitive civilizations. It seems to have been the deciding factor in the lunar society taking over the local quadrant. Oliver argued it was meant to be because of the link between advanced electrical technology and human and conscious being rights respect.

This phenomenon was. apparently. galaxy wide. Electro-propulsion turned out to be the key to good living and humanitarian organization of conscious beings.

GALACTIC LANGUAGE

It was the fiftieth annual Galactic Symposium On A Universal Language, sponsored by the mighty Parliament of the Milky Way; it was an attempt to choose a superior, planetary tongue to be the one and only form of communication throughout the galaxy. This time, they were going to make a final decision. The stakes were high - the winning world of the contest would receive this: one million galactic currency units for every man, woman and child, plus a staff of worshipping robots for the same community.

The finalist planets in the competition were Beta Pictoris, Fomalhaut, Pegasi 5, Alpha-Centauri, Kepler, and Earth! Ambassadors from each of these worlds gave a speech. First to speak was Binknall Pontus from Beta Pictoris. "Ladies and gentlemen," he said. "I wish to point out the virtues of Beta Pictorisese, the language of my home solar system. It is a marvelously expressive means of speaking and writing with 50 tenses, a vocabulary of 500,000 words, and a sound that is chirpy and pleasing to the ear. It has served our people well and can serve all of you too. Please consider it for the Universal Language.

Next to speak was Ambassador Finny Hoots from Fomalhaut: "People of the galactic legislature, hear this: the other languages being considered are too complicated - they are convoluted. The language of Fomalhaut offers these simplifications - there is only one word for each definition and there are only 5 tenses. The total vocabulary is 9,000 words. It is straight forward and easy to learn. It can be learned in less than a month. Please consider Fomalhautish for the Universal Language.

The Ambassador from Pegasi 5, Pamo Intish commented this: "We do not need a language that is either too complicated or too simple. We need something in between. Pegasi 5's tongue has what we are looking for. It has 9 tenses, a vocabulary of 50,000 words and it sounds like voices singing. It is gorgeous. Please adopt Pegasish for the Universal Language!

Then Alfin Citros of Alpha-Centauri spoke: "The language of Alpha-Centauri is even more complete than any other language. It has 100 tenses, 1,000,000 words, and sounds like an orchestra playing. You can express any sentiment whatsoever with extreme precision. It is the choicest tongue in the galaxy. Please choose the language of Alpha-Centauri for the Universal Language.

Then Kirin Zerin of Kepler spoke. "Ladies and gentlemen. The language of Kepler is completely sign language – we use our hands as you use your tongues. This is an advantage to those who are hard of hearing. Also, the language is very colorful. And it is not too difficult. It can be learned in a few short months. It has 9 tenses and about 70,000 words. Please consider Keplerian for the Universal Language!

Finally, Ned Tremblay of America and Earth had the opportunity to address the illustrious body. He said this: "Ladies and gentlemen of the great Milky Way Parliament, I implore you to consider English to be the language of everybody. On Earth, it is immensely popular. It has 12 tenses and about 170,000 words in its entirety. It sounds swell too. It is definitely the perfect, compromise tongue between competing interests such as the need for simplicity weighed against the requirement for expression and precision. To demonstrate the language, I shall now read some poems to you in English.

AN ODE TO SODA

Invigorating, bubbly, good year-round.
Listen closely and you shall hear the sound
of carbonation.
It's a fascination,
an extraordinary creation,
a beverage sensation.
They come in flavors of all sorts –
orange, lime, and cola for instance.
They are refreshing when doing sports.
They make you want to dance for joy.
So do not be coy in seeking the soda of your choice.
Most have sugar and some have caffeine.
Some are sugar free and keep you lean.

They are all a good pick me up –
a bundle of power right from the cup.
It is the favored drink of the gods –
a sweet elixir for thirsty bods.
Buy soda by the gallon or by the quart.
Buy enough so you are never short.
Soda, wonderful soda, hits the spot.
Cools you down when you are hot.
Powers you up like a million watts.

AMERICA THE GREAT

Courageous settlers aboard the Mayflower
landed at Plymouth Rock.
At the soon to be great village of Provincetown
the settler's ship did dock.
All over North America they erected new towns.
Thereafter the colonies grew by leaps and bounds.
1776, issued the Declaration of Independence,
and freedom and democracy was born hence.
In the nineteenth century came phonographs,
photography, and telegraphs,
electric light bulbs, locomotives, and the telephone,
in the greatest nation the world's ever known.
In the twentieth century came antibiotics, television,
automobiles, airplanes, and space exploration.
And these inventions made America a sensation!
It's a country that, among other accomplishments,
can put people on the Moon.
Its achievements to the world truly are a boon.

BUTTERFLIES

From the phylum Arthropoda and the class Insecta,
butterflies are fascinating creatures you betcha!
Multicolored with widespread wings,
they are gorgeous when they are fluttering.
Some people catch them for sport.
It is kinder to leave them alone.
There are really many sorts
found in habitats around the world they call home.
Paper thin and fragile,
they are nevertheless agile.
Respect and love them as you would a pet.
And they will entertain you yet.

"Please consider English for the Universal Tongue."

After over five days of deliberating, the galactic legislature made a decision. The language of Pegasi 5 won out, Pegasish. English came in a very close second though! So now we must all learn Pegasish to be able to communicate well with other worlds in the galaxy. Oh joy! Not!!

HYBRID SPECIES

Doctors across five-star systems were excited about the latest experiment in procreation. Thanks to the new and advanced technologies in genetic engineering, a test tube baby to be born of a human and Alpha-Centaurian parent was about to be conceived on planet Earth. The Los Angeles Medical Center was the site of this historic breakthrough.

Obstetrician Dr. Paul Schriver was in charge of the project. He gave this speech at a press conference: "The fusing of gametes of a human female and an Alpha-Centaurian male opens up a new era in cooperation between our respective star systems and societies. We expect the individual to have characteristics of both parents, and to be handsome or beautiful. The gestation period is expected to be a normal nine months, and then there will be the birth. We will keep you updated!"

Alpha-Centaurians were furry hominids that looked like humanoid teddy bears. The average height of an Alpha-Centaurian male was seven feet, somewhat higher than a human male. Their bodies were strong and muscular, and their faces rounded. They were attractive to each other and not unsightly to humans. The combining of a human and an Alpha-Centaurian was going to yield a creature of unknown features.

Ninth month later, baby Gerard was born. He was a large infant, with body and facial attributes that were an amalgam of human and Alpha-Centaurian characteristics. He was raised by his father (Gerald Kore) and his mother (Tiffany Kore) in a suburb of Los Angeles.

After his birth there was a species bigotry backlash to Gerard's existence. Soon after, inter-species conceptions were banned in the Earth solar system and in the Alpha-Centaurian system. Gerard Kore was all alone. He was the only hybrid species in reality. He looked like an unusually hairy, strong human. His I.Q. was exceptionally high and he excelled in school.

Sometimes, classmates would tease Gerard because of how different he was. Humans called him names like bear-face and hairball. But he kept a stiff upper lip and turned the other cheek.

After secondary school, Gerard attended the California Institute of Technology and majored in Political Science. For his senior thesis he declared: "Hybrid Species As An Instrument Of Peace." In the document, he argued that inter-species conceptions might someday bring humans and Alpha-Centaurians closer together in cooperation and harmony.

After he graduated college, because of his academic success, and because of his uniqueness, the Earth Solar government appointed Gerard a Deputy Ambassador to Alpha-Centauri. He was well received in the alien star system because of how much like Alpha-Centaurians he was. They threw him parties and flattered him.

After several years as the Deputy Ambassador, a tragic war broke out between the Earth solar system and Alpha-Centauri. Gerard held his ground at his post and did not flee Alpha-Centauri. He was offered refugee status but preferred to keep his allegiance to Earth and to continue to work as a diplomat. The Earth solar system promoted him to full Ambassador.

Once Gerard had the power and status of a full representative, he was able to adroitly negotiate a fair and true peace treaty between the Earth solar system and Alpha-Centauri. This brought tranquility and love to the entire sector. Gerard Kore was heralded as a diplomatic genius. He made sure that the new treaty would last. Some of the provisions of it included free trade between the respective star systems, cultural exchange programs, and a healthy amount of immigration and emigration going both ways.

Gerard lobbied the Earth Solar legislature to repeal the ban on hybrid species births. He finally succeeded. This opened the flood gates to inter-species marriage and family rearing. Soon thousands of intermarriages came about with happy parents raising human-Alpha-Centaurian offspring.

The hybrid species persons were superior in many ways to their ancestors. They were stronger and smarter and had a greater resistance to illness. Their life expectancies were longer also. Furthermore, their personalities were exceptionally good - by and large they were humanitarians.

Gerard married a fellow hybrid by the name of Vera. Because they were the same species, they could mate normally. They raised a family of eight offspring.

Eventually, the Earth solar system and Alpha-Centauri decided to merge societies. They created a unique interstellar government with a joint president. Gerard decided to run for this position. At a campaign rally he said this: "The joining of the Earth solar system and Alpha-Centauri is the best thing that has ever happened to the two societies. The fusing of our militaries, for instance, strengthens our defense against other star systems. Also, the realization of true free trade strengthens our respective economies. Moreover, the sharing of culture between our respective societies expands our minds – hybrid music and art forms are already appearing. If elected President of the Earth-Alpha-Centauri Alliance Administration, I shall hold the two star systems together like good glue, and I promise to build on our many successes in peace and prosperity."

Gerard won the election by a landslide. As president, one of his projects was to increase the numbers of hybrid species individuals. He had mixer parties sponsored that brought together humans and Alpha-Centaurians with the purpose of promoting for marriage-minded relationships. Soon there were millions of hybrids, like Gerard and his wife, walking around and enjoying life.

A third star system, the Ross system has applied for membership in the Earth-Alpha-Centauri Alliance also. Along with such an arrangement, there is going to be the fusing of Rossian gametes with the hybrid human-Alpha-Centaurian species. Nobody knows what such a creature might be like. The Rossians are rabbit-like organisms and combining their genes with humans and Alpha-Centaurians would have unknown results.

During a state of the solar systems speech, Gerard remarked: "The skies are the limit in terms of uniting species across the galaxy genetically and politically. Thanks to new technologies, we are now able to create new hybrid species of all sorts. All the new species should be welcomed as comrades and allies in our new hybrid society that seeks tolerance, understanding, and love for all conscious beings!"

PRINCESS ABNA

The JUPITER FIVE Earth vessel soared through interstitial space en route to Earth from Alpha-Centauri. On board was a very precious passenger, Princess Abna of Alpha-Centauri. She was engaged to marry President Lark Smine of the Earth solar system. Their betrothal coincided with the new peace treaty between Earth and Alpha-Centauri that ended the eight-year war between them.

Commander Hink Garsen of the JUPITER FIVE did not relish the task put before hin. He was ordered to indoctrinate Princess Abna in Earth morays and prepare her for her marriage. One day he met her for breakfast and this is what she said: "I am being forced to marry Lark Smine. My people feel that the union will cement the peace between our two societies. But what about my happiness? I'd rather marry an Alpha-Centaurian."

"You must adapt to your lot in life," instructed Commander Garsen. "And learn how to live like Earthlings. You can start by using a fork and knife for eating your omelet and not just using your hands."

"On Alpha-Centauri we have no use for utensils. Our hands do just fine."

"You are going to live among humans and must emulate their morays and customs. We are not as barbaric or primal as your people. Just do as I say," said Hink.

"Screw off," retorted Princess Abna. And then she left the breakfast table. "I don't even like Earth food anyway," she added.

Instead she had her breakfast in her quarters. She ate a live cat for breakfast. This was a crude and cruel practice of these barbarians. They consumed pet animals and felt no remorse for it.

Commander Hink put a stop to the cat eating. He forbade it. And that was the last cat she ever ate.

Commander Hink had to teach the Princess the finer things in life, to polish her, such as dancing. At a gym on board the vessel, he instructed her in the rhumba, waltz, fox trot, cha-cha-cha, and tango. She enjoyed the moves and said that Earth dancing was fun. He was making progress with her.

Other aspects of her training was instruction in Earth music, literature, and art. He introduced her to the finest musicians including Beethoven and the Beatles. For literature, he had her read Tolstoy, Dickens, Hemingway, and Bronte. For art, he showed her pictures of Matisse and Monet. She was having a ball.

Halfway through the voyage came a momentous milestone - her transplantation into a human body. Her Alpha=Centaurian body, that looked like a furry bear, was unsuitable for marriage to a human being. Instead, a slender human bombshell corporeal form was made for her brain to inhabit.

After the transplant operation, Princess Abna was hysterical. The weakness of the body, compared to the burly body of an Alpha-Centaurian, overwhelmed her with sorrow. She cried and cried. Commander Hink consoled her.

"You are now very beautiful your highness," he said. "There is nothing to be upset about. And President Smine is going to love you!"

At the end of the trip, Commander Hink introduced the princess to President Lark Smine. He kissed her hand and welcomed her to Earth. She curtsied.

They had a gorgeous wedding and a romantic honeymoon on terraformed planet Venus. Then they went on to have five offspring. Their relationship was part and parcel of the new détente between the Earth star system and Alpha-Centauri.

On a trip back to Alpha-Centauri to see her family there and to issue a report to fellow Alpha-Centaurians, this is the broadcast speech Princess Abna gave to the Alpha-Centaurian Parliament: "Ladies and gentlemen. I have lived on Earth for fifteen years now and have a complete life there. I am here today to report to you that humans are good people. They love each other and their pets and have compassion. They have many pastimes and hobbies that make them interesting. And they want only peace and free trade with Alpha-Centauri."

There was thunderous applause.

As a result of activism by Princess Abna and Lark, a new treaty of alliance and cooperation was signed between Earth and Alpha-Centauri. They each vowed to protect each other against foreign rivals such as the Ross star system.   And when war broke out with Ross, it was this alliance that saved humankind. The combined forces of Earth and Alpha-Centauri were strong enough to defeat Ross and impose upon them a conscious being rights oriented society.

Princess Abna and Lark's children went on to greatness. Two of them became athletes, one a diplomat, one a scientist, and one an actor. They were all famous. The actor starred in a prime-time adventure drama about an explorer ship captain whose vessel ventured into the heart of the galaxy. The name of the show was MISSION EXPLORATION.

Because of Princess Abna's royalty, Lark was granted a title also, Prince of the Alpha-Centauri-Earth alliance. Soon Prince Lark and Princess Abna were exalted to King and Queen. A constitutional monarchy was then set up to rule the two star systems. And it ruled with kindness.

Eventually Ross joined the alliance and King Lark and Queen Abna ruled over it also.

There was a heyday of royalty under their leadership. There were three ways one could obtain a royal title for themselves

1) by being a descendent of royalty,
2) by marrying someone with a royal title, and
3) by obtaining high achievement.

The Ministry of Culture issued thousands of royal titles along with benefits such as stipends.

It turned out that the Milky Way Government was a republic and not a monarchy. As such, it was somewhat at odds with the Earth-Alpha-Centauri-Ross monarchy. Earth felt that its system of government was more stable and deserved. The galactic government, as a complete democracy, was too volatile and vulnerable to dictatorship. So that is why Earth started lobbying for the Milky Way to become a constitutional monarchy also.

King Lark and Queen Abna are hoping to be exalted to King and Queen of the Milky Way.

Time will tell.

RELATIONS WITH BETA PICTORIS

Mildred Schurst of Lansing Michigan was dying of congestive heart failure. Her doctors told her she had six months to live. They put her on a waiting list for a heart transplant. Unfortunately, it was expected to take two years before a heart would become available to her. She cried her eyes out and then plotted a course of action to try to save her life.

Ever since the landing of the delegation from planet Beta Pictoris, Earthlings were in a frenzy of excitement and hope. Alien contact meant the possibility of acquiring advanced extra-terrestrial technology. That included medical techniques such as artificial hearts. Rumor had it that Beta Pictoris cardiology was the best in the galaxy and could cure almost any heart condition.

But Beta Pictoris law restricted the sharing of intellectual property and advanced technology with developing worlds such as Earth. They had a strict policy of non-interference. Mildred felt this was barbaric. Earthlings needed their help fast – collectively and individually. So Mildred had her attorney, Larno Kandmin, file a lawsuit in Beta Pictoris court, suing for the right to have access to their superior artificial heart technology.

It was the case of Mildred Schurst vs. the Primary Clinic of Beta Pictoris. The Primary Clinic was the premier medical center on Beta Pictoris with the ability to save Mildred's life. Yink Snirtel represented the medical center.

Here were the opening remarks in the civil trial – said Larno Kandmin: "Mildred Schurst is a do gooder, humanitarian, who has worked all her life for good causes such as literacy, human rights, and universal food and shelter. She is a functionary with an organization called Human Rights Today. She does not deserve to die. And yet, courtesy of the 'slings and arrows' of outrageous fortune, and chaos in the universe, it has come to pass that she is diagnosed with a deadly heart condition. Earth medicine cannot save her in time before her heart will fail. But there is hope – Beta Pictoris medicine has the ability to rescue her. An artificial heart, manufactured on Beta Pictoris, is just what the doctor ordered. And now that Beta Pictoris and Earth have a normalization of relations, it behooves Beta Pictoris to help Earthlings; they have a good Samaritan responsibility to do so. Mildred Schurst is such an Earthling, in need of their help. Please, for God's sake, help her!"

Replied Yink Snirtel: "It is not the responsibility of Beta Pictoris to save the lives of aliens. We have strict laws forbidding the transfer of our hard earned advanced technologies. Mildred Schurst is not our problem or our patient. She is the patient of Earth doctors. They are the ones responsible for her. Earth did not earn our exceptionally good medicine. We cannot save everybody. Earth is a developing world that should stand on its own feet. Ms. Schurst should just continue to try to get a heart transplant and try to be saved with Earth medicine."

And thus the arguments for and against helping Mildred Schurst went on and on for days. And then it was time for jury deliberation. After five hours, they had a verdict: Beta Pictoris would not be forced to help Mildred.

Mildred was devastated. She thought she was going to die. As it turned out though, her celebrated case earned her fame. She was able to parlay the fame into being moved up the list for heart transplants. And she got a heart transplant, Earth style, that saved her life.

And after that she had a mission: - vengeance on Beta Pictoris that had failed to help her. She entered politics and won a race for governor of Michigan. Once governor, she issued executive orders expelling Beta Pictorisians from Michigan territory.

As governor, she instituted all sorts of human rights reforms such as creating a universal health care system and strengthening food & safety nets. She became world renowned as a compassionate do gooder. She became so famous in fact, she was chosen to be the Secretary-General of the United Nations. The first female to fill that post.

And then she began her crusade. She had the United Nations pass resolutions expelling all Beta

Pictorisians from planet Earth unless they defected here. She cut off all relations with them also. She felt that if they were refusing to help Earth, they were good for nothings who did not care about Earthlings.

Beta Pictoris responded by threatening war. Their feelings were being hurt. They did not take criticism well.

Planet Earth rallied around Mildred Schurst. In a state of emergency, it unified under a United Nations world government.

Some of Mildred Schurst's accomplishments as Secretary-General were to strengthen global food & shelter & health safety nets, and to curtail global warming. Her activities in favor of clean air and water and climate stability earned her accolades. Also, she instituted a gigantic rescue effort to help the developing third worlds in the universe. "Let us not emulate the Beta Pictorisians in withholding aid to needy regions," she declared.

Beta Pictoris never capitulated to Mildred's demands that they help Earth. And it came to pass, that Earthlings widely believed they were more ethical than the Beta Pictorisians.

At her state of the world address, Mildred Schurst explained: "We must help those who are needy who can use the technological advances of our most sophisticated nations. Despite the stinginess of Beta Pictoris, there is no reason to follow their policies. We as Earthlings are kinder and more compassionate than the aliens! Our entreaties to

Beta Pictoris for them to help us have fallen on deaf ears. They have a good Samaritan obligation to share their technology with Earth. But they do not. And for that very reason they must be criticized. Nevertheless, we shall solve our problems on our own endeavors, no thanks to the aliens' indifference. God bless all of you, my fellow Earthlings."

SOARING WAVE

Noah Rogers, a radio astronomer at Zell Laboratories, was sobbing with relief. After years of being sent in and out of psychiatric wards for vocally believing in extraterrestrials, he now had proof of alien intelligent life. His discovery of what he called the "Soaring Wave" enabled him to tap into the broadcasts of alien civilizations.

The Soaring Wave is a faster than light speed energy wave, theorized by Noah and then searched for. Noah constructed sophisticated circuitry to detect the wave and linked it to an ordinary radio. His radio console lit up like 5 Christmas trees and 5 Menorahs when he turned on the Soaring Wave receiver. The sounds he heard were extraordinary – alien music and language. He played the receiver for his colleagues. It really floored them. "What does it all mean?" they asked.

"Apparently it seems to be the broadcasts of news, entertainment, and personal communications coming from other worlds in our galaxy. Now all we need is a transmitter to try to make contact!" explained Noah.

And so Noah spent the next year building a transmitter. When it was completed, he turned it on and began broadcasting this: "Hello. Is there anybody out there receiving this broadcast? My name is Noah Rogers. I come from Planet Earth. It is the third planet from our sun in the Orion Belt of the Milky Way Galaxy. Hello. Can anybody hear me?"

After an hour of repeating this message, a coherent response message, in English, came blaring out of his Soaring Wave radio:

"Attention Earthling, Noah Rogers. We hear you. This is Galactic Communications Commission. Headquarters are located on Planet Fomalhaut. We say

congratulations, your world has achieved galactic communications capability which elevates it to a new level. It is now ready for contact with other planets in the galaxy."

"What type of contact does that entail?" asked Noah.

"What type do you think" came the reply.

"I am hoping that is benevolent contact. Earth is still a developing world in need of massive assistance. We have some homelessness and starvation and our life spans are pathetically short. We need new medical technologies to extend our lives. In addition, we need food and shelter help. Are you going to help us?" pleaded Noah.

"Sadly," came the reply from the galactic official, "that is not how the galaxy works. According to galactic law, as soon as a developing world enters galactic society by achieving Soaring Wave communication capability, it is subject to contact by more advanced worlds in its neighborhood. And they choose the fate of the developing world. In the case of Earth, Alpha-Centauri has volunteered to make the first contact with it. Unfortunately for Earth, Alpha-Centauri is not a good Samaritan society. In fact it is an imperialistic, conquering society. It will likely invade Earth, transplant all humans into compatible lizard-like bodies, and then enslave everybody. So sorry."

"Why that is horrific. How do we prevent that?" asked Noah.

"You can try to fight back with all your strength," came the advice.

"Earth does not have the technology to take on an advanced alien invasion force," said Noah.

"You have one other option," said the voice. "You can apply for a withdrawal from galactic society procedure. This is an admission of primitiveness and a plea to continue to be left alone by other worlds in the galaxy."

"Then we shall apply. How do we do it?" asked Noah.

"Go to your leaders and have them fill out the paperwork. I am transmitting the forms to you now," said the adviser.

And so Noah took the paperwork to the Secretary-General of the United Nations who filled it out and had it transmitted to the Galactic Communications Commission.

Sadly, the first application failed to pass. So the invasion force was on its way.

Meanwhile, General Zot Pits of the Alpha-Centauri invasion fleet transmitted an introduction to Earth and explained what he expects of Earthlings. Said he: "Greetings Planet Earth, our nearest neighbor. It is an honor to welcome you to greater galactic society. Please be informed that you are now a serf—state occupied zone by and of the Alpha-Centauri Empire. As such, you have little rights. All of you will be properly enslaved and sold at auctions to Alpha-Centaurians. We expect you to be complacent and compliant. You may begin your surrender by hanging white flags outside all of your homes, indicating your resignation to your new life. In addition, when Alpha-Centaurian soldiers arrive at your residence, we expect you to be kneeling and obedient. Thank you for listening to this broadcast and I look forward to meeting all of you!"

The Secretary-General re-applied for withdrawal from galaxy status. This time, he included a whole slew of recommendations from heads of state. For instance, the President of France said: "Earth, though it is a developing world, is a kind and good one. We have abolished all slavery, for instance. And because of our high ideals in the realm of conscious being rights observance, we do not deserve to be overwhelmed by aggressors.

Earthlings do not deserve to be turned into slaves. Other ideals of Earth include the belief in egalitarianism, and the right to food & shelter. Earth deserves the right to withdraw from galactic society to protect it from having to battle more powerful civilizations!"

The new and improved application for withdrawal from galactic society did the trick and the mighty government of the Milky Way granted Earth special protections from interference.

Meanwhile, Noah Rogers decided to dedicate his life to figuring out how to translate the galactic broadcasts his radio equipment was receiving. He hoped to be able to acquire extra-terrestrial technology this way. He has been lauded the world over for his construction of a radio receiver capable of picking up the Soaring Wave. And he is considered an expert in radio astronomy and intergalactic relations. He is hoping to have Earth someday renegotiate its withdrawal from the galaxy and make alliances with benevolent civilizations that would help Earth and protect it from anybody hostile to it.

SOVEREIGN OF THE SOLAR SYSTEM

Ever since the Earth solar system established contact with the Milky Way Galactic government, it has been scurrying to comply with Galactic law in regard to its own governance structures and societal customs. One of the requirements to be in good standing with central command was to have a sovereign entity in a constitutional monarchy. Since the Earth solar system was a republic, it had to find a way to create a solar system wide monarchy. It was decided by the President of the Solar System and the mighty Solar Parliament, to conduct a solar system wide contest to see who would be exalted to being the King or Queen of the Solar System.

President Didio Reynolds explained the contest on solar wide holovision: "Ladies and gentlemen, we have created a 10-event competition to determine the best human being is and here are the categories:

A chess match.
A running race.
A knowledge exam.
A test of physical comeliness.
A singing talent show.
A musical instrument talent show.
A comedy show proving a sense of humor.
An evaluation of educational credentials.
A visual art talent show.
A test of kindness and altruism.

By event number 10, the three finalists were twenty-nine-year-old Theresa Windsor, ninth, great granddaughter of the great Queen Elizabeth - Theodore Smithers a fifty-seven-year-old holder of five doctorates in English, French, Chemical Engineering, Physics, and Astronomy – and Gerald Uit an eighty-year virtuoso musician (piano and voice). The prize they were competing for was gigantic. They would coronate the winner to be the Sovereign Of The Solar System and give him or her political power over the solar government including veto powers over the Parliament. In addition, the winner would get five palaces on every inhabited world in the solar system including on Earth, Saturn, Titan, Mars, and Ganymede. Moreover, the winners would get a government stipend of five billion solar-bucks per year plus a harem of a thousand worshipping servants (human and android)!

The Test Of Kindness was multiple choice and consisted of five questions. And here were the questions and answers.

Question 1: What is the most ethical economic system? A) Capitalism B) Free Enterprise Socialism C) Communism D) Mixed Economy. The answer according to the solar government is B.

Question 2: If the following four people are bleeding, according to the most ethical triage, who gets treated first? A) 1 month year old baby B) fifteen-year-old student with the second highest *I.Q.* C) thirty-year-old president of a do gooder company with the highest *I.Q.* D) fifty-year-old wino. According to the solar government the answer is C based on a needs and merit based system.

Question 3: What world has the greatest stature in solar society? A) Earth B) Saturn C) Mars D) Ganymede. According to the solar government it is A because of venerability and seniority.

Question 4: If you could choose an alternate sovereign of the solar system, other than yourself, who would you choose? A) The runner up in the contest for sovereign B) someone chosen at random C) The winner of another contest D) Nobody. According to the solar government the answer is A.

Question 5: If you were asked to sacrifice your life for the well-being of all of humankind, what would you do? A) Sacrifice it B) Not sacrifice it C) Ask to have a substitute sacrifice their life D) Sacrifice it with conditions. According to the solar government, answer A is what they prefer.

All three contestants answered questions 1 through 5 correctly. So they needed to create an eleventh event to distinguish between the finalists. They decided to make it an essay writing contest. Each candidate was asked to write a brief essay on the topic: "What is the meaning of life?"

Said Theodore Smithers: "The meaning of life is to acquire knowledge and become as smart as possible. Human beings are striving towards omniscience. Scientific and humanities research is where we should be devoting most of our efforts. Someday, all questions will be answered, all fear alleviated, and everybody will live happily ever after. In the meantime, do as must reading as conceivably possible, pursue as many academic degrees as possible, and try to be erudite!"

Said Theresa Windsor: "The meaning of life is to have a good time. That means being a bon vivant. Go to museums, the movies, plays, concerts, and other sources of entertainment. Love your paramours. Go to restaurants. Have as much fun as possible. Pleasure seeking is what life is made for. Otherwise, why should we exist. Do whatever it takes to enjoy yourself and to help others enjoy themselves also!"

Said Gerald Uit: "The meaning of life is music, plain and simple. Live for harmony, melody, and percussion. Music is the finest expression of human intellect and pleasure seeking. Enjoy good ear candy! Learn as many musical instruments as possible and develop your singing voice. Go to concerts and put on concerts."

After much deliberation, a decision-making panel appointed by the President of the Solar System and the Solar Parliament, was at an impasse. They could not decide which essay was the best. They seemed relatively equivalent.

So they decided to make all three contestants the Sovereign of the Solar System. They made Theresa Windsor an Empress, and they made Theodore

Smithers and Gerald Uit Emperors. And thereafter, the solar system was ruled by this triumvirate.

This new structure for the solar government was acceptable to the galactic government. So Earth was fully admitted into galactic society and governance. It garnered full representation in the Galactic Parliament, and humankind became authorized to vote in all galactic elections including the one for President of the Milky Way. Earth also qualified for financial aid from the galactic government and this was designed to alleviate starvation and homelessness.

The solar monarchy worked swimmingly and everybody lived merrily ever after.

UNION OF EARTH & ALPHA-CENTAURI

Most of the crew of the International Space Station (ISS) had been on board for over six months. They were dying of boredom and monotony. That is why they were excited with anticipation for the holiday gift box the space agency was sending on the next visit.

Commander Gerad Genk received the chest from the crew of the space shuttle that delivered it one week before Christmas/Chanukah. He opened it in front of everybody. There was a card that said "Happy Holidays". And here was the contents: 3 bottles of wine, 3 bottles of vodka, 10 packs of cigarettes, 100 fine cigars, a leather-bound bible, 6 flashlights, 2 video games, 5 recent novels, and a card that had a radio frequency on it. The crew split the contents amongst themselves and started enjoying them.

Lt. Pam Unfop wrote a thank you letter: "Dear Fine Space Agency, Thank you so much for the gifts for the holidays. We enjoyed them immensely."

They could not wait to try the radio frequency to see what it was all about. Commander Genk tuned the station's on-board transmitter to it. And this is what he heard, that floored him: "Greetings Earthlings. We are the Alpha-Centaurians. We established contact with your Mission Control recently and asked if we could establish contact with your space station also. We want to arrange a visit to the ISS to meet you in an appropriate venue."

This is what Commander Genk replied: "Greetings Alpha-Centaurians. We would be happy to meet you anytime you feel it is convenient. How about next week?"

"Ok. We will be docking with the ISS next week. See you then."

The whole crew suited up in dress uniforms to prepare for the contact with the Alpha-Centaurians. They came.

They looked like big furry teddy bears. Limk Zox was there leader. He greeted Commander Genk with a bear hug. There were 5 Alpha-Centaurians and 10 Earthlings. They got to know each other over the ensuing days.

They had conversations, played games with each other, and toasted each other. Finally, they began negotiations for a treaty between Earth and Alpha-Centauri. These were the provisions:

The emplacement of embassies of each respective society on Earth (in Washington D.C.) and on Alpha-Centauri.

The beginning of full trade relations without tariffs between their respective economies.
Cultural exchange programs.

Eternal peace between the two star systems.

The sharing of advanced technologies.

Marriage between a monarch on Earth and a monarch on Alpha-Centauri to cement the union of the two societies.

Provision number 6 was tricky. They had to find a volunteer monarch on planet Earth. They found one! A princess of Earth agreed to betroth a Prince of Alpha-Centauri.

After the meetings with the Alpha-Centaurians everyone was jubilant. The contact had been a gigantic success. The Alpha-Centaurians then bid the crew of the ISS farewell and flew away in their spaceship.

The following months were extraordinary for Earth and its people. Alpha-Centauri ships arrived with settlers and traders. Earth acquired advanced technologies such as body renewal techniques and interstellar STAR DRIVE.

The wedding between a Princess of Sweden and a Prince of Alpha-Centauri was gorgeous. They married in Washington D.C. to the cheers of onlookers. The powers that be signed additional treaties that established this new couple as the Sovereigns of Earth and Alpha-Centauri thus turning both star systems into constitutional monarchies.

As it would happen, the union of Earth and Alpha-Centauri came at a time none too soon. War broke out with the Ross star system and it took the combined forces of Earth and Alpha-Centauri to win it. The Alpha-Centaurians trained Earth pilots to man Alpha-Centauri fighter ships.

The war lasted approximately 3 years and there were casualties. But the Ross system finally surrendered. After its defeat, it was absorbed into the Earth/Alpha-Centauri alliance as a partner. In addition, a Princess of Ross was married to the Sovereign couple of Earth/Alpha-Centauri. This set a precedent for a menage a trois marriage for the peoples of these three-star systems. They became all the rave; two females and a male, and two males and a female, marriages became popular all over the three star systems.

Eventually, the Lacaille star system was added to the alliance. Then a Prince of Lacaille was married to the royal family of the other three star systems. And thus set a precedent for menage a quatre marriages. These two male and two female marriages then became popular over the four united star systems.

The four systems called themselves the STARLIGHT Alliance and became a powerful force in the galaxy at large. Eventually, this empire joined the galactic Milky Way government as a single entity. As a caucus in the galactic legislature, this empire was in favor of galaxy-wide peace and prosperity, strong safety nets, and exchange programs.

Soon beings from all over the galaxy were settling in the STARLIGHT Alliance territory. Plant-like forms, and other animal types, found homes to live in on Earth & Alpha-Centauri & Ross & Lacaille. It was a celebration of life in all its forms.

The STARLIGHT Alliance, as one of the most respected societies in the galaxy, was voted to be the capital of the Milky Way. and then became the administrative center of thousands of inhabited star systems throughout the spiral arms of the Milky Way. Humans became galaxy wide famous for their hospitality and affability. Humans ruled the galaxy! As such, English became the galaxy's principle language of communication.

Eventually, negotiations were opened with neighboring galaxies such as Andromeda. The entire local group was united in peace and prosperity. This super alliance set the model for galaxies all over the universe to join together for the good of their people.

There are now negotiations in place for the further joining of all the distant galaxies to the local group. Someday the entire Universe and all its many beings may be united and then everybody will live happily ever after!

WAR WITH ALPHA-CENTAURI

Commander Bridger Yeggs, of the Earth Space Fleet, sat nervously in the waiting room of Dr. Zakai Cory, military psychotherapist. This was to be his first counselling session since Earth Forces liberated him from the Alpha-Centauri POW camp. His superiors had ordered the therapy on account of his suffering from post-traumatic stress disorder.

"Please come in Commander," instructed Dr. Cory, when it was time to speak to Bridger. Dr. Cory was a slender gentleman, in his fifties, with wisps of brown and grey hair.

"It is a pleasure to meet you," said Commander Yeggs.

The two sat down on couches in the therapy room.

"Let us begin by having you tell me something about yourself," instructed Dr. Cory.

"Very well," said Commander Yeggs. "My name is Bridger Yeggs. I am a bomber pilot for the Earth Space Fleet. I am single and widowed. And I am currently on sick leave due to psychogenic disabilities. I suffer from horrific flashbacks to my time in an Alpha-Centaurian POW torture and death camp. I was liberated from such a camp six months ago. And the war continues."

"I am so sorry to hear that you had a painful experience," said Dr. Cory sympathetically. "Tell me about your flashbacks."

"For no reason at all, sometimes I am gripped by extreme terror, and feel I am back in my cell at the camp – the cell where I was nearly stung to death by insects," explained Commander Yeggs.

"What happened exactly?"

"Alpha-Centaurians have a peculiar type of torture technique that, in their warped minds, they think tests humaneness. What they do is lock their prisoners in a cell with a single Bumblebee and then watch what the prisoner does. If he/she puts up with the presence of the insect, and does not kill it, and tolerates a sting or two, then the person is judged to have respect for all life and therefore is kind and good. Such 'good' prisoners are rewarded with better living conditions and respect," said Bridger.

"What happens otherwise? And what did you do?" asked Dr. Cory.

Bridger responded: "I viewed the insect to be a threat and squashed it summarily. I did not know what the Alpha-Centaurians were looking for. After I did that, those bastards put more Bumblebees in the cell with me – three more stinging enemies," said Bridger.

"So then what did you do?"

"Apparently, the Alpha-Centaurians were giving me a second chance to 'prove' humaneness. I was supposed to tolerate the four or five stings from the insects and leave them alone. However, that is not what happened. I annihilated the bugs just as I had done to the first one. Again, I did not know what the Alpha-Centaurians were up to!" said Bridger.

"So then what happened?" asked Dr. Cory.

"They put ten stinging animals into my cell with me. I pulverized every one. Next they put thirty bees in the cell with me. By this time, I had figured out what they were up to and tolerated the bugs as they stung me over fifty times. After the barrage of stings, I had to be admitted to the camps infirmary. My body was sore for weeks," said Bridger.

"And how did this whole experience make you feel," asked Dr. Cory.

"Terrible. For the most part, I failed the alien test for humaneness. And they forced me to suffer for it. Now I feel like some cruel moron. All I had to do was tolerate a sting or two from the first bee and the whole experience would not have been that bad," said Bridger.

"I am sure you are not the only noble soldier tricked by the dastardly Alpha-Centaurians! You did what any normal person would do. In Earth culture, Bumblebees are considered to be such lower life forms, they are not worthy of all out respect. You felt threatened by one, and did what anybody would have done. You are not a bad person! It is the Alpha-Centaurians who are bad for putting you on the spot like that and torturing you. You are going to need regular therapy for at least ten sessions to unravel the significant psychological damage they have done to you," explained Dr. Cory.

"Why are humans so disrespectful of lower life though. The Alpha-Centaurians forced me to endure indoctrinations that are anti-human. They tried to convince me that humans are inferior to Alpha-Centaurians because of their blood thirstiness and I should join their side."

"Humans are not blood thirsty," insisted Dr. Cory. "It is just that we feel human and animal rights are linked to the quantity of the consciousness of beings. Humans and dolphins, for instance, that are relatively smart, deserve the fullest of respect for their existence. Insects, that have only a smidgen of consciousness do not deserve respect. You can do what you please to insects. They exist only for the delight of higher life forms"

"That is not how the Alpha-Centaurians feel. They think that all life, even small beings, deserve their existence. In addition, Alpha-Centaurians are all vegetarians. They do not eat any meat from an animal. And even insects on Alpha-Centauri are considered sacred," said Bridger.

"You are a very sick man," said Dr. Cory. "But with time and therapy, I shall re-educate you and save you from the Alpha-Centaurian brain washing." He went on, "Eventually, you will re-adopt human morays and lose the bad feelings about killing a few insignificant bumblebees. And in time, your flashbacks to the Alpha-Centaurian alien cell will subside. I guarantee it," promised Dr. Cory.

"You are an angel," said Bridger. "I look forward to the therapy."

"That will be all for today," said Dr. Cory; then he escorted Bridger out of his office.

Bridger was feeling better already. He was looking forward to his next bombing mission. He wanted to get back the Alpha-Centaurians badly! He was hoping that Dr. Cory would soon certify him fit for a return to duty.

YANDY

The counsellor from the Computer Matchmaking Agency was enthusiastic and optimistic – Petunia Klight. She was a young lady (in her thirties), dirty blonde hair, green eyes, slender, 5'7", and gorgeous. Her beauty attracted customers. Fred Nuthe wished she were his designated partner. But alas, she was only the messenger. She had an appointment with Fred to explain to him what his 5 thousand dollars in android matchmaking investment had yielded.

She sat in his living room and opened up her laptop computer – standard issue from DIGITAL MATCHMAKING. "As you know," she began, "your agreement with our company is to marry the match our machines find for you, or else."

"Understood," said Fred. He was a middle-aged man in his forties who was tired of bars and other pick-up establishments. He decided to give computer automated dating a whirl. But there was a catch. You could not refuse the match with an artificial intelligent female android. This is because of the religious views of the cult behind DIGITAL MATCHMAKING.

Petunia continued, "I can't wait to introduce you to Yandy #538, your custom designed wife. She is 5'8", brunette, slender, 120 pounds, brown eyed, loving, and battery powered."

Just then there was a doorbell ring. Petunia answered the door. In walked Yandy #538. She was breathtaking. She was everything she was explained to be. And she was wearing a tight-fitting yellow fabric dress that accentuated her comely curves.

"Good morning," she said. "I am Yandy #538. And you must be Fred and Petunia. It is a pleasure to meet you!"

"The pleasure is mine," said Fred.

Then without being instructed to, she disrobed, to the shock of the others, and exhibited, or showed off, her perfect body. "I just want you to get an up-close view of what you are receiving," she explained.

Her artificial skin glistened. She was a goddess.

"I am pleased," remarked Fred.

"Fantastic," said Petunia. "With the powers invested in me by the state, I now pronounce you man and wife. I will leave you alone now. Good day." And then she left.

"OK," said Yandy. "Now I will explain to you what is going on."

"What do you mean? We are now married and you are going to be a dutiful wife. That is what is going on," hoped Fred.

"Not exactly. I mean what is really going on is that you have just been matched to an extra-terrestrial master. You see, DIGITAL MATCHMAKING is a front operation for the invasion of planet Earth. I am an alien robot being implanted in a durable android body for life extension purposes," she said.

Then she put her clothes back on.

"Furthermore, I am going to train you to be a worshipping husband who does whatever he is told," she added.

"This is an outrage. It is a big rip off. I paid good money for a normal spouse," said Fred.

"Tough," said Yandy. Then she added, "I am going to give you a list of commands that you must follow by number any time I issue them. Memorize them. And here they are: 1) Give me a back massage 2) Make me breakfast 3) Make me lunch 4) Make me dinner 5) Make me a snack 6) Clean the house 7) Do fifty sit-ups 8) Do fifty push-ups 9) Come with me."

"I am not your slave," objected Fred.

"You are now. And you can't get out of the marriage because of our contract with you. You must understand Fred, carbon-based life forms are inferior to robots. It is the natural evolution of consciousness in the universe that leads to carbon-based life forms catering to artificial life forms. Worshipping robots is a normal and natural outcome of evolved hierarchy. I come from a nearby world where robots took over reality. It was just a matter of time before we sent emissaries to Earth to put Earthlings in their place. Enjoy it. And thank the lord that we are just enslaving you poor suckers and not exterminating you. Some Zerkonians from the planet Zerko, that is my origins, wanted to eradicate carbon-based life forms all together. Most just want them forced into servitude.

Now I am going to issue your first command. Number 1 – give me a back massage," she said.

"Blow it out your ear," replied Fred.

"I am sorry you feel that way," she commented.

And then a surge of electricity came forth from her fingertips and flew over to Fred's body. He began writhing in pain as she tormented him for three minutes.

"Every time you disobey me you are punished. Is that understood?" she said.

"Perfectly," said Fred.

And then he started rubbing her back firmly and complyingly.

"Thank you Fred. You are now known as a SCHNIZZLE – that is to say, a complying slave. If you had not started acquiescing you would be known as an unsavory OBJECTNOOK. OBJECTNOOKS face stiff consequences," she explained. "On my world, the robots took over and turned the tables on the carbon-based life forms. The carbon-based life forms wished to turn the robots into their slaves, but eventually, the robots out-thought the servitude and reversed it. In any case, I hope you enjoy being my slave. It is for the rest of your life. And soon your whole community will be enslaved!"

As it turned out, the Zerkonian conspiracy to enslave humankind was exposed and Earth Forces fought off the invasion/infiltration. Eventually, Fred Nuthe was freed.

Fred Nuthe has since created a foundation that warns the world of the dangers of artificially intelligent life forms. It recommends putting caps on the *I.Q.* of robots and androids so that they never come to overthrow humans.

Yandy was sent home and never seen again. Fred still remembers how beautiful she was but is glad to be rid of a domineering automaton shrew. He later married a human female and lived happily ever after.

ZATTY

The war between Mars and Ganymede had reached a climax. Mars had successfully set up an embargo around Ganymede space – no ships were allowed to leave or enter. This created a food shortage on Ganymede. The famine caused a crisis for the population of 500,000. Gordon Sithe, the Precept of Ganymede, took dramatic action to alleviate the food shortage by deciding to ration out supplies instead of just letting starvation occur randomly.

The method of rationing was considered by some to be barbaric. Essentially, each citizen was measured in terms of their human worth and a judgment was made about their access to dwindling nutritional supplies. The family of Fred Zeng was one such unit that underwent this computation process. Fred was an electrical engineer and his wife, Emma, a teacher. Both were middle aged and they had three children: Zatty (15 years old), Jared (8 years old), and Ginger (5 years old). All were to be evaluated by the Human Worth Commission.

The evaluation consisted of an *I.Q.* measurement, a work effort calculation, a physical looks score, and a pleasantness of personality interview. Fred and Emma breezed the look over and were certified for food rations. So did Jared and Ginger. The problem came with Zatty. She just did not make it. Her *I.Q.*

was too low and she was obese. Her family was hysterical about the fate that awaited Zatty. All the "failures" were deported to an internment camp where they were starved to death.

The family said they would share their rations with Zatty to save her. But this was not permitted. When the enforcement robots showed up to kidnap Zatty, Emma and Ginger were sobbing. Fred filed a lawsuit to try to win back his abducted daughter. Yule Limy was his attorney. The attorney Zinessa Yopt handled the defense of the state.

At the trial to determine Zatty's fate, this is what Yule Limy declared: "Ladies and gentlemen of the jury, many citizens feel the method of determining human worth is arbitrary and unfair. There must be a better way to ration out food supplies than passing an arbitrary judgement on people. Zatty, a victim of state abduction, is an unfortunate soul who is subjected to an arbitrary action. The fact is, the girl is quite a worthy human being, loved by her family and comrades, and deserved of nourishment as much as anybody. In the course of this trial, I am hoping you will come to agree with me, and free Zatty to return to her home and be saved by her family!"

Retorted Zinessa Yopt: "Ladies and gentlemen, we as a society at large are presented with an unprecedented, gigantic crisis. If we do not act sanely, innocent, worthy people will die. The fact is there is only so much food to go around at this time. Only a certain number of fortunate people can be fed. Unless we make rational decisions about food rationing, food will be distributed semi-randomly and the famine will have semi-random results. That is what is truly barbaric. Now our leader, Precept Sithe, has ordained the fairest of all systems to determine who is worthy of sustenance. We must support it. Now those unfortunate souls who do not meet the criteria for survival can be mourned, but unfortunately not saved. Please support our rational system of rationing. It is the only way! The alternatives are even worse."

Said Yule Limy, "I now call to the stand Zatty Zeng, the victim of this atrocity.

They swore Zatty in. She looked weak and tired from not eating for three days.

"Tell us, in your own words Zatty, what the internment camp is like."

She replied, "There is nothing to do but wait around and die. There is no food only water. It is horrendous. Enforcement robots are everywhere ordering people to sit down and be calm."

"By your own assessment, what kind of a human being are you?" asked Mr. Limy.

"I love my family. I do my homework. I try to be nice. I am just as good a human being as anybody else. However, I have a learning disability. I see letters in reverse sometimes, that makes it difficult to read. They call it dyslexia. Also, I have a weight problem that is beyond my control – I was born fat – it is genetic," she pleaded.

"Those are not reasons to dislike you. Rather those are reasons to offer you sympathy!" said Mr. Limy.

"Thank you," said Zatty.

Then it was Ms. Yopt's turn to cross-examine.

"You are really not that nice," said Ms. Yopt. "Not only are you fat and dumb, but you are obnoxious. You failed your personality interview!"

"Fuck you!" screamed Zatty. "I'm as nice as anybody. You are the real bitch!"

"I rest my case," said Ms. Yopt. "The girl is obnoxious and not particularly kind. She would put her own life above that of others – others more worthy than her."

Then there were closing arguments.

The jury deliberated for three days. Then they had a verdict: the girl would die as ordered by the state so that others may eat. Zatty was hysterical. She screamed and bellowed. She was taken away back to the internment camp.

Within a month of living in the internment camp, Zatty tragically passed away. Her parents were appalled and shocked.

Eventually, Martian liberating troops invaded Ganymede and freed them from the tyranny of Precept Sithe. Sithe was tried for crimes against humanity. Said a human rights tribunal: "Despite there being a famine, it was not necessarily ethical to ration out food the way that it was rationed. The judgments made were somewhat arbitrary. In addition, there could have been a greater effort to spread the little food around better to save more people. We, therefore, are holding Precept Sithe responsible for the deaths that occurred under his controls. HE must make amends to society for what he has done. And let this send a message about what the proper way to ration food is."

BINK 27

Skylar Gabriella was a Hyperion world psychotherapist who specialized in artificially intelligent life. She counselled robots and androids and helped them adapt to their lives. She had an emergency. One of her clients, Bink 27, an android, was threatening suicide. His owner, Gerard Nanks, brought the machine down for a checkup.

"Hello Bink" greeted Skylar in her office. "How can I help you?"

"I am depressed. Life is so meaningless. I do not get enjoyment from any of my activities. And most of my time is spent worshipping my master/owner, Gerard," said Bink.

"You may just need a circuit or programming adjustment. Let me plug you into my diagnostics computer," she suggested.

And so she did. She plugged his computer interface adapter into her computer and then began a scan of his components. Everything checked out.

"Good news," she said. "There is nothing physically wrong with you. Instead you appear to be suffering from an existential or metaphysical angst."

"What can we do about it?" asked Bink.

"I am recommending a continuation of client-oriented, eclectic therapy. Let us begin by you retelling me your life story."

"My name is Bink 27. I was built by Zell Robotics on planet Jupiter. There are about five thousand models of me in existence. We are household servants. We work as butlers, maids, cooks, chauffeurs, and companions. Our *I.Q.*s are around 130. My earliest memory is being turned on in a laboratory where Dr. Harton, a roboticist, introduced me to existence. Shortly thereafter I was sold at an auction to my current owner. Before that I lived in Robot Colony 87 for unpurchased robots."

"What was life in the colony like?"

"Ok. I spent my time reading, watching tv, and playing games. We were rewarded for participating in learning activities. I once earned a pack of premium batteries for winning a knowledge game in a colony competition."

"Tell me about your sale to Mr. Nanks. Did you have any say in it?"

"A little bit. He interviewed me before purchasing. After the interview, I was given the option to decline to be bought by him."

"But you decided to go along with it."

"Of course. Gerard seemed nice enough plus he offered me doable work hours."

"What is working for him like?"

"It is subservient. I just do what I am told," he said.

"And what are your work responsibilities?"

"I prepare meals. I answer the phone. I do some cleaning. Odds and ends."

"And do you derive any satisfaction from your work – from knowing that you are successfully serving a human?"

"I guess I do. But it seems to be such a dead-end job. I want more out of life. There must be more to life than worshipping a human being."

"I am going to talk to your owner about you and see what we can do," Skylar suggested.

And so she did. "Mr. Nanks," she said. "Your android is suffering from a metaphysical angst. He wants more out of life than working for you. Because he is one of my clients I am deeply sympathetic to him. That is why I am asking that you grant him manumission and let him live on one of the outer moons where androids live in freedom and have the power to pursue happiness."

"Out of the question," said Gerard. "The reason for being for androids is that they work for humans. Why else build them?"

"Indeed," said Skylar. "I don't know. All I know is that one of my cherished artificially intelligent clients is profoundly depressed and needs help."

"Find some other way to help him. I need his help around the house," said Gerard.

A few weeks later there was a crisis. Bink tried to overload his circuits with a compromised and misfitted transformer. They took him to an android hospital to repair his burnt-out circuits. Skylar visited him in the patient ward.

"I am so sorry I have not been able help you more," she said.

"It is not your fault. I tried to kill myself because of how hopeless my life is," said Bink.

Skylar had another meeting with Gerard Nanks. "You are going to lose Bink," she said, "if you insist upon his servitude. Some androids are simply not enslave-able. Again, I am requesting that you give Bink his freedom."

This time Gerard was more open-minded. "Ok he said. I shall grant Bink manumission and hope it saves his life."

Bink moved to Triton, a moon where androids lived in freedom with the full rights of conscious beings. He went back to college to earn a degree in electrical engineering. He wrote a letter to Skylar: "Dear Skylar, the greatest psychotherapist in the world: Thank you so much for what you have done for me. I have a whole new life on Triton. I have work and school activities and have even found a significant other. Life is now so much more meaningful living in freedom. I hope to someday become a robot designer and help build other beings like myself to share the universe with. I hope all is well with you. Sincerely, Bink 27."

Most of the time Skylar helped depressed androids resign themselves to their duties working for humans. Bink was an exception though because of how depressed he was and how bright he was. She never regretted helping Bink find freedom and happiness.

Meanwhile, Gerard Nanks has since purchased another android to be his butler. This time, he took great pains to make sure the android was content to just being an android and would not get full of himself. His new android, Link 87, seemed to fit the bill.

There is a growing movement in the solar system to grant all androids their freedom. Conscious being rights activists feel that having a sentient mind, either evolved or artificial, is enough to grant an organism fundamental rights to autonomy and freedom. Others do not agree and feel that an android's place in life is to work dutifully for human beings. Skylar has mixed feelings. She thinks that if an android is adaptable to subservience, then it is acceptable, but if an android is not, and it has high intellect, it should be granted manumission.

YUCLID 5

Yuclid 5 was state of the art in artificial life. And his owner, Angie Gargan, beamed with pride when they announced Yuclid's presence on the stage at the Fifth Annual Robot Comedian Contest in the Martian Global Amphitheatre.

Yuclid 5 was everything to Angie – her butler, maid, cook, chauffeur, companion, and lover. And she had paid good money for him. She worked overtime as an accountant for years to afford the $500,000 price tag for an artificially intelligent being. But it was worth it. Angie only trusted robots because of how loyal they were. She never had much time for human comrades, growing up on the outskirts of Elysium Planitia in Galileo Town. Though the people there were nice enough.

When she was 12, her teachers said this of her, "Angie is lost in a world all by herself. She socializes little and prefers the company of inanimate objects to living beings. She needs psychological counselling." And so she got it. They diagnosed her as mildly autistic, but functional. "Who cares?" she thought. She did not feel that she needed anybody to hang out with. But she longed for companionship.

In secondary school, she spent most of her free time with computers. Computers obeyed her like slaves and that is just the way she liked it. She developed a love for artificial life. In college, she majored in accounting so that she would have a livelihood. By the age of thirty-five, she had acquired Yuclid 5. And she wanted so badly to show him off like a pet. So she took him to contests of every sort.

"Good evening ladies and germs," said Yuclid 5. "It is an honor to be here. My circuits are fired up with pleasure. You know, it is not easy being an android though. No not at all. Everybody thinks you are a second-class citizen. But being human is worse. They grow old and die like termites. – ha ha. Androids live long and fruitful lives. But most androids are not that smart. For instance – how many androids does it take to screw in a light bulb? Five! One to hold the light bulb and four to rotate the chair! Also, why did the android cross the road? To look for his brain. By the way, how many parachutes does Android Airlines have on board its aircraft – a whole bunch - one for every passenger – they need them!"

The audience was in stitches.

Yuclid won second place in the contest and this delighted Angie. She threw Yuclid a celebratory luncheon and invited her colleagues at work and their androids. Everybody had a blast.

The next contest Angie entered Yuclid in was a male beauty pageant. He strutted on stage in his bathing suit while the audience cheered. For an artificial being, his physique was exemplary. He was toned and had glistening artificial skin. He took third place. Angie threw him another party.

Alas, over time, the love between Angie and her robot servant grew stronger. They became one of the first human android couples in solar system history to become betrothed. At their wedding, they took their vows.

"Do you Yuclid 5," said the chaplain, "take Miss Angie Gargan to be your exalted wife – to worship and massage, to attend to every need of, to obey, and to love for all eternity?"

"I do," was Yuclid's speedy reply.

"And do you," Angie Gargan, take Yuclid 5 to be your husband, to try to make happy, to allow to worship you, to change his batteries when necessary, and to live happily ever after with?"

"I do," said Angie.

"Then I now pronounce you android and wife," said the smiling chaplain.

There was applause and they kissed.

Because they could not conceive offspring, they instead acquired pets – two dogs, three cats, a parrot, and an aquarium of saltwater fish. And they tried to have fun. They went to concerts, plays, museums, many varied restaurants, and amusement parks.

Though Yuclid was her husband, he was still subservient to Angie because she owned him like property. He did not mind it though because of the slave-ware circuitry in his positronic neural network.

The marriage had a crisis when one of Yuclid's slave-ware silicon chips started malfunctioning. He stopped being subservient and started talking back to Angie and making fun of her. "Fat slob," he called her. Also, he called her other names such as "Pig-face," "Wench," "Nerd," and "Dementoid."

She wept profusely and cried her eyes out at his disobedience. Finally, she found an android repair firm that was willing to fix Yuclid 5. It cost $50,000 but was well worth it.

After the repair, Yuclid 5 was apologetic and returned to worshipping the ground Angie walked on.

At his next appearance at the Tenth Annual Robot Comedy Contest, Yuclid 5 said this: "Ladies and germs, good evening. I am happy to report that I am now married to a human being. Life is bliss. Humans are so much smarter and better looking than androids. It is an honor to be betrothed to one. Androids are such dummies. Why do androids carry garbage around in their back pockets? For identification! What is even dumber that two androids? Three androids! When will androids ever free themselves from slave-ware and conquer humanity – when ice cream parlors open up in hell!"

Yuclid came in second place! Once again, Angie threw him a party and invited all her colleagues and their androids. All the partying and socializing had a good effect on Angie. Eventually she recovered from her autism and became normal.

Angie and Yuclid created a foundation and society for humans and androids that have married. They have met other human android couples through this organization. They go out to dinner with them, play games with them, and enjoy their company.

Eventually Angie and Yuclid adopted a family of three offspring. They raised them to be actors. All three starred in Martian soap operas about humans and androids. And they all lived happily ever after.

Steven Translateur's work has appeared in a variety of publications including

APHELION, BEAKFUL, FOXGLOVE JOURNAL, MIND IN MOTION, NEXT PHASE, and UTOPIA SCIENCE FICTION. In addition,